JOHN O'B

TIPPING POINT:
OPENING
SHOTS

BOOK I OF TIPPING POINT

Other books by John O'Brien

A New World Series

A New World: Chaos

A New World: Return

A New World: Sanctuary

A New World: Taken

A New World: Awakening

A New World: Dissension

A New World: Takedown

A New World: Conspiracy

A New World: Reckoning

A New World: Storm

Companion Books

A New World: Untold Stories

A New World: Untold Stories II

The Third Wave: Eidolon

Ares Virus

Ares Virus: Arctic Storm

Ares Virus: White Horse

Ares Virus: Phoenix Rising

Red Team

Red Team: Strigoi

Red Team: Lycan

Red Team: Cartel Part One

Red Team: Cartel Part Two

A Shrouded World

A Shrouded World: Whistlers

A Shrouded World: Atlantis

A Shrouded World: Convergence

A Shrouded World: Valhalla

A Shrouded World: Asabron

A Shrouded World: Bitfrost

A Shrouded World: Hvergelmir

A Shrouded World: Asgard

Lifting the Veil

Lifting the Veil: Fallen

Lifting the Veil: Winter

Lifting the Veil: Emergence

Lifting the Veil: Risen

Author's Note

First, I want to say that this is a much different series than I've written in the past. There are no monsters, no initial apocalypse, no transformed mutants. And, I want to warn you off the bat that this first book isn't my usual action-oriented tale. There is action, but it's sparsely scattered throughout, picks up at the end, and will continue into the second book. But this is a political-military styled story that has been running around in my mind ever since I read about China's militarization of the Spratly Islands. However, it needed something else—a spark. Well, as much as COVID-19 has slowed down our lives, it has also provided the catalyst I had been searching for. The story began to click as my meager brain cells bounced around inside my skull, starting as a low, dull hum that rose to a crescendo that roared to be written.

Now, I expected a difficult time writing a story with so many moving pieces. In that, I was not disappointed—it turned out to be even more complicated than I thought. I can't even begin to convey how much research it took.

There were days spent doing nothing but hunting down a certain element or fact, and there were more times than I can remember when I seriously contemplated just tossing the whole concept. But then I would lie awake at night—a common occurrence—and there would be a break as if the walls of Jericho came tumbling down. A piece that I had worried over would click into place and the story would flow like a dam had broken. However, I now have bald spots on top of my head where I pulled many a tuft out. I also have a permanent keyboard impression on my forehead from banging my head on it.

In this book, you will find a lot of semi-fictional news articles. You may get tired of them and not see the reason for so many, but I did this to really hammer in the current geo-political nature of what China and the United States are currently experiencing. Sometimes it's so much easier to place information in a news article rather than write the information in story form. So, accept my apology in advance for the seemingly tedious nature of the first half of this book. The Action does pick up later in this one and the next.

I want to thank my mother for her tireless editing. As she labors over the first rounds of my work, she does her magic and turns my cave paintings into works of art. I also want to thank Vanessa McCutcheon for turning the works into their final form.

So, I want to say that this story is just that, a fictional tale. It doesn't depict any political leanings I might have, nor any feelings toward another nation. I ask that you read this as a tale of fiction meant for enjoyment and not as some sort of manifesto. But, if you still want to crucify me after you read this first installment, the line starts at the door.

In this book, I suggest a manmade origin of the corona virus. I want to iterate strongly that this is purely for the sake of the story and not to allude to or to blame anyone for the current pandemic. So, I ask that you not supplant truth for fiction here.

I'd like to note here that Chinese conventions are to call someone by their full name instead of the single-name convention familiar in the west. For that reason, I have opted to go with the western naming conventions for ease.

I want to thank all of you who pick up my stories. I can't tell you enough how much I appreciate and love you all. When I first began writing, I had no idea where it would take me. I just had a story that needed to get out. Thank you so much for making it possible to continue sharing these stories. You are awesome!

–John

Cast of Characters

US Personnel

Presidential Cabinet

Jake Chamberlain, *Secretary of the Navy*
Tom Collier, *CIA Director*
Elizabeth Hague, *Ambassador to the United Nations*
Imraham Patel, *CDC Director*
Aaron MacCulloch, *Secretary of Defense*
Bill Reiser, *NSA Director*
Joan Richardson, *Homeland Security Director*
Fred Stevenson, *Secretary of State*
Frank Winslow, *President of the United States*

Joint Chiefs of Staff

Phil Dawson, *General, USAF – Joint Chiefs of Staff Chairman*
Kevin Loughlin, *General, US Army – Joint Chiefs of Staff Vice Chairman*
Tony Anderson, *General, US Army – Army Chief of Staff*
Duke Calloway, *General, US Marines – Commandant of the Marines*
Brian Durant, *Admiral, USN – Chief of Naval Operations*
Mike Williams, *General, USAF – Air Force Chief of Staff*

SEAL Dive Team 1

Paul McIntyre, *Commander, USN – SEAL Dive Team 1 Commander*
Chris Newsome, *Lieutenant, USN – Seal Dive Team 1 Alpha Platoon Commander*
Peter Fields, *Chief Petty Officer, USN – SEAL Dive Team 1 Alpha Platoon Chief*

SEAL Dive Team 1 Gold Team

James Baldwin, *Lieutenant (j.g.), USN – SEAL Dive Team 1 Gold Team Leader*
Bill Collins, *Petty Officer Second Class, USN*
Scott Renton, *Petty Officer Third Class, USN*
Ted Riker, *Petty Officer Second Class, USN*
Sam Vangle, *Petty Officer Third Class, USN*
Tyler Welch, *Petty Officer Second Class, USN*

SEAL Dive Team 1 Blue Team

David Hawser, *Petty Officer First Class, USN – SEAL Dive Team 1 Blue Team Leader*
Ken Bollinger, *Petty Officer Second Class, USN*
Allen Crimson, *Petty Officer Second Class, USN*
Rick Dewey, *Petty Officer Third Class, USN*
Joel Infelt, *Petty Officer Second Class, USN*
Matt Longe, *Petty Officer Second Class, USN*

US Naval Personnel

Jerry Ackland, *Commander, USN – Captain of the USS Texas*
Charlie Blackwell, *Vice Admiral, USN – Third Fleet Commander*
Kyle Blaine, *Lieutenant, USN – F-35C pilot*
Shawn Brickline, *Admiral, USN – Pacific Theatre Commander (USPACCOM)*
Ralph Burrows, *Captain, USN – Captain of the USS Abraham Lincoln*
Chip Calhoun, *Rear Admiral, USN – Carrier Strike Group 5/Task Force 70 Commander*
Bryce Crawford, *Admiral, USN – Commander of the Pacific Fleet (COMPACFLT)*
Sam Enquist, *Lieutenant (j.g.), USN – F/A-18F Electronic Warfare Officer (EWO)*
Ed Fablis, *Rear Admiral, USN – Carrier Strike Group 9 Commander*

Scott Gambino, *Commander, USN – Captain of the USS* Ohio

John Garner, *Captain, USN – Captain of the USS* Theodore Roosevelt

Steve Gettins, *Rear Admiral, USN – Carrier Strike Group 1 Commander*

Matt Goldman, *Lieutenant, USN – F/A-18F Pilot*

Myles Ingram, *Commander, USN – Captain of the USS* Howard

Tom Jenson, *Lt. Commander, USN – Executive Officer of the USS* Howard

Zach Keene, *Lieutenant (j.g.), USN – F/A18-F Electronic Warfare Officer (EWO)*

Tyson Kelley, *Captain, USN – Captain of the USS* Ronald Reagan

James Munford, *Lt. Commander, USN – Executive Officer of the USS* Texas

Michael Prescott, *Rear Admiral, USN – Carrier Strike Group 11 Commander*

Carl Sandburg, *Rear Admiral, USN – Carrier Strike Group 3 Commander*

Kurt Schwarz, *Captain, USN – Captain of the USS* Nimitz

Nathan Simmons, *Commander, USN – Captain of the USS* Preble

Chris Thompson, *Lieutenant, USN – F/A-18F Pilot*

Warren Tillson, *Vice Admiral, USN – Seventh Fleet Commander*

Chris Walkins, *Captain, USN – Captain of the USS* Carl Vinson

Tony Wallins, *Lt. Commander, USN – Executive Officer of the USS* Preble

US Air Force Personnel

Wayne Blythe, *Major, USAF – B-52 Pilot*

Vince Rawlings, *General, USAF – Air Force Pacific Commander (COMPACAF)*

US Army Personnel

Sara Hayward, *Colonel, US Army — USAMRIID Commander*
Charles Warner, *General, US Army — Special Operations Command (SOCOM) Commander*

CIA Personnel

Andreas Cruz — *CIA Operator*
Felipe Mendoza — *CIA Operator*

NSA Personnel

Allison Townsend — *NSA Analyst*

Philippine Personnel

President Renaldo Aquino — *Philippine President (as of 17 May, 2021)*
General Ernesto Gonzalez — *Philippine Rebel General*
President Andres Ramos — *Philippine President*

Chinese Personnel

Wei Chang, *Minister of State Security*
Sun Chen, *Admiral, PLAN — Captain of the* Shandong *aircraft carrier*
Hao Chenxu, *President of People's Republic of China (PRC), Paramount Leader of China*
Tan Chun, *Commander, PLAN — Captain of* Changzhen 17
Lei Han, *Minister of Finance*
General Quan, *General, PLAN — Fiery Cross Commander (as of 30 May, 2021)*
General Tao, *Fiery Cross Commander (prior to 30 May, 2021)*
Liu Xiang, *Minister of Foreign Affairs*
Zhou Yang, *Minister of National Defense*
Lin Zhang, *Admiral, PLAN — Southern Fleet Commander*

Introduction

Chinese Expansion into South China Sea

South China Sea, Spratly Islands
June, 2015

The echo of shouting men carried across the sea, rising above the surf as it rolled across the shoal. Water stretched across the horizon, the small boat riding up crests and down into the next trough. Near the edge of the reef, waves slapped against the side of the boat as the crew wrestled to tie off a large floating tube that ran across the water to a large spool assembly covering the entire back end of a barge.

Finally securing the tube's end, they revved the motor, and the shallow-bottomed boat heeled over, heading toward where the top of the reef rose above the waterline. Behind, the long tube slowly unwound from the spool and unfurled its large diameter into the water to drift on the surface of the sea. Steadying the boat in the occasional gust, the crew secured the end of the conduit in the shallows at the top of the shoal.

Once the first process was complete, another weighted tube descended from the bottom of the barge. The operation of building a manmade island had begun. Sand and debris were suctioned from the seabed and then run through the floating tube to spill out in a gout before being deposited atop the manmade shoal, the excess water running back into the sea. Sailing back and forth, the single barge slowly built up the shoal until a tiny island of sand emerged.

Another barge joined the first, and then a third. As the island expanded, more ships were added to the process. When there was enough solid ground, landing ships were brought in and equipment delivered. Bulldozers began to level the increasing heights of the sand deposits. More ships appeared around the expanding island until the surrounding scene looked like a harbor, each one adding yet more floating conduits and sand. This enabled increasing operations ashore, and soon, structures and then roads.

China was turning these shoals into an island, even though varying nations had claims to the area. However, it would be China who settled them and turned them into military bases.

* * * * * *

Spratly Islands (NY Times) 27 Oct, 2015 — Straining regional tensions even further, China has been quickly turning reefs into islets in the South China Sea. Over the past two years, seven new islands have been created.

Other countries with regional claims have become alarmed by both the speed and magnitude of China's island-building spree. In May, China announced that their efforts to move sediment from the seafloor to a reef would soon be completed. In addition, China has begun the construction of port facilities, military buildings, and an airstrip capable of supporting military aircraft on the islands. Satellite footage shows evidence of more airstrips currently under construction. These installations will reinforce China's claims and foothold on the hotly contested Spratly Islands, a scattering of reefs in the South China Sea. This has the potential of extending China's territorial waters more than 500 miles from the mainland.

…the United States sent a Navy destroyer near the islands, entering the disputed waters.

…Defense Secretary Aaron MacCulloch voiced criticism over China's actions in the region, stating that, "The United States will fly, sail and operate wherever international law allows, as we do all around the world." Sending China a statement to that effect, the United States reinforced its position by sending a guided-missile destroyer within 12 nautical miles of the island, the normal convention for territorial waters, angering the Chinese.

...the Fiery Cross Reef is the most strategically significant new island, with an airstrip that is long enough to allow China to land any plane, from fighter jets to large transport aircraft.

For years, China maintained smaller buildings before beginning the massive increase in construction. By preserving these initially isolated buildings, China can claim that it is merely expanding its earlier facilities.

Two of the largest island-building projects were completed in recent months. Satellite images depict the likelihood of China building additional airstrips on the long, straight sections of Mischief Reef and Subi Reef. When completed, that would give China three airstrips in the region.

*   *   *   *   *   *

US-China Economic and Security Review Commission
12 April, 2016

In the two years prior to October 2015, China has constructed close to 3,000 acres of artificial islands. These islets were built on seven coral reefs and now occupy territory in the Spratly Islands that is located in the southern part of the South China Sea.

...Moreover, China's island building activities may have violated international law. The World Court in The Hague is currently hearing a case presented by the Philippines at the Permanent Court of Arbitration regarding China's claims and activities in the South China Sea.

* * * * * *

Hong Kong (*CNN*) 12 July, 2016 — The World Court in The Hague today ruled on a maritime dispute between the Philippines and China. The international tribunal concluded that China doesn't have a legal basis to claim historical rights to the bulk of the South China Sea.

Chinese President Hao Chenxu immediately sent a statement rejecting the decision by the Permanent Court of Arbitration. This action is likely to have long-lasting ramification for the hot spot, which sees nearly $3.7 trillion of shipborne trade pass through its waters. Recent calculations range from 20% to 33% of all global trade.

"China will never accept any claim or action based on this decision," Hao said. It should be noted that China boycotted the proceedings.

The tribunal concluded that China doesn't have any territorial rights to their claims, which includes the island chains of the Spratly Islands and the Paracel Islands.

China's Ambassador to the United States accused the tribunal of "professional incompetence" and "questionable integrity." He also accused the United States of engaging in military exercises that constituted "military coercion."

A State Department spokesman responded to the Chinese claims by stating that the United States, and the world, expect China's commitment to nonmilitarization of the islands. "The world is watching to see if China is really the global and responsible power it professes itself to be."

The tribunal also deemed that China's man-made islands in the Spratly Islands were illegal and did not constitute islands, but were instead rocks or low-tide elevations. Territorial waters could not be applied to natural formations such as reefs that were artificially expanded.

Rulings in The Hague are regarded as legally binding. However, there is no current mechanism to enforce it.

*   *   *   *   *   *

NEAR MISCHIEF REEF, South China Sea (*NY Times***) 20 Sept, 2018** — As the United States Navy P-8 Poseidon flew near Mischief Reef in the South China Sea, the radio crackled with a Chinese warning.

"US military aircraft," an English voice blared over the speaker. "You have violated China sovereignty and infringed on our security and our rights. You will immediately depart and remain outside of Chinese territorial airspace."

Aboard maritime reconnaissance aircraft, flying in what is widely considered to be international airspace, personnel captured video showing the dramatic changes of Mischief Reef.

Until five years ago, only tropical fish and turtles populated the underwater atoll. Now Mischief Reef has been transformed into a Chinese military base, complete with radar facilities, surface-to-air missiles, and an airstrip long enough for fighter and transport aircraft. Six other shoals nearby have undergone similar transformations due to Chinese dredging.

The aggressive territorial claims and the militarization of these islands have put neighboring countries and the United States on the defensive…

In congressional testimony, Admiral Brian Durant, Chief of Naval Operations, issued a stark warning about China's power play in a sea through which roughly one-third of global maritime trade flows.

"China is now capable of controlling the South China Sea short of war with the United States," Admiral Durant said. This statement caused some consternation in the Pentagon.

Meeting with Defense Secretary Aaron MacCulloch, Chinese president Hao vowed that China "cannot lose even one inch of the territory" in the South China Sea. This came even though an international tribunal at The Hague dismissed China's territorial claims to the waterway.

The reality is that neighboring governments lack the firepower to challenge China. The United States has long fashioned itself as a keeper of peace in the Western Pacific.

"As China's military power grows relative to the United States, and it will, questions will also grow regarding America's ability to deter Beijing's use of force in settling its unresolved territorial issues," said Admiral Durant.

There always exists the fact that an encounter in the South China Sea could set off an international incident, bringing China and the United States into a confrontation. The busy waterway hosts a shifting array of variables. There are hundreds of disputed shoals, thousands of fishing boats, shipping vessels, and the warships of various nations. Of late, that collection now includes an increasing array of Chinese fortresses.

in 2012, the Philippines were forced off

Scarborough Shoal, a reef just 120 nautical miles from the main Philippine island of Luzon, by the Chinese Coast Guard. A similar incident in 1995 allowed the Chinese to plant their flag on Mischief Reef, another location well within what international maritime law considers a zone where the Philippines has sovereign rights.

Where will the Chinese strike next?

To date, major confrontations have been avoided, but there's always the risk that a relatively minor incident in the remote waters will escalate into something much larger, either through miscommunication or a mishandling of a situation. The region is a dangerous place and not just a pile of rocks that can be ignored.

"United States aircraft, Leave immediately!"

The challenges issued by the Chinese kept coming over the speaker. Chinese radio operators queried the P-8A Poseidon eight times. Twice, the Chinese accused the American military aircraft of violating its sovereignty.

A spokesman for the United States Pacific Command said that challenges issued to the aircraft were becoming routine as military aircraft and naval vessels conducted Freedom of Navigation operations in the South China Sea.

"What they want is for us to leave, and then they can say that we left because this is their sovereign territory," he said. "It's kind of their way to try to legitimize their claims, but we are clear that we are operating in international airspace and are not doing anything different from what we've done for decades."

Three years ago, President Hao visited the White

House and promised that "China has no intention to militarize" the Spratly Islands, a collection of disputed reefs in the South China Sea.

However, since then, Chinese vessels have dredged mountains of sand onto Mischief Reef and six other Chinese-controlled features in the Spratly Islands, adding at least 3,200 acres of new land in the area.

Footage has showed the length of China's construction on the islands. On Subi Reef, a construction crane is positioned next to a shelter designed for surface-to-air missiles. In addition, there are barracks, bunkers and open hangars. At least 70 vessels, some of them warships, surround the island.

On Fiery Cross Reef, giant radar domes protrude like giant golf balls across the northern end of the reef. A military-grade runway spans the length of the island as army vehicles cross the completed tarmac. The entire island bristles with antennas.

It's impressive to see the Chinese building, given that this is the middle of the South China Sea and far away from anywhere, but the imagery shows that the Chinese claim that the islands are not militarized is clearly not the case. The military equipment is in the open for anyone to see.

American military officials have stated that China deployed anti-ship and antiaircraft missiles on three of the islands: Mischief Reef, Subi Reef, And Fiery Cross. A recent report issued by the Pentagon mentioned that with Chinese forward operating bases constructed on the artificial islands in the South China Sea, the People's Liberation Army was expanding its capability to strike at the U.S. and allied forces and military bases in the Western Pacific.

Beijing responded by claiming that it is the United States that is militarizing the South China Sea by sending surveillance flights over Chinese islands and American warships into Chinese territorial waters.

"Certain people in the US are staging a farce" said Liu Xiang, the Chinese Foreign Minister. "It is self-evident to a keener eye who is militarizing the South China Sea."

It should be noted that an international tribunal dismissed Beijing's claim, deciding that China has no historical rights to the South China Sea. The case was brought by the Philippines after Scarborough Shoal was commandeered by China.

The landmark ruling, however, has had no practical effect. One part is because there is not currently any means to enforce the rulings. But Andres Ramos, who became president of the Philippines less than a month before the tribunal reached its decision, chose not to press the matter with Beijing. He declared China his new best friend and dismissed the United States as a has-been power.

* * * * * *

The South China Sea is home to many scattered island groups, some of them mere reefs or shoals. Several nations — Taiwan, Vietnam, China, the Philippines, and Malaysia — all lay claim to some or all of the disputed chains, none of which have been rectified in the World Court. However, these nations claim the rights to resources and name these as territorial waters.

Beginning in 2013 and proceeding through 2015, China began expanding seven locations in the Spratly Islands (located in the southern entrances to the South China Sea) and twenty sites in the Paracel Islands off the coast of Vietnam. Over a period of two years, they dredged sand from the sea floor and deposited it on the shoals to create actual islands. There, they built small buildings in an attempt to establish territorial rights to the newly created land masses.

In 2013, they expanded these islands and structures, further enhancing their claims to the territories and developing exclusive economic zones. In 2016, the World Court in the Hague ruled that China could not claim territorial or economic zone rights to these manufactured islands because an artificial island did not meet the required definition of an island. For any rights to be established, an island needed to be a naturally occurring phenomenon.

China rejected this ruling and continued building facilities on the islands, eventually creating military bases with runways capable of landing any aircraft on four islands in the Spratlys. In addition, they installed anti-air and anti-ship missile batteries as well as lagoons and docks for naval ships.

The addition of naval and air bases in the Spratlys effectively seals the southern entrances to the South China Sea and places Chinese forces within striking distance of the Philippines.

In response to these Chinese expansions, the United States regularly conducts "freedom of navigation" passages with its naval ships and aircraft, bringing about heated Chinese reactions. This region is volatile, and every small incident has the potential to turn into a larger engagement.

Spratly Islands and the South China Sea

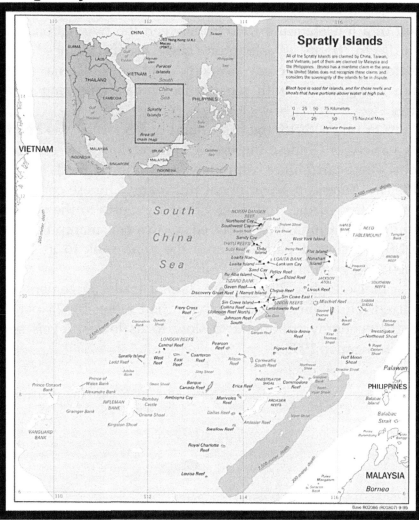

US-Chinese Trade War and Agreement

The trade war between the United States and China is the result of a longstanding friction between the two nations with regards to trade. Washington cites unfair Chinese trade practices and intellectual property violations. China asserts unfair US practices with regards to China's emerging nation status.

On July 6, 2018, the first round of US tariffs was applied on a variety of Chinese imports. China retaliated on American goods. These tariff hikes continued on additional goods through 2018. The American government put many Chinese companies on a ban list, further reducing China's exports to the country. Additionally, China was declared a currency manipulator by the US Treasury department, and the yuan sank to its lowest value in eleven years.

In December 2019, Phase 1 of a trade agreement was finalized. However, Chinese exports had fallen by 25 percent and the economy continued to slow to its lowest levels since records began in 1993.

Chapter One

Beijing, China
21 July, 2019

The click of booted heels reverberated down the enormous corridor. The large oil-brushed paintings portraying heroes of the revolution and various other battlefields along one wall and the heavy drapes hanging like red and gold waterfalls of cloth on the other were not enough to absorb the sounds. Sunlight streamed through tall, narrow windows, dappling the floor in alternating stripes of light and shadow, fading into each other. Motes of dust were stirred by the man's passage through the bands of light, reforming into their lazy dances once the air currents were stilled again.

Antique vases perched on pedestals kept him company as he continued his march. They were reminders of China's rich heritage and its timeless empire. Monarchs and governments had come and gone, but the empire always remained—and always would, even through the difficult times they were currently experiencing. China wasn't going broke, but their goal of becoming *the* world's greatest economic power seemed to be slipping from their grasp.

The ornate ceiling looming twenty-five feet overhead and the wide hallways always made Hao feel small. Walking along this hallway for the past ten years hadn't negated the intensity of this feeling, even as he rose in power. As China's paramount leader, Hao Chenxu shouldn't experience smallness in any room, but he could never shake that feeling as he walked to the conference room where the Standing Committee meets. He felt like he was in some underwater cathedral venturing into a lair of giant sea snakes.

The building had a way of making one feel isolated, and he had to keep reminding himself that nearly 1.35 billion Chinese people lived on the other side of those windows—he was responsible for nearly 20 percent of the world's population.

The polished teakwood doors at the end of the hallway

grew larger as Paramount Leader Hao walked through light and shadow. Soldiers posted to either side of the doors snapped to attention, one reaching for a door handle to allow Hao entrance. A man of his level usually ignored soldiers of such low rank, never making eye contact or acknowledging their presence.

Hao caught the soldier's eye and gave him a brief nod. The reaction lasted just a millisecond, the man's eyes widening before he regained his composure. Hao knew that the action would ripple outward, whispers voiced in corners during illegal dice or card games. That ripple would spread and grow, the story becoming grander with each telling. By the time it reached several rings outward, the ripple would become a crashing wave extolling that the paramount leader was one of them. That nod would be worth the undying loyalty of a division's worth of men and women.

His position was assured, but even that security always seemed fragile enough that it could break at any moment. Members were constantly jockeying for increased power, and some compromises had to be made to keep the Politburo happy. If Hao had learned anything in his years of maneuvering, it was that nothing was so stable that it couldn't come tumbling down. It was a balancing act of exhibiting force and placating, and it required knowing which one to use in a given situation.

The door swung open and Hao felt, as he always did, like he was pulled into the room more than he was entering it. Each time, it seemed as if the conference room yawned open, suddenly coming to life and inhaling to sweep him inside. The clicking of his heels came to an abrupt stop as he crossed the threshold and stepped onto the plush dark red and gold carpet.

Men seated around the polished teakwood table rose as Hao entered, the shuffling of chairs and feet adding to the feeling of the room coming alive. As happened every time, Hao found his gaze straying to a mural that encompassed one wall. Depicted there was a lone farmer, steadfastly plowing his field behind his trusty water buffalo. Nearby the aging man, a gentle stream wandered lazily through a valley with a backdrop of snow-covered peaks rising majestically.

It presented a scene of peace, of simpler times. The farmer wasn't enmeshed in politics, didn't care about territorial disputes. He worked hard, languished on the bank, and dipped his toes in the cool water when he became too warm. At the end of a day toiling in the fields, he retired to his home to enjoy a hearty meal. The mural told a rich story, and Hao found himself inwardly sighing each time he entered the room, envious of the man and his peace and the serenity of the valley.

But that life of peace wasn't meant for Hao. He had made a different decision early on, one that had swept him onto his current course and into this room.

"Thank you for waiting," Hao said, nodding to each of the other members and continuing to his own chair.

The creak of worn leather squelched through the room as the elder statesmen took their seats. Hao pulled his chair out and sank into the plush comfort at the head of the table. Moving the folders that had been placed on the table to his front, Hao couldn't possibly understand what all the old teak table had witnessed. It had seen many older men sitting around it, all driving the course of a nation toward prosperity. It had heard plots that would shock a world's populace, heard decisions that had made many shake their heads. It had witnessed much and would witness more, this day being no better or worse than the many before.

With another nod, the financial minister cleared his throat and opened a series of folders. Hao knew they were here to discuss in what direction to proceed with the trade war between China and the United States. Although there were additional pressing issues that required discussion in the near future, this was the issue at hand, their highest priority.

"… so, as you can see, the tariffs imposed by the United States are hurting our economy more than we're publishing. We have lost approximately 18 percent of our exports in terms of gross revenue, and our economy has slowed. We're beginning to see the largest slump in growth since 1993, and our forecasts are even more dire. We can expect up to a 28 percent loss in exports and a growth percentage that may dip under 6 percent."

"You can't paint the picture of slowed economic growth in the same brush stroke with the US tariffs. Our economy has been on a downward trend for a number of years. Yes," Hao stated, raising a hand to forestall the finance minister's interjection, "the trade war has perhaps accelerated that downward trend, but we can't pretend that it hasn't been here for a while now. That is what needs fixing. Fix that, and we fix the problem with the shrinking exports."

The finance minister blanched at the implied threat. When the economy was robust, his position of power was nearly insurmountable. But when the treasury dollars and reserves began diminishing, then it was his head thrust out for the chopping block. Even in light of China's growth and increased financial influence throughout the world, his position ebbed and flowed with the economy. He also knew that Hao occasionally purged his cabinet members to consolidate power so as to remain unchallenged, and if matters continued on their current path, a scapegoat would be required. He suddenly viewed the others around the table as hyenas waiting to pounce on his corpse before it even cooled.

What wasn't being said, at least not yet lest the utterance bring it to reality, was that the Chinese stock market was heading toward a full recession. The early morning trading had demonstrated a 16 percent decrease. Sure, it had rebounded by the early afternoon, but the signs were all there. The 2015 recession had driven a 19 percent loss across the board that they were still attempting to recover from. Another recession might well drive back China's emerging status as a world economic power.

Hao looked down the length of the table, catching each man's eye. One, sitting at the other end of the table, was not an active member of the Standing Committee, making Hao wonder why he was here. And perhaps more importantly, who had invited the man without Hao's permission? With the economy on the downturn, Hao envisioned a rival emerging from within the cabinet. So far, he had managed to quash any threat to his leadership, but that required a constant vigilance that slowly consumed him from within. One of these days, he'd miss a sign, and then greater compromises would have to be made in order to remain in power. At some point, those would become impossible to uphold and he'd be out.

The stranger sitting at the table had wiry hair that seemed to defy physics, the strands standing up in every direction. The round wire spectacles caught the light when he glanced up from his papers, which he appeared more interested in than the current discussion. Hao figured the man had to be a member of the science ministry, and wondered why he was here. Everyone else in the room pointedly ignored the individual, and for a long moment, Hao wondered if he wasn't a ghost of some past meeting.

Refocusing, Hao continued, "How are the trade talks with the Americans?"

The finance minister, Lei Han, paled even more, his eyes glancing to the side and his cheek twitching.

"Not very well, I'm afraid. We'll reach an agreement, most likely by the end of the year, but it won't be as favorable as we hoped. There are several points on which they aren't budging and won't, just as there are points we won't move from. I think we can expect our exports to drop by 20 percent overall, a number that will be difficult to overcome in the short term."

"So, you're saying we can just expect another recession and should be okay with that?!" Hao asked, glaring at Lei.

Hao wondered if this was the right time to replace the minister. It wasn't that long ago that Lei had wielded considerable power in this room and had hinted that compromises needed to come from Hao. However, he was still somehow attached closely to the foreign affairs minister, Liu Xiang, who still held considerable clout. Removing him could bring a confrontation hovering at the edges into the light, and Hao wasn't ready to face that yet. For one, the military alliance seemed to be distancing themselves, and he needed to bring them onto his side first.

"Well, um, of course not," replied Lei. "But there will be little we can do from an economic standpoint that will alter the trends we're seeing. The margins on manufactured goods are already low. We have already attempted to disrupt the other market economies but were labeled 'currency manipulators' and had to pull back our efforts along those lines."

"Well, we need to find other means to disrupt their economies, then—don't we? If we could send other stock markets into decline globally while ours remains relatively stable, then other nations will have no choice but to trade with us. That will drive up our exports and restore our economic growth. That's what this meeting is about: determining a course of action that will drive the world's nations to buy from us," Hao said, his stern tone menacing.

"Perhaps I could help with that," the foreign affairs minister offered. "Allow me to introduce Yao Fan."

All eyes turned to the bespectacled man who seemed oblivious to the attention suddenly directed his way. Hao's stomach knotted; he felt like he had just plunged headlong into a trap.

"Yao, if you please," Liu said, his voice rising.

The scientist appeared to come out of a trance and noticed all eyes boring into him, singling him out and making it seem as if he were suddenly separated from the group.

"What?...Oh yes, here we are. Um, we are working on a mutated version of the original SARS virus and are quite close to having a stable working solution figured out," the man stated, his eyes roving to the paper he was holding. "You see, the trick is in the stable configuration of the–"

"I don't think we need those details, doctor, thank you," Liu interjected.

"SARS virus? We're here about economic matters, not some awful creation manufactured in an underground lab," Lei complained.

Hao kept his peace, letting his ministers argue, purposefully remaining out of the conversation. He knew his questions would be asked by others, which would make him appear to be both in control and knowledgeable about the discussion.

"You have your nose too deep inside your books and numbers to understand, minister. This conversation is about taking care of our economic concerns. Allow me to explain," Lei replied, looking toward Hao.

Hao nodded for the man to continue, unable to shake the feeling that the finance and foreign affairs ministers had orchestrated this change in direction. Although the tone did imply that Lei was frustrated by Liu, Hao would have to look into this further at a later point.

"We need to disrupt the foreign markets and economies, and there are many ways to accomplish that goal. We can create the conditions whereby we can manipulate the strength of the dollar, but what we've attempted so far can only be viewed as a failure. In a similar move, we can work to lower the economic values of the foreign markets. That is a lengthy process, and usually a short-lived outcome."

The foreign affairs minister leaned forward, warming to his subject.

"Now, we can also interfere with the manufacturing process, sometimes through hacking. But what we really need is to hit their labor force, eliminate a greater number of them for a long period of time, driving their stock markets into decline while holding ours stable."

Hao watched recognition dawn in the eyes of the men around the table—the potential impact of a contagious virus hitting foreign labor forces. This would require purposely spreading a virus throughout the world while hiding the fact that it was of Chinese manufacture, perhaps that it was yet another accidental result of the live marketplaces scattered throughout the nation. The trick would disguise the fact that the virus was manmade.

"Minister Lei, can we brace the stock market for a period of time? Should we decide on this course of action, we will need to look strong," Hao responded.

The finance minister mentally sighed with relief as the

danger of his removal passed. "We can for perhaps six to eight months, but without significant changes, it will fall regardless of what we do."

"Unless we are able to substantially increase our exports, in effect replacing the losses brought by the American tariffs," Hao summarized.

Lei nodded. "Yes, unless we can strengthen our economy."

"Tell me more about this virus," Hao requested, turning his attention back toward the scientist.

"Ah yes, well, you see, it's quite a nasty little bugger — not so much the mortality rate, which is quite a bit lower than the original, but in the long-run, you see, it infiltrates the body and infects a variety of organs, most predominantly the lungs. The most common ailment is pneumonia, with digestive issues a close second. The symptoms can last a month or longer, and here's the big breakthrough: a host can be contagious while being asymptomatic," the wiry-haired man said in a low, conspiratorial tone. "Asymptomatic means–"

"I'm aware of what the word means," Hao interjected.

"Oh, well, yes — so the contagion will spread without anyone being the wiser. And with an incubation period of up to fourteen days, the virus will spread across a larger area before anyone is aware…at least for the initial exposures."

Yao's voice grew quieter as he begins to voice something seldom said, even in his lab.

"As far as long-term ramifications, the virus will leave scarring in the affected organs, and the hosts have a tendency to develop neurological issues, twitching muscles, muscle decay, sensory degradation, and the like. It mutates quickly, and there are no antibodies that last more than a few months, so reinfection becomes a probability, and developing a vaccine will be difficult at best."

"Like the seasonal flu?" Liu questioned.

"Um, yes, but it could be that it's an all-year-long infestation at first. Some of the mutations can become quite nasty, but those require very special and rare circumstances."

"So, what could we be looking at a year down the road? Two years?" Hao queried.

"Well," the man said, pushing his glasses further up his nose, "that all depends on how the virus is dispensed and the initial range. But, some of the models we've run estimate a 65 percent infection rate."

"Sixty-five percent of the world's population?" Lei exclaimed, his brain crunching through the numbers. "You're talking nearly five billion infected. What's the mortality rate?"

"We had to tone down the mortality rate in order to increase the infection rate and stability, but we're looking at around 2 to 3 percent."

"One hundred and fifty million dead?" Lei said, whistling.

"And is this virus ready?" asked Hao.

"Oh, my goodness no. We still have a year of work ahead–"

"You have three months," Hao stipulated.

The man looked at the president as if he hadn't heard him right, but wilted under the stare boring into his soul. That look spoke of ill tidings should the virologist say the wrong thing. He gulped and shuffled his papers.

"Sure, sure…we'll have to take some shortcuts and forgo extensive testing, but I should have something viable in that timeframe."

"Very well," Hao said, turning to speak to the foreign affairs minister. ""I'm assuming you already have a plan in mind or you wouldn't have brought it to the attention of this table."

"I do."

"I hope this plan takes into account that we will recover quickly from the spread of the virus and have our industry ready to respond," Hao said, his tone conveying a warning.

Lui nodded, knowing that China had to suffer as the rest of the world did, but perhaps not to the same degree. There would need to be controls in place to ensure that the viral spread was contained within certain regions. For a brief moment, Lui pondered what this kind of containment might look like and how it would be achieved. Although he had ideas that had been discussed, he banished any further thought along those lines. That was to be for others to decide. He vaguely pondered where those that gave the orders for containment would lose any sleep over their decisions.

As the meeting continued, a plan slowly developed that would hopefully catapult China into the leading global economic power. The virus, an engineered form of the SARS virus, would be less deadly but more contagious than its predecessors. According to the virologist, it will be an airborne virus, spreading via water droplets that lingered in the air. The main reason the virus wasn't currently ready was the need to hide the genetic markers that would betray its man-made origin.

The market could be supported for six to eight months, long enough to ready the virus and prepare for its dispersal. After that, there would need to be a huge economic infusion in the form of increased exports or an increased valuation of the yuan against the dollar. The final plan would need to be completed by the end of the year, with the initial implementation scheduled for October, 2019. With a slight smile of satisfaction on his lips and a cunning gleam in his eyes, Hao imagined what was to come. Bringing China to become the world's largest economic power might elevate his status near to that of Mao's.

They discussed the steps necessary for the recovery of the Chinese market following its own epidemic, and the steps to achieve world dominion—a place for the continuation of the empire forged so many millennia ago. As the talks went on, Hao kept glancing up to the farmer working his field. The farmer, Hao knew, couldn't make the tough decisions that were necessary to run a world power, couldn't even fathom the depths leaders needed to go to in order for their nations to survive. No, the world where Hao had made his home was far more complex than the farmer's. The man in the field wouldn't be able to comprehend the decisions that Hao and his cabinet were making. And yet, Hao thought, for the briefest of moments, that the farmer, for all of his simplicity, was the stronger person.

*   *   *   *   *   *

Beijing, China
17 October, 2019

The mural of the farmer again caught Hao's attention as he entered the room. However, it didn't linger long in his thoughts as he marched to his chair and sat down without acknowledging the other men present, letting his lack of eye contact inform them he was upset. Perhaps there would be a need for additional warnings or shouting to force the Standing Committee down the path he chose, but it was enough for now that they knew he wasn't pleased.

He grudgingly gave Finance Minister Lei a nod before only partially listening to the older man speak; he had heard the numbers before. There were continued signs of a failing economy looming everywhere.

Perhaps not quite a failing one, but certainly not one that is poised for growth, Hao thought.

Hao always tried to be honest with himself and his reality, thinking of himself as a tough realist. One could not base decisions on illusions or delusions and expect for them to work out as planned.

The economy had been propped up as best as it could be, but the tariffs imposed by the United States, responsible for nearly a 20 percent loss in exports, had hit China hard. They were poised to break out as a major world economic power and had placed resources accordingly—resources that could not easily be diverted. The last thing they needed now was to sink into another depression as they had in 2015. Two coming so close together could set China's economic advances back a decade or more.

The item that lingered in Hao's mind and hovered over every head in the room, like a sword poised to swing—was the delay in getting the virus ready. This would mean pushing back the operation to disperse it across the world, which would have a domino effect of stalling the subsequent recovery. If they didn't get the virus ready soon, then the entire plan would fall apart and there would be nothing to prevent China from sinking into another depression. That couldn't be allowed to happen as the Americans would then be able to negotiate from a stronger position, further stunting China's growth as a world power.

Hao motioned with his hand, cutting off the finance minister's ramblings.

"Enough of this. We know where we stand. Where are we with the virus?" Hao asked, directing the question toward Liu Xiang, his foreign affairs minister. It was he who had suggested the idea in the first place and it was up to him to decide which way the sword would swing, and when.

"I am assured that they are close to having the virus ready. Unfortunately, it will take a little while longer as they keep having problems stabilizing it. I'm told it is rapidly mutating, and it's unknown where those mutations will lead," Minister Liu answered.

Of course, Liu wouldn't mention that they had been told not to expect the virus to be ready until the end of the year. He wasn't suicidal, but everyone understood that it was Hao who had insisted on the target date being moved up.

"Are we assured that the virus can't be determined to have been manmade?" Hao inquired.

"That's what I'm told," Liu replied.

Liu didn't quite squirm while replying. He was too disciplined for a tell like that. However, it wasn't easy to maintain eye contact. He knew that nothing was foolproof, but didn't want to voice his hesitation about believing the scientists. Plus, it might distract from the path of the conversation.

"Very well," Hao nodded. "If scientists had their own way, nothing would ever get made."

Hao's voice rose, perhaps reflecting his frustration at the scientific community, or maybe exhibiting a touch of fear. "Only through insisting on timelines to light a fire under them do they ever make progress. Well, I'm here to tell you that we can't wait for perfection. There is no such thing. We have no choice but to move forward. We will begin operation in December whether the virus has been perfected or not."

The finance minister felt that he had to be the voice of reason in a cabinet that seemed more and more determined to use biological warfare in their quest for dominance. While he is in step with the others with regards to becoming the world power, his hesitance stems from what could happen in the future if this sort of action became commonplace. Where do you draw the line?

"With all respect, paramount leader, I feel it's my duty to say that we may not reap the intended benefits if we don't wait until the virus is ready. I understand the urgency, but someone has to argue against deploying too early," Lei stated, despite Hao's tone.

Hao thought for a moment and then stood. With his hands behind his back, he began walking around the table.

"Gentlemen, I hear your arguments, both voiced and silent. We are placed in the unfortunate position of having to act. If we do not, then our economy may be set back ten years or more. We owe it to our countrymen to keep progressing—we owe it to ourselves. From this point forward, we will not retreat, we will not give another inch," Hao stressed, his voice back in control.

Those in the room knew that their illustrious leader wasn't only referring to the current economic concerns, but also to China's other areas of expansion—all of them.

* * * * * *

Wuhan, China
14 December, 2019

Hu Huize stared at the tiny monitor, the video of the streets and marketplace slipping past the edges. The faces of the shoppers didn't betray any notice of the drone zipping down the narrow roads as it worked its way nearer the open-air markets. Blustery winds swirling around tall apartment buildings made control difficult, and Huize had to wrestle with the drone several times in order to avoid slamming it into concrete walls and panes of glass. Rain showers helped calm the smells of the inner city, but the droplets splashing against the camera made navigating even more difficult.

The background din of car horns, the shuffling of thousands walking the sidewalks, the muffled conversations mixing together to reverberate off the enclosed towers of concrete suddenly grew in volume as the drone exited the enclosed city streets and entered the open market. The waves of sound from the yelling hawkers and haggling marketgoers ebbed and flowed. People gathering fish, monkey meat, and an assortment of other foods were oblivious to the buzzing in the air overhead.

Huize brought the drone lower and adjusted its speed. Even if those below noted the flying object, it would take a very close observation to see how this drone was different than any other hobbyist's toy. Thin aluminum fingers extended to the side as if it were an old crop duster coming in for a pass over a fertile field.

Reaching up, Huize pushed a switch on the controller, relieved to see the small green light activate. Huddled in a doorway in an effort to escape the worst of the wind gusts, his face faintly illuminated in green—the only real color in this world of gray squalls—Huize's finger hovered over a button, not knowing that with a single press, he would change the world.

As a gofer in China's Ministry for State Security, Hu Huize was often assigned tasks without explanation that he knew better than to question. He just did as he was told and proceeded home to his wife and child without another thought about his actions. Curiosity was a good way to end up dead or in prison, and Huize had no intention of following that path. He was paid, the work was stable, and that was enough for him.

There was no desire to work his way up through the chain, as that was a good way to develop enemies. Nope—just be a mouse, don't screw up his missions, and live to be old. That was his goal.

Huize pressed the button, pleased when a second green light illuminated. His task was just about complete. It wouldn't be long before he could get out of the cold and warm up with a bowl of steamed noodles.

Aboard the drone, the signal was received. Valves opened from a small tank slung beneath the body and liquid under pressure began pouring through thin tubes before being forced out of small holes to form a vapor. As the drone motored slowly down one street of the open market, the liquid mixed with the small drops of the misting rain and was slung about on the swirling winds. Several blocks later, the liquid had been disbursed and the lack of pressure caused another signal to be sent.

Huize saw the second green light turn red and he closed the switch. Both lights extinguished and he turned the drone around, retracing the flight back to his position. Landing the drone on the sidewalk next to him, Huize reached down and picked it up, tucking it back into its hard case. For a brief moment, he wondered if he had just videoed the marketplace and why he would be sent to do that, but his defense mechanisms kicked into place and that thought was quickly pushed from his mind.

The blustery winds continued to swirl through the marketplace, leaving behind a trail of contaminated water droplets on stalls, food, and door handles. Shoppers bickering over a few yuan were unaware that each indrawn breath ingested a previously unknown pathogen, taking it home to spread to family members.

Walking back to the ministry building, Huize had no idea what he had unleashed upon the world. Nor would he really find out the true extent of his actions as the flu he caught that day would turn deadly two weeks later. Huize wouldn't realize his dream of a long, easy-going life, living out his later years together with his wife. He wouldn't get the chance to see his child grow up. Both Huize and his wife would be dead and their child orphaned. Huize also wasn't aware that his wasn't the only drone buzzing the open markets on that dreary day.

Two weeks later, the world watched as Wuhan's medical services were swamped with clusters of pneumonia cases that swept through the city.

* * * * * *

Beijing, China
Beijing Capital International Airport
1 January, 2019

A masked Hou Chingming walked down the empty aisles of the Boeing 767. The cleaning crew with him had already finished their task and were waiting on him at the end of the breezeway. As the supervisor, Chingming was responsible for signing off each flight. His signature on the yellowed parchment certified that they had cleaned the aircraft.

Unknown to the airline agents, the passengers eager to escape the frigid winter holding Beijing in its grasp, and pilots studying the route charts, Hou Chingming and his crew were not the usual cleanup people. As a matter of fact, and a detail unknown to Chingming, none of the crews cleaning any of the aircraft were the usual personnel.

Chingming hoisted the spray bottle clenched in his hands. Starting at the back of the aircraft, Chingming sprayed the armrests of every third aisle. The drops glistened as they settled onto seats that would be fought over in a short time, the residue fading as the liquid slowly evaporated. When the flight crew and passengers boarded the international flight in less than an hour, the contaminated droplets would no longer be visible.

Finishing with the aircraft, he gathered the waiting crew. Together, they worked their way to the next aircraft in the international terminal. Like Hu Huize, Hou Chingming never questioned the tasks he was given, knowing that to do so would invite the wrong eyes to turn in his direction. That was how you vanished and more than likely died in a very painful way.

Day after day for a week, Chingming and his crew showed up at the international terminal and cleaned the aircraft, with Chingming giving each one his special treatment after they finished. Unlike Huize, Chingming wondered to himself, what in the hell he had been assigned to do. It didn't take much to put two and two together: he was infecting the aircraft with something that was to be spread throughout the world. With each squirt of the nozzle, he flinched, wondering if the protective gear was enough to keep him from harm. However, he went about his task quietly. To voice any concern was a sure way to disappear.

But he wasn't completely quiet. In the dark hours of the night, he whispered his deep misgivings to his girlfriend. The two talked in the early morning hours, sharing heroic moves each of them would make to alert others to what they believed was occurring. However, when it was time for Chingming to head for the airport and for his girlfriend to go to her hotel job, the heroic words of the night vanished like smoke.

Chingming died alone in a crowded quarantine center. His family would have visited him if they weren't also fighting for their lives behind welded doors. His girlfriend made a single post on Twitter, the many evenings of bedroom talk finally finding action. However, the post was quickly deleted and she disappeared after a knock at her door.

One by one, aircraft pulled out of the international gates and taxied out to runways. Inside, passengers settled in for the long flights back home or on to another leg of a business trip. Water whipped behind the airplanes as they turned onto the runway and ran up the engines. Slowly, each aircraft gained speed as it powered down the runway before lumbering into the air. With the gear tucked away, the graceless tube of metal was transformed into a thing of grace, slicing through the moisture-laden air.

Passing through ten thousand feet, the veteran travelers pulled out phones and laptops, each finding their own way to while away the hours to their destination. The viral droplets, manufactured to remain active for days on hard surfaces, became attached to sleeves, to skin, and to the accoutrements of civilization. Across the world, the hosts delivered and spread their stowaway cargo.

All eyes turned to China, where the pneumonia cases turned out to be something more severe than the usual winter illnesses. Several days later, it was revealed that a new virus was responsible for the outbreak in Wuhan. Health officials in China said that they were monitoring the situation to prevent it from turning into something more serious. Again, the world looked to the unfortunate city, unaware that they also had boils festering in their own backyard.

Chapter Two

China extended their timeline for the dispersion of the viral packages prepared at the Wuhan Institute of Virology. The cluster cases originally diagnosed as pneumonia quickly became something much worse—an outbreak of an unknown SARS-CoV virus. The WHO was too quick to rely on the information they received from the Chinese authorities, telling the world that they would soon get the outbreak under control.

Wuhan became the center of attention on the world stage as medical facilities were rapidly overwhelmed. Quarantine centers were established and packed with anyone exhibiting the slightest symptoms. Doors to tenement buildings were welded shut, and several quarantine centers collapsed under the weight of those forced inside with limited supplies and sanitation. Those crushed in the collapsed buildings no longer had to worry about the choking coughs or difficulty breathing; the survivors' strained breathing was no longer due to a viral condition but tons of concrete and rebar.

The world waited with bated breath to see if such drastic containment procedures would be enough to prevent the virus from escaping into their countries. Little did they know that the virus was already happily spreading from one to another. The realization that any measures to prevent the spread of the virus were too little and too late came when the first symptoms began to appear in their own countries.

The virus, now named SARCoV-19, proved to have an initial contagion rate of nearly 5.7. That meant that every person who had the virus infected nearly six others. That was far above any flu virus, and ranked up there with MERS. Those numbers dropped to around 2.2 once the symptoms began to appear in each country and varying preventative measures were put into place.

True to its intent, the world's economies were thrown into turmoil as the virus spread rampantly. Manufacturing lines couldn't be fully manned, restaurants were closed, distribution methods were hampered. Stock markets dropped sharply and continued to bounce as various measures were implemented to bolster the flagging economic indicators.

As the world turned their attention to their own nations' survival, they didn't seem to notice that Wuhan and the vicinity were the only parts of China that had been affected. The virus hadn't spread to Beijing or any other large cities. The lockdown of Wuhan and the draconian measures put into place prior to the dispersal of the virus had succeeded in saving most of China, just as planned.

However, China's economy continued to decline as nations curtailed their imports, using funds and other measures to shore up their markets. Even though Phase 1 of a trade agreement with the United States was signed in December of 2019, there wasn't enough time for any truly measurable results benefiting the Chinese economy to be realized.

* * * * * *

The creak of leather was abnormally loud in the conference room as Hao Chenxu settled in, alone in the room with just the image of the farmer for company. The room with its dark paneling and thick drapes weighed heavily on the decisions made within its confines. President Hao stared at the farmer as if an answer to his difficulties would come from the wizened mouth.

The Chinese leader had read the reports coming out of Wuhan. Although he knew the city would be heavily struck by the virus, he hadn't envisioned just how hard. Heavy equipment dug trenches for the mass burials; the crematoriums worked day and night in attempts to keep up with the dead piling up in the city. And all of that came at his utterance.

The weight and guilt of his decisions came at him when he had moments to himself. And the plan seemed to be coming apart at the seams. The focus was on Wuhan rather than being directed away. If it became much worse, he would have to evict all of the news media and go dark. While that would draw additional attention, it would be short-lived. No, part of his worry came from the reports being leaked by his own doctors. Several had "succumbed" to the virus, but he couldn't afford to have many more leaks, or the plan he had set in motion would come tumbling down around his ears.

No words of wisdom came from the farmer, no solutions to Hao's problems. For a moment, Hao wondered if he had allowed evil to surface in his eagerness to push China to the forefront. He had unleashed a terrible contagion upon the world, one that might now forever become a part of it, as his scientists were now beginning to tell him.

President Hao sat in his chair in the empty room, thoughts racing through his mind. Should he have waited to achieve his aims through normal channels? Did his impatience threaten the livelihood of his wife...of his son? What of the thousands already dead? Should he announce to the world what had happened in a drive to stop what he had initiated?

Coming out of a trance-like state, the weight of his actions heavy on his shoulders, Hao shook his head. He sought to push off the demons that seemed to crowd his head during silent moments.

Now is not the time to falter, Hao thought.

Pushing himself out of the chair, the Chinese leader walked across to the mural.

"You wouldn't understand the decisions that must be made in order for your life to be as it is," Hao said, addressing the farmer.

With that, he turned on his heels and strolled out of the room. A moment later, the sound of his heels clicking on the polished floor echoed in the wide passageway.

* * * * * *

China's economic recovery bleak

17 April

Beijing (BBC)—For the first time in decades, China has experienced a year-on-year economic contraction. The second-leading economic power saw its GDP shrink by 6.8% in the first three months of this year.

China has announced that the community lockdowns has created unavoidable and significant pain on their economy. And economists are predicting that conditions will worsen before getting better. According to the World Bank, the best-case scenario for China will be a growth to 2%, down from 6% last year. If conditions continue to deteriorate, then that growth could fall to 0.1%. 20% of China's economy is comprised of exports. With most of Europe—its biggest customers—also experiencing lockdowns and decreasing consumerism, there isn't much optimism of seeing increase in global demand.

Varying reports say that foreign demand will slump this quarter as SARCoV-19 weighs on economic activity outside China.

Inside of China, there isn't any use in hoping that Chinese consumers will shore up China's economic woes and the global economy. The lack of demand due to the global pandemic is holding back China's hope of a recovery in the near future. With economies across the globe suffering and on the verge of collapse, the worst is yet to come for China's exports.

China has received short-term loans to corporations from the central bank, in addition to seeing lower interest rates. But more help is required to give these companies a lifeline.

China has spent nearly $600 billion on stimulus packages to bolster their flagging economy, a move that has assisted the global economic engine. However, that places China with a large debt risk in their system, something which they simply cannot afford right now.

Banking on China to pull out of their worst economic downturn in generations is not realistic, and the methods China is using to stimulate their recovery is risky.

* * * * * *

China's economic woes

21 May, 2020
Beijing (*BBC***) —**
For the first time since China began publishing goals in 1990, they have announced that it would not be setting a target for economic growth. This move is unprecedented and abandoning a targeted growth is an acknowledgement of the difficulties facing China.

Sales have continued to slow and are nowhere close to where they need to be for China's economy to be running on all cylinders. Worried about future waves of infection due to the global pandemic, consumers are holding onto their disposable incomes and aren't spending as much in the marketplace as they used to.

Beijing can't be sure of how deep this crisis will go or how long they will be able to bolster their economy with stimulus injections. It's then not a surprise that they have chosen to abandon any idea of growth targets.

In the past, China has always given a growth target to show how well they are doing, but this year, there isn't any way to get away from the fact that China is facing a tremendous challenge with their economy.

This year is different than other downturns. The

rest of the world's economies are also in a downturn, so there is no consumer demand and foreign trade has fallen off. The trade war with the United States put a hardship on the economy, but now that has been compounded by the viral pandemic.

For the past decades, China's government has had a simple contract with its citizens: we'll keep the quality of life improving and you fall in line so that we can keep China on the right path. In the past, they've been able to fulfill that promise, but with these recent downturns, that contract is in jeopardy.

This social contract has drawn the nation together in order to obtain China's grand plan—that China would eliminate absolute poverty and raising the standard of living for millions of people. Now, the viral pandemic is threatening to put that social contract at risk.

It could be argued that this economic crisis is more than just a health crisis for China, but is a major threat to the country's social stability. The younger generations may not be guaranteed the same degree of successes that their parents have experienced. In order to keep the current Chinese government's legitimacy, they will need to keep the contract of wealth, employment, and stability. China needs their economy to recover and not announcing a growth target gives them more flexibility to work out a plan.

* * * * * *

Oval Office
Washington, DC
12 February, 2020

With a heavy creak of leather, Frank Winslow settled into the plush chair. Outside, winter winds gusted against the windows and rattled the side door. The steely grey clouds whipping past the gardens had brought with them the promise of the forecasted sleet, subduing the usual green of the lawn, bushes, and trees.

Picking up several folders on the table in front of him, Frank leaned back with a heavy sigh. The SARCoV virus had crossed the oceans on both coasts and was slowly but surely sweeping across the nation. The stock market was taking a hit due to the fear of the virus and the varying solutions put into place. It wasn't that they were going to stop the pandemic — only slow the spread so that medical services weren't overwhelmed. SARCoV was here and it wasn't leaving anytime soon.

As much as Frank wanted to, there was no way he could enact the same harsh measures the Chinese had put into place. Well, not if he wanted to survive the upcoming election. That was another goal — being elected — and the reason why many of the responses he wanted to make had to be delayed until afterward. Besides, there wasn't any use in a major initiative, especially one that would take a while to implement, only to have it reversed should his party lose. Yet it was also important to look like he was doing something to address the problem.

Looking up and around to the others gathered in chairs and sitting on the couches, Frank thought about the perceived power residing in the room. The room itself held a power, but it was just a room. What gave it power was the universal perception that it was indeed the seat of power. It was the same with the men in the room, including himself. He was just a human like everyone else in the world. He was born, grew up, and would eventually die. But as leader of the free world, he was given an authority that few had held.

As he pondered the nature of power, he thought also of the term "free world": a misnomer. Very few people in the world were actually free. Sure, those on the North American continent and Europe were freer than most, but they still carried so many obligations. They had taxes and bills, worried over their children's educations, and had so many stresses placed upon the family that the term "free" came with an asterisk. The men in the room had obligations and worries too, but none of the same as the people they led. Not one of them had to worry about money, and their children would be accepted into any university or college without a blink. Their stresses centered around policy considerations and diplomatic maneuverings.

"Okay, gentlemen, where shall we start?" Frank asked, holding several folders in each hand.

"Mr. President, if I may," General Williams answered, "I had Colonel Hayward from the USAMRIID fly in this morning; she's waiting in the lobby."

"Well, this sounds like it should be interesting. By all means, Mike, show her in," Frank responded.

General Williams, the top Air Force general and chairman of the Joint Chiefs of Staff, rose and strode toward the doors leading to the lobby.

"If you'll remember, sir, we had some hint that the SARCoV virus may have been manufactured. Colonel Williams has an update on that information."

Frank held up the folders in his hands with a questioning look on his face.

"It's the blue one, sir," General Williams answered.

"Blue it is, then."

General Williams cracked the door and poked his head through, his words lost as he spoke to someone outside. A woman with her hair tied up in a bun, nary a strand out of place, stepped into the room.

"Sir," she acknowledged the General and then President Winslow as she strode into the room.

General Williams resumed his seat, leaving Colonel Hayward standing at the open end of the couches.

"Sara, why don't you tell the rest of us the information regarding SARCoV that you briefed yesterday," General Williams said.

Colonel Hayward cleared her throat and opened the

folder she was carrying.

"Hang on a second, Colonel," President Winslow interjected. "Why don't you have a seat before you start your brief."

"Thank you, sir, but I'll be fine. I've actually been sitting for most of the day already," Sara replied, knowing full well the reputation the president had for making all members of the armed services comfortable in his presence. This was no different than the first day she had met the man, when he insisted on sharing his limo for a ride from Andrews Air Force Base to the Pentagon.

"Very well, what do you have for us?"

"Sir, as you will recall, we had some reservations about the SARCoV-19 virus deriving from the open-air live markets scattered throughout Wuhan. So, we took it on ourselves to test the virus separately from the CDC and WHO.

"SARCoV-19 shares 96 percent of the genetic sequences of other coronaviruses coming from bats, and initial assumptions were that we were looking at a new mutation of SARS. However, a couple of sequences caught our attention, but they were very difficult to locate. Our analysis indicates that these sequences were spliced in, thus giving this SARCoV virus its unique qualities," Colonel Hayward briefed.

President Winslow held up a hand, forestalling anything further from the Colonel in charge of the USAMRIID office.

"Are you saying that the virus is manmade?" President Winslow inquired.

"I am, sir. It was difficult to find the markers, but I'd stake my career and reputation on the fact that SARCoV-19 is a manufactured virus. I won't head down the path as to the why's or what-for's, but I believe the nature of the virus answers those questions for themselves."

The colonel hesitated, nearly adding onto what she was saying, but choosing instead to keep it to herself.

"Feel free to share anything you have, Colonel," Frank said.

"Well, sir, I was just going to add that it appears that

whoever made this virus either made some mistakes or was pushed into its early release."

"And what makes you say that, Colonel?" Frank asked.

"It's just that the virus was built almost perfectly, but then there are parts, or sequences, that, well, are sloppy. If I were to hazard a guess, and that's what I'm paid to do, I would say that corners were cut with SARCoV-19. For one, it mutates quickly. We already have over sixteen different mutations, and there will be more. If I were to put out a virus like we're seeing, I would make sure it was stable enough to predict where it was going to end up. This virus does not have that quality."

"Could that be to cover up its manmade quality? If it were too perfect, would that also indicate that a virus was manufactured?"

"While that may be true, sir, this virus mutates too rapidly. I can't see any carefully planned scientific endeavor releasing this virus in its current state. I can only say that it appears the virus was rushed. The other thing of note is that they could have easily hidden the last few genetic markers that show its manufactured nature. The only thing they would have needed was time, and it appears to me that's the exact thing they didn't have," Colonel Hayward iterated. "I will add, sir, that there is one additional aspect to SARCoV-19 that demonstrates its manmade quality. The virus has hooks that allows it to attach more readily to tissue. That wasn't observed in any other coronaviruses, and it makes the virus more contagious."

"Colonel, are you able to prove this beyond a shadow of doubt?" Frank asked.

"We're not at a hundred percent as yet, but we'll arrive at a definitive answer one way or the other," Colonel Hayward answered.

"When do you think you'll have that information?"

"That's tough to say, sir. If I was forced to, I'd say by the end of the year."

"If you knew before then, let's say late October, that would be ideal."

Colonel Hayward nodded. "I'll do what I can, sir."

"That's all one can ask," Frank commented.

"Colonel, you keep saying 'they.' Do you have any idea who 'they' are?" Bill Reiser questioned.

As head of the NSA, Bill had a reasonably good idea whom they were hinting at, but wanted it voiced out loud. For the past two months, he had been adamant that the Chinese government was responsible for this virus. It wasn't based on anything other than a few vague intercepts his agency had acquired, none of them amounting to much if taken individually. However, Bill's job was to take in seemingly obscure data and present a larger picture. The intercepts he had been briefed on showed that the Chinese were up to something far larger than what the NSA was currently seeing.

"Every manufactured virus has a certain 'signature,' if you will, much like a bomb manufacturer. I have seen this signature once before, and I believe that doctor is currently working for the Wuhan Institute of Virology. Now, keep in mind that we're looking at only a couple of sequences, and those could have been taken from previous works by the doctor in question," Colonel Hayward answered.

"I knew it," Bill breathed.

Eyes around the coffee table strayed toward the NSA director for a brief moment before returning to the colonel standing at the end.

It became apparent that Hayward had completed her briefing and was waiting on questions. Frank was reasonably sure that any questions he'd have were already answered in the blue folder that lay still unopened on his lap. He looked around at the other seated members of this meeting, each giving a small shake of their head to indicate they didn't have any questions.

Frank nodded toward General Wilson, who then addressed the colonel.

"Thank you, Sara. If you wouldn't mind waiting in the lobby in case we have further questions."

"I promise we won't keep you long," Frank added.

Colonel Sara Hayward nodded once to all in the room,

spun on her heels, and strode out of the room, quietly closing the door behind her.

"We're going to need positive proof that it was the Chinese that did this all," Frank said once they were all alone again. "And that it was done on purpose."

"I think she just provided that answer. With the information the colonel and I have provided, there can't be any doubt who did it. I don't need to add the criminal nature of this," Bill replied.

Frank nearly laughed out loud, hearing his NSA director talk about criminal activities. If anyone in the room were to be held accountable for what they'd done in the last three short years, none of them would ever see the light of day. But that was one of the differences between those sitting in this room and those working their nine-to-five jobs.

"We need to be absolutely positive about this before we can even think about disbursing this information," Frank iterated.

"What about an anonymous leak?" Fred Stevenson suggested.

That was in the purview of his State Department, and they had certainly given many a leak to the media. It was their way of letting the other kids on the block know that the United States was onto their games. Many scrambled to cover up their activities in response to the anonymous leaks. Others that had been banging loud on their drums grew quiet.

"I'm okay with that," Frank responded. "But, I want this to be only a one-and-done thing. Let's get it out that the virus looks to be manufactured and let the populace draw their own conclusions. They're already thinking it was China's fault. We can let this start a wave of patriotism and buy American. After all, we were discussing how we can bring back American manufacturing and jobs before this virus hit. That's what the whole trade war with China was about. Let's use this to start a low-grade fervor for American goods."

"We'll need to be able to manufacture those goods before we can start the whole buy American thing," Fred stated.

"And let's start that with guarantees. I want us in talks with Apple, Nike, Google, and Microsoft to bring some of their manufacturing back into the US. At a minimum, let's broach them diversifying to other countries. The last thing we need is for China's economy to prosper. This trade agreement was only a forestalling endeavor to retard their growth. That won't last and we can't afford to drop any further behind in our trade disparities.

"I also want to be in discussion with the pharmaceutical companies to bring the manufacture of medicines back into this country. We grew lazy, and that laziness created this situation. Now is the time to rectify it. Promise them first crack at a vaccine for this SARCoV virus and give them monetary incentives."

Those seated around the coffee table all nodded.

"Again, none of this gets out for now. We'll save what we know for an opportune time. Don't forget, we also have an election to win. Okay, what else do we have on the agenda for today?"

* * * * * *

Apple searches to find new manufacturing outside of China

Apple is considering relocating its supply chains as key manufactures for the company are also considering relocating their production centers outside of China. According to one report, the move is being considered because the SARCoV pandemic is upsetting current supply chains.

Apple partners, Wistron Corp. could move half of its production into other countries within a year, the report stated. Many of Apple's other partners are also talking about reorganizing their supply chains.

The trade war between China and the US became a serious consideration, forcing companies to reconsider where to locate their manufacturing locations. The ramification of the trade war and the viral pandemic demonstrate the risks of relying on a single country to manufacture a product.

Many of Apple's partners have already begun their moves. Some producers have started their expansion into Vietnam, Mexico, and India, with some moving into Taiwan as well.

* * * * * *

Apple, Microsoft, Google looking to move out of China.

March 4, 2020

KEY POINTS

- Apple, Google and Microsoft have looked to move some hardware production from China. Countries currently under consideration include Vietnam and Thailand.

- Assembly of products such as phones could feasibly be moved quickly, experts told CNBC.

The trade war between the US and China and the SARCoV pandemic have forced major American technology firms to look at moving more of their hardware production out of the world's second-largest economy. Reports show that Apple, Google, and Microsoft are moving production of their hardware into Vietnam, Thailand, and other parts of Asia.

Google is set to begin production of an upcoming low-cost smartphone in Vietnam in the coming months. The company has also asked a manufacturing partner in Thailand to prepare production lines. In the meantime, Microsoft is poised to start production of its Surface line of notebooks and desktop PCs in Vietnam.

Both of these companies' hardware has been mainly produced in China, until now. Microsoft declined to comment while Google did not respond to two requests for information when contacted by CNBC. Apple also did not respond to a request for comment when contacted by CNBC.

Chapter Three

By July, the worldwide number of infected had crept over 17 million, with cases spreading exponentially in all nations. Markets fluctuated daily as nations struggled to meet demands. Manufacturing plummeted, with priority given to what were deemed essential supplies. Stores had a difficult time keeping shelves stocked, and many people relied on home deliveries for fear of the virus.

In the turmoil, China attempted to jumpstart their economy to bring themselves out of the forming depression, but the international community was in no position to resume their pre-virus imports. Consumer consumption within China also dropped as people began hoarding their yuan in uncertain times. Large conglomerates continued diversifying their manufacturing, further compounding China's economic woes.

The leaked information regarding the belief/fact that SARCoV-19 was manufactured by the Wuhan facility and unleashed upon the world, whether accidental or not, drove a wave of national furor toward buying American products. Other nations began to find alternate suppliers for their imports. Driven by the promise of federal funding and incentives, pharmaceutical companies began the process of creating their manufacturing plants in Canada, the United States, and Great Britain.

*   *   *   *   *   *

Fiery Cross Reef, Spratly Islands
South China Sea
15 June, 2020

Spray glistened in the morning sun as the Arleigh-Burke-class destroyer carved its way through the deep blue swells of the South China Sea. A warm sun beat down on the decks, the bleached blue skies contrasting sharply with the waters the warship was navigating. Trailing by a few miles, another nearly identical ship followed in the white wake.

Like dogs making sure the sheep don't stray, a pair of different steel-gray warships plowed the seas to the sides. Bows rose and fell as the players danced to a tune they'd heard time and time again, like some strange courtship ritual. Those in the combat information center aboard the USS *Howard* thought this mission would be no different than on other occasions.

"Commander Ingram, we're approaching the twelve-mile line," Lieutenant Commander Jenson stated.

"Copy that, Tom. I'll be right in," Commander Myles Ingram replied.

Hanging up the handset, Lieutenant Commander Jenson turned back to the vertical plot that was the centerpiece of the CIC. On it was depicted the radar plots of other ships and the island the ship was approaching. As part of the continued freedom of navigation sorties the United States Navy had been conducting, the USS *Howard* was tasked with a freedom of navigation pass by the Fiery Cross Reef.

"Captain in the CIC," a voice rang out.

This call was for information only; no one left their post to stand at attention as they might have in the olden days.

LCDR Jenson turned as Commander Ingram joined him in front of the plot.

"Busy sea," Ingram commented after studying the ships plying the same area.

"Aye, sir. We're currently thirteen miles from the shores of Fiery Cross, sailing at ten knots. The *Fitzgerald* is following at five miles. Those riding our flank two miles out are two Type 052D Chinese destroyers: the *Kumming* and the *Hefei*. So far, they seem content to shepherd us," Jenson briefed.

"Thanks, Tom," Commander Ingram said, taking a sip from the thick sludge generously called coffee. "Let's go to general quarters."

"Aye, sir. Sound general quarters," LCDR Jenson called.

Claxons rang throughout the ship, followed shortly by the sound of boots clanging on the decks and scrambling up ladders. More sailors hurried into the CIC and took their stations. Within several seconds, departments began calling in ready.

"Twelve miles out," a voice in the CIC called.

Commander Ingram smiled. He and his crew had conducted several of these patrols and he was adamant on the terminology. When someone had called out that they were crossing the twelve-mile boundary, Myles corrected them: there wasn't a boundary because these waters weren't part of anyone's territory. He felt it was an important distinction. If he didn't correct it, then the arbitrary line the Chinese had drawn in the sea might become real.

"Sir, the *Kumming* just increased speed and is taking an intercept angle."

"Copy that. Maintain course and speed. Let's get the cameras rolling," Ingram ordered.

He watched the plot as the Chinese warship angled away from its compatriot and began to close in on the *Howard*. On one of the large monitors, he was able to see the bow wave arching away from the destroyer. It wasn't easy to watch a dangerously armed warship bearing down on you without targeting it with your own powerful arsenal. However, having played this game numerous times, Commander Ingram knew this was just for show; the Chinese wouldn't do anything but put on an antagonistic display.

"US warship, you have entered the territorial boundaries of the sovereign nation of China. You are ordered to immediately turn around and depart," the radio blared, the broadcast coming from the approaching vessel.

Commander Ingram grabbed a handset and nodded to the radio operator. "This is the USS *Howard*, a United States naval vessel on a peaceful mission sailing in international waters."

Myles handed the phone back. "You know the procedure. Just keep answering the same."

This was the standard ritual: China exhorting over the radio that the United States was illegally entering Chinese waters, and the United States answering that they were legally allowed to be there as they were in international waters.

"Sir, the *Fitzgerald* has closed to three miles."

"Thank you," Commander Ingram answered, gathering the same information from the plot.

The entire sequence was a dance of sorts, the picture constantly changing as the players changed positions. Staring at the plot board, the dance became three-dimensional as Chinese aircraft from the island appeared overhead and began conducting flybys.

"*Kunming* is four hundred yards and still closing; speed twenty-five knots."

Commander Ingram glanced again at the monitor to see the white arcing bow wave spraying outward as the ship closed in. This was usually where the approaching ships veered off and shadowed the offending vessel, occasionally making threatening moves without getting much closer. The Chinese destroyer didn't change course and continued angling toward the *Howard*'s bow.

"Three hundred yards."

"Steady. Maintain course and speed," Commander Ingram ordered.

"Two hundred yards," the same voice called out in a nearly monotone manner.

Commander Ingram could readily see the fine details of the Chinese warship that came into view. The Type 052D destroyer drew abeam of the *Howard* and then began to draw ahead, still proceeding on its current course.

"Fuckers," Myles muttered.

At one hundred and fifty yards, the Chinese warship didn't alter course and seemed hellbent on colliding with the American destroyer. Ingram, along with every man and woman in the CIC, felt a jolt of adrenaline surge through their systems as the gray hull of the *Kunming* crossed dangerously close to the port bow. Lieutenant Commander Jenson could almost hear the grinding metal and feel the jolt of the impending collision.

"Sound the collision alarm. Rudder hard to starboard, full reverse on the engines," Commander Ingram shouted.

The ship shuddered as the gentle ten knots of thrust suddenly altered to a hard reverse of the propellor. Slowly, the *Kumming* and the *Howard* steadied their distance and then started to draw apart. The Chinese warship then made a turn to parallel the *Howard*'s previous course.

With the danger of an imminent collision over, Commander Ingram ordered the ship back to its original course and speed. To be pushed away from the island would set a dangerous precedent, and Ingram wasn't going to be the one to do it.

"Chinese vessel *Kumming*, you are endangering the peaceful progress of a ship sailing in international waters. Cease and desist your maneuvers. If you do not, we will be forced to respond in a defensive manner," Commander Ingram broadcast once the situation had stabilized.

"US warship. You are violating the territorial waters of the sovereign nation of China. Turn around immediately," the response came.

The USS *Howard* responded as they always had, repeating that they were on a peaceful passage in international waters.

"Make sure that video gets back to DESRON 23 and the *Lincoln*," Commander Ingram said, keeping an eye on the Chinese destroyer now pulling away from the scene.

* * * * * *

White House
Washington, DC
6 July, 2020

The Marine posted at the cherry-red door came to attention and then bent to open it. Entering, President Winslow waved those already inside the room back into their seats. It wasn't often that he found himself in the Situation Room for meetings, preferring the comfort of the Oval Office. However, there were times when it was necessary to conduct meetings with the use of multimedia, and the Oval Office wasn't the place for that.

Seated around the polished conference table, each place with its own rubberized mat, were most of the rest of his cabinet. Secretary of State Fred Stevenson looking his usual frazzled self, the NSA and CIA directors, Bill Reiser and Tom Collier, respectively, appearing smaller than they were as if intentionally attempting to become invisible. Frank Winslow knew Fred to be a well-organized man behind that frayed exterior. No one else could truly keep all of the state's activities in place. Bill was an ex-spook who rose through the ranks of the NSA, so his demeanor of secrecy was expected. On the other hand, Tom was an ex-Navy admiral who had made his mark in the intelligence field and had been boisterous in his beliefs. Now, that part of his personality had nearly vanished over the time he had spent in his current position.

The others around the table included the secretary of defense, Aaron MacCulloch; the chairman of the Joint Chiefs of Staff, Phil Dawson; the JCS vice chair, Kevin Loughlin; and the chief of naval operations, Brian Durant.

Many of the black leather chairs positioned around the table were filled, the empty ones neatly arranged. Monitor screens surrounded the entire room with the largest centered at one end of the table. They didn't show real-time situations, but switched between varying pictures. The main one hosted the presidential seal with "White House Situation Room" in white lettering underneath.

Winslow nodded at everyone as he took his seat, the leather crunching as he sank in. He noticed Colonel Hayward from USAMRIID and Imraham Patel, the CDC director, sitting near the far end. Multiple folders were arranged on the table in front of him as they were for nearly everyone else, with only Hayward and Imraham less encumbered, a single file in front of each.

"Okay, ladies and gentlemen, we have a long day ahead of us so let's begin. Seeing we have Colonel Hayward and Director Patel with us today, let's begin with the topic of SARCoV. We have to come up with a definitive answer on what we're going to do in the long run. I had the opportunity to speak with both of our experts prior to this meeting, and we have three basic paths we can take.

"One, we take the harsh measures imposed by China and lock down our cities. Two, we take the opposite approach and open up the economy. Three, we take a route somewhere between those extreme measures. Each has associated pros and cons. But, instead of listening to me prattle on, I want to hand this part of the meeting over to the experts. Imraham?" President Winslow said.

Clearing his throat, the tall man with short hair, graying at his temples, opened the folder in front of him and looked down the length of the table.

"As the president mentioned, there are three basic avenues we can proceed down. The first one, a complete lockdown of the cities and work force, the establishment of quarantine lockups for those infected, isn't truly feasible. The differences in our work force versus that of China won't allow for the results we'd be looking for. For one, the Chinese don't have the migratory work force that we do here in the United States.

"We may be able to keep the city streets clear, but that won't do much for those who make their living roving from orchard to orchard, field to field, or moving between processing plants. A total lockdown won't eliminate the virus from our populace, especially if we keep our borders open with the rest of the world. I probably don't have to mention the blowback that would roll through the country were we to lock people in their homes. I would recommend that we don't pursue this method. It will only anger the populace without managing to contain and eliminate SARCoV-19.

"Alternatively, if we open the economy and let the virus spread at will, we'll find two major things. The first is that our medical services will quickly become overwhelmed, especially in major metropolitan areas. Although not entirely in my purview, there's a good chance that we'll find the economy suffer rather than recover as a large percentage of the work force becomes sickened.

"So, that leaves us somewhere in between. I recommend that we open the economy wide enough to allow us to absorb the infections and keep the pandemic contained to an extent that the medical services are able to handle the inflow of patients. The death rates with option two and three will generally be the same, but the last one will spread those deaths over a longer period," Imraham briefed.

"Colonel Hayward," President Winslow responded, "do you have anything to add to what Doctor Patel stated?"

"No, sir. I believe the good doctor covered the options pretty well. SARCoV-19 is here to stay and it's now a part of our lives. Over time, depending on the mutations, the current outbreak will decrease. But I believe we're looking at years rather than months. It's best that we adapt and employ mitigating measures. We have evidence that the degree of illness depends on several factors, one of which is how much viral load one receives. The greater the load, the more ill one becomes."

"What about the endeavors toward developing a vaccine?" Winslow asked.

Hayward gave a slight shake of her head, the motion coming from her personal thoughts regarding the feasibility of creating a vaccine rather an answer to the question.

"You don't think a vaccine is feasible, colonel?" Winslow queried.

"I think Doctor Patel might answer that question better than I," Colonel Hayward replied.

"Doctor?"

Imraham again cleared his throat. "Yes, well, in answer to that. I think it will be difficult to develop a vaccine on short notice, but rest assured, we'll work diligently to bring one about."

President Winslow chuckled. "That sounds like something I might say at one of the debates. What you're truly saying is that you doubt we'll find a working vaccine."

"I'm not exactly saying that. I'm saying that it will be

difficult. We tried to find a vaccine for the original SARS virus and were unsuccessful. The virus mutates so quickly. We may be looking at annual injections," Doctor Imraham answered.

"It also appears that we won't be able to develop a vaccine that will provide lasting antibodies. If we are able to effect a vaccine, it may turn out to be one that will have to be given multiple times...booster shots if you will, sir," Colonel Hayward chimed in.

"Okay, thank you both. Let's keep this under wraps for now and focus on our current undertakings with the pharmaceutical companies. Our official recommendation will be mitigation while partially opening the economy. I believe this is the only way our economy will recover."

With that, knowing they were being silently dismissed, the colonel and doctor rose from their seats and exited.

"Anyone have any questions on our policy regarding SARCoV-19?"

No one said anything.

"Very well, let's move on. Next on our agenda is the South China Sea. Fred, will you catch us up with what we're doing regarding the aggression demonstrated by the Chinese with the near collision in the Spratlys?" President Winslow asked, leaning back in his chair and directing his attention to the secretary of state.

"We've put in an official condemnation of the act to the UN. In addition, there's an article submitted asking to put some teeth into the World Court's decision regarding the illegality of the Chinese territorial claims in the Spratly and the Paracel Islands in the South China Sea. It's a resolution asking for the Chinese to remove their military additions by the end of the year. Failing that, the resolution adds sanctions against China to be imposed by the UN. We're citing the increased aggression in international waters exhibited by China and how dangerous these moves made by the Chinese are to all nations traveling through the South China Sea. I don't expect this resolution to pass, but it serves notice to China that we aren't going to let the incident slide.

"We have contacted China and directed that they cease these dangerous maneuvers. The message is that our forces will defend themselves in international waters when confronted. Hopefully that will give them pause before they do something like that again. I don't have to remind everyone here that this is the second time we've had a close call. Now, we can impose sanctions despite the recent trade agreement, but that's about all we can do from a diplomatic position."

"Thank you, Fred. Anyone else care to chime in?"

"We can authorize the firing of warning shots across the bows of the Chinese if they stray too close again," stated Admiral Durant, the chief of naval operations.

President Winslow inwardly smiled, expecting nothing less from the grizzled admiral who looked like he'd be better suited in a dockside brawl than squeezed into the formal whites of the US Navy's highest office.

"While I have no doubt that the idea has merit, I think the idea is to keep the escalation to a minimum," President Winslow responded.

"I don't know, maybe it's just me, but it's pretty difficult to be aggressive when you're trying to find a piece of floating debris to cling to," the admiral grumbled.

Chuckles emanated from around the table, CIA director Tom Collier nearly spraying coffee out of his nostrils.

"I'm just saying it would unmuddle things were we to send those scrap heaps to the bottom," Admiral Durant added.

He then smiled, knowing full well his reputation and his expected response. It wasn't that he didn't feel that way or wasn't ready to jump should he be given the order, but it was also a game he played with everyone else. He was the one who kept the politics out of war matters. Although he had a gruff exterior, he had a sharp mind for strategic and tactical operations. President Winslow was aware of his top admiral's talents and knew there wasn't any other man he'd want in the position, especially when it came down to a shooting match.

"So, let's go with the idea that we aren't going to shoot at any Chinese ships in the near future. Is there anything we can add regarding the incident?" President Winslow asked.

With everyone shaking their head, Winslow then turned their attention to further actions in the South China Sea to keep pressure on the Chinese.

Phil Dawson, the chairman of the Joint Chiefs of Staff and the top Air Force general, chimed in: "Well, sir, the Chinese are currently running both of their carrier battle groups in the South China Sea. While the *Shandong* is operational, the *Liaoning* is really nothing more than a training platform. They've had to tow that aircraft carrier back into port twice now. It's really at sea for show, even though they are conducting flights from it. In addition, they have deployed several destroyer squadrons.

"We have two carrier strike groups also in the South China Sea, the *Nimitz* and the *Abraham Lincoln*. The *Lincoln* is scheduled to depart at the end of the month; we haven't scheduled her replacement at this time."

"I highly recommend that we keep two strike groups in the area," Admiral Durant commented following General Dawson's quick brief. "That means we need to arrange for another carrier strike group to ready itself for sea."

A map of the South China Sea flared to life on the main screen.

"Four carrier groups in the same area seems a touch crowded and creates a recipe for a disastrous incident. That aside, I see the need," President Winslow said, holding up a hand to forestall the expected countering argument from Admiral Durant. "We've had this conversation several times, but I want to ask it again. If we come down to a shooting match, won't our carriers become trapped in those waters?"

"If that happens, we'll need to extricate them immediately, but they'll be able to fight their way out. We have their patrols arranged so they can quickly join forces to become mutually supportive," Admiral Durant answered.

"I also want to remind everyone that we won't have immediate support from the bombers out of Guam. If you'll recall, we opted to remove them in April after the base came within range of both North Korea's and China's ballistic missiles. We didn't want to run the risk of the aircraft becoming first-strike targets and losing them permanently. It was also to remove them due to current tensions in the South China Sea should China opt to strike first and launch SLCMs from their submarines," General Dawson commented.

"So, for the time being, we run two carrier strike groups continuously in the region and keep with the freedom of navigation overflights and ship passages?" President Winslow asked.

Admiral Durant nodded.

"That would be our recommendation," General Dawson answered.

"What about our responsibilities in the Strait of Hormuz?"

"We handed over most of that to the Brits since the beginning of the year and moved the strike group into the South China Sea. We still have a destroyer squadron in the area but can recall them if you think we need to," General Dawson responded.

"I'll leave that up to you. After all, it's not like the Iranians will suddenly decide to quiet down if we become enmeshed with the Chinese. Let's make sure we have contingency plans in our back pocket just in case. I wouldn't put it past the Chinese to escalate this before the election as they know we won't be as decisive.

"While I want to keep up the pressure so we don't seem weak, I want to strongly iterate that there can't be any accidents that ramp up the action. Now, I also want the media involved in what we're doing. We have a tight election coming up and I want to be seen as continuing to take a tough position against Chinese aggression. There's a wave of patriotism and 'American made,' and I plan to ride that furor all of the way to a new term," President Winslow stated.

"Very well, sir. The *Theodore Roosevelt* and Carrier Strike Group 9 will be notified for a duty rotation, and we'll keep up with our FONOPS missions," General Dawson said.

There was a slight pause; all of those around the table

were party to an earlier decision to leak to the media that one of the United States' strike group carriers was down due to a SARCoV outbreak and the intimation that there were similar problems among other navy vessels. This was to done to garner a Chinese reaction. While there were cases, the *Roosevelt* was in no way out of action. They had established rigid quarantines and, in many cases, the crew was replaced from stateside.

"Now, China's economy is hurting worse than ours, so we need to keep up the pressure on both fronts without seeming to be pressuring them. We cannot let them overtake our economic power or they'll be able to set the terms of trade. That will drive our economy into something we may not be able to fully recover from. So, pressure on all fronts without truly pushing them over a line. Once we're through the election, we can push on with further plans," President Winslow stated.

"Provided we're all still here," Secretary of State Stevenson said.

"Yes, providing we're all still here," President Winslow agreed.

They broke for lunch and pushed on through the afternoon with plans and signals they wanted to send the Chinese through the media and other means.

*   *   *   *   *   *

The bustle of people gathering their belongings filled the situation room, idle chit-chat and scheduling discussions dominated the space as folders were stuffed into satchels. One by one, the staff departed. President Winslow waved away the security details that had shown up to escort him back to the Oval Office, leaving him alone in the room.

He glanced over the seats and along the polished table, thinking over the decisions that had been made in this room. Some had far-reaching ramifications, while others were difficult to think about even to this day. The ones that held lives in the balance seemed the hardest to make.

Frank wondered how much longer he would have to be a

part of it. A part of him wanted for it to continue, for him to win the upcoming election. But there was another part that was eager to cast this life aside and head for an easier one outside of politics. He envisioned lounging on a boat with a line in the water or spending an entire day doing nothing but sitting in a rocking chair on the porch with his wife.

Now, that would be something, he thought, inwardly sighing.

Directing his tired thoughts to the campaign, he wondered if he was doing enough to actually win. The polls showed him close to his opponent. The downturn in the economy due to the pandemic wasn't helping, nor was the actual viral outbreak. But he'd spent more time dealing with matters of state than being out on the campaign trail. He wondered if perhaps he wasn't subconsciously sabotaging himself in order to leave behind the problems currently overflowing his plate.

Mulling his options and the battleground states that required his presence, the thought of even more travel drained his energy. He now understood why previous presidents came into office looking healthy and full of vigor only to limp away after their terms with graying hair and a mind turned to gruel. Sitting in the top chair of the United States wasn't easy, and it was not for the weak-minded.

His thoughts returned to the decisions made in the room, how all of his cabinet would be crucified in the streets of DC were the public to know the discussions that had taken place at this table. Frank enjoyed making the difficult decisions. He had what it takes to sit in the Oval Office, and he'd do it for another four years. There were plans in motion that he wanted to see fulfilled. Somehow, he'd harness the energy necessary to sit here for another term.

Frank gathered the folders and placed them in his bag. At the door, he glanced back into the room and smiled. He had a feeling that the situation room wasn't done with him as yet.

Continuous Bomber Presence on Guam Comes to an End

In a dramatic and unannounced shift in policy and regional posture, the Air Force has ended its uninterrupted rotation of bombers to the island.

April 17, 2020

Guam (*The War Zone*) — In a move to shift to a less predictable concept of operations, The United States Air Force has abruptly ended the uninterrupted rotation of bombers to Andersen Air Force Base that has been in place since 2004. Yesterday, five B-52H Stratofortresses departed Guam without any replacements arriving. This move brings to an end what the service has named the Continuous Bomber Presence Mission. Notably, this came just days after the bombers were involved in a readiness operation designed to be a significant statement of American resolve directed at China.

Using the callsign "SEEYA," the bombers departed Guam for the long transit flight to their new home at Minot Air Force Base located in North Dakota.

"In line with the National Defense Strategy, the United States has transitioned to an approach that enables strategic bombers to operate forward in the Indo-Pacific region from a broader array of overseas locations, when required, and with greater operational resilience, while these bombers are permanently based in the United States," a US Strategic Command (STRATCOM) spokesperson, confirmed in a statement. "US strategic bombers will continue to operate in the Indo-Pacific, to include Guam, at the timing and tempo of our choosing."

The Continuous Bomber Presence Mission began in 2004 with the Air Force deploying B-52 Stratofortress, B-1B Bone supersonic bombers, and B-2A Spirit stealth bombers for six-month deployments to Andersen Air Force Base. The mission was to ensure that the United States had a task force of heavy bombers in position to respond immediately to contingencies in the Pacific Region. The deployed bombers on Guam were the cornerstone of America's projection of power and deterrence.

It is hard to overstress how significant a development this is, despite STRATCOM's view that it will not impact its ability to employ bombers to respond to contingencies in the region. The potential for major crises to erupt in the Pacific remains very real.

North Korea is continuing to work on expanding and improving its nuclear arsenal and delivery platforms. The northern regime is also continually testing new and improved conventional weapons. Bombers flying from Guam have always been a major component of show-of-force and deterrence operations directed at North Korea.

Tensions have been simmering between the United States and China over a host of issues, including China's vast territorial claims in the South China Sea, the renewed closer ties between the US and Taiwan, the US support for the pro-democracy protesters in Hong Kong, and the ongoing trade and economic disputes. The SARCoV-19 pandemic has only served to aggravate these frictions. As of late, there have been numerous engagements between the United States and Chinese military forces, especially in the South China Sea. Recently, a near-collision between a US Navy destroyer and a People Liberation Army Navy (PLAN) destroyer nearly sparked a dangerous encounter. Other incidents within the region, dangerous jamming and the lasing of American military aircraft, threaten to escalate into a greater regional conflict.

In addition to challenging US forces in the region, Chinese security forces are taking increasingly aggressive stances with other foreign military aircraft and civilian ships as it asserts its claims in the South China Sea. The Pentagon recently issued a sharp criticism of Chinese authorities when a Chinese Coast Guard vessel rammed and sunk a Vietnamese fishing boat near the Paracel Islands, one of the hotly contested islands in the South China Sea.

Challenging China's territorial claims in the region, B-52H bombers flying from Andersen Airfield in Guam, among other US military aircraft, have been flying patrol in the South China Sea as part of Freedom of Navigation Operations. US Navy vessels have also been operating near the shores of the contested islands as part of these ongoing missions.

Several questions have been raised about the United States ability to project military power in the region in light of the major SARCoV-19 outbreak among the crew of the *Nimitz*-class aircraft carrier *Theodore Roosevelt*. The carrier is now indefinitely berthed at a pier in Guam. This has forced the Navy to redeploy one of the carriers positioned in the Middle East, another hotspot where tensions are high with Iran, and redirect it to the Pacific. This is in addition to the redeployment of the rotating bomber squadrons away from Guam.

In response, China recently deployed one of its carriers, the *Liaoning*, and sent it on a mission near both Japan and Taiwan. Accompanying the Chinese carrier were two destroyers, a pair of frigates, and a supply vessel. This Chinese excursion demonstrated China's increasing ability to conduct carrier operations.

It remains to be seen what ramifications will follow the decision to end the Continuous Bomber Presence Mission, but it's easily apparent to see that the US military's posture in the Pacific has undergone a major shift.

* * * * * *

Laser Weapon Test Successful

May 23, 2020
Hong Kong (*CNN*) — The US Navy issued a statement indicating that its test of a new high-energy laser weapon was successful in downing an aircraft in mid-flight.

The USS *Portland* executed the first system-level implementation of a high-energy solid-state laser to disable an aerial drone. Images and video show the laser firing from the warship's deck followed by a video of what appears to be a burning drone.

"By conducting advanced at sea tests against UAVs and small crafts, we will gain valuable information on the capabilities of the Solid-State Laser Weapons System Demonstrator against potential threats," the commanding officer of the *Portland* said. "With this new advanced capability, we are redefining war at sea for the Navy."

Directed energy weapons can be effective against drones, small armed boats, or as additional defensive measures against missile attacks. Earlier, the USS Ponce successfully conducted a live-fire exercise using a 30-kilowatt laser weapon.

"It is throwing massive amounts of photons at an incoming object," a Navy spokesman said. "We don't worry about wind, we don't worry about range, we don't worry about anything else. We're able to engage the targets at the speed of light."

* * * * * *

US aircraft carriers conduct a show of force against Beijing

July 7,2020

In order to prevent China's unsupported claims to territorial waters in the South China Sea from being enforced de facto, the US Navy frequently sends patrols through the contested areas in what they call Freedom of Navigation Operations (FONOPS).

China recently issued an outcry against the two US Navy carriers sent into the South China Sea and are now on an extended cruise in the region. While the rhetoric issued by both sides may sound like saber rattling, the US are upholding their commitment to defend common global good of allowing all countries the freedom to navigate the seas. These FONOP missions demonstrate a rare case where international law, the defense of weaker nations, and the pursuit of a national interest all align.

These patrols involve US military ships deliberately cruising through waters that China has claimed jurisdiction over to make the point that they are not, legally, under Beijing's exclusive control. The policy of dispatching ships on these freedom of navigation operations is an enduring one — going back to 1979 — so it also testifies to the benefit of continuity in national security.

These continued patrols both reassure friends of our commitment and keep enemies in check without engaging in an actual conflict. However, there is an inherent risk of a violent and dramatic escalation when two opposing forces operate in close proximity.

The accepted law of the sea as per UN conventions is that a country has territorial rights into adjacent oceans and seas out to 12 nautical miles. That means any foreign nation can legally send spy ships 13 miles away from sensitive military installations.

However, China believes that principle should apply to the contested area in the South China Sea. Vietnam, Malaysia, and the Philippines all have claims to the areas in question. To further complicate the situation, China constructed multiple islands from reefs and shoals, turning them into military fortresses. An international tribune ruled that China's territorial claims to the man-made islands are illegal. China refuses to accept the World Court's ruling on this matter and has continued to place military weapons on the islets.

Beijing therefore asserts that it has jurisdiction over large swaths of ocean in the southern section of the South China Sea, hundreds of miles from China's shorelines. Many of these contested lands lie near the coasts of foreign countries. This serves as a pretext to claim that US military patrols are violating Chinese territorial waters. In addition, many of these Chinese military bases are placed close to shipping lanes, through which passes 20% to 30% of the global trade.

This places China's maritime military forces and militias — civilian boats under government control — with the ability to harass commercial and military shipping of any nation daring to travel through the South China Sea. There have been multiple instances of foreign commercial boats being driven away by Chinese vessels, even to the point of ramming and sinking them.

Accordingly, Chinese military craft have used their continued claim to the region to justify its harassment of US ships and aircraft. This includes unsafe intercepts by Chinese jets and the use of damaging laser against US military pilots.

The two-carrier patrol coincided with a large Chinese naval exercise near the Paracel Islands. This action was met with threats that the carriers could be sunk by China's vast armada of aircraft carrier killer missiles.

There's more than just international law at stake; China's expansionist claims come at the expense of countries with far less military and economic clout. The US presence and patrols make it feasible for those countries to stand against Chinese pressure and defend their rights.

It isn't just about international law. There is a direct American national security interest at play. The United States Navy has freely navigated and controlled the breadth of the Pacific Ocean since the end of World War II. They have enjoyed the unparalleled ability to conduct logistical operations and its network of regional allies — Australia, Japan, South Korea, the Philippines, and potentially Taiwan — rely on the ability of the United States to counter China's regional might. The question then comes into play about how much of the Pacific will be dominated by the Chinese rather than the United States.

From China's point of view, they are sensitive to the threat of American bases on their Pacific flank. Guam, Japan, Okinawa, and South Korea all serve to hem in China. In early years, China suffered a series of disastrous foreign invasions. Therefore, China would like to push the United States away from their shores and eastward by 2,000 miles. This would put the US beyond a defensive line of the island chains formed by Japan and the Philippines, essentially forcing them away from the Philippine Sea.

It is important to mention that China is not the same country when foreigners preyed upon a weak nation or in the mid-90s when the presence of two US carriers constituted enough of a threat to make Beijing back down during a crisis. China has built up a formidable arsenal of its own. They have constructed numerous long-range anti-ship missiles, nuclear attack submarines, large warships, and naval aircraft capable of providing the ability to threaten ships and safeguard islands hundreds of miles from its own coastline.

While the United States continues to conduct its Freedom of Navigation operations to prevent China from getting its territorial claims by de facto, they have not been sufficient to prevent China from reinforcing their positions militarily, and in particular, they haven't stopped the Chinese government from creating and expanding their artificial islands.

US changes policy toward Beijing in South China Sea

After years of neutrality, the US issued a warning to China over its claims in the region.

July 15, 2020

Washington, DC (*Fox News*) — For years, the United States and China have been involved in a clash over maritime freedoms in the South China Sea. However, this week marked a change in the usual rhetoric with Washington clamping down on Beijing's activities in the region. This is the first time they've called it "illegal." According to many strategists, this opens the legal gateway to a potential military response.

The Secretary of State issued a statement that the United States is making it clear that China's territorial claims of many contested islands in the South China Sea are completely unlawful, as is its bullying measures exerted to control them.

"Beijing uses intimidation to undermine the sovereign rights of Southeast Asian coastal states in the South China Sea, bully them out of offshore resources, assert unilateral dominion, and replace international law with 'might makes right.' Beijing's approach has been clear for years," he stated. "The People's Republic of China (PRC) has no legal grounds to unilaterally impose its will on the region."

The issued statement underscored the US position that Beijing has offered no coherent legal basis for its territorial claims in the South China Sea since formally announcing them in 2009.

In 2016, an Arbitral Tribunal at The Hague

unanimously judged that the People's Republic of China's maritime claims had no basis in international law, upholding the 1982 Law of Sea Convention—to which the PRC is a state party. The Philippines brought this arbitration case before the World Court, who sided with the Philippines on all claims.

Washington could double-down with additional sanctions against Chinese officials and corporations that are involved in malicious activity in the South China Sea. Another State department spokesperson vowed that the US is no longer remaining neutral on these maritime issues.

Making these explicit claims and verbiage allows the US to penalize any destabilizing Chinese behaviors. They are particularly referring to the interference and bullying behavior demonstrated by China toward other regional claimants, notably the Philippines, Vietnam, Malaysia, Brunei, and Indonesia. The State department also hinted that closer ties with Taiwan could be realized in the future.

In the past, the US policy was to publicly condemn Chinese territorial claims and aggressive expansions in and around the South China Sea, but has always called for peaceful resolutions for disputes involving regional players. This latest change and wording outright rejects this past policy and puts the US into the center of the conflict.

As a show of force and to demonstrate its resolve and commitment to freedom of navigation, the US sent the warship *Ralph Johnson* to muscle its way through the waters China is claiming as its territory. This further adds to the seriousness of the situation.

For the past ten years, China has become more aggressive with its claims that the entire region belongs to them, reinforcing its military presence and pushing aside weaker nations that get in its way. In addition, China has busily constructed military bases on manufactured islands in the contested regions that include hangars, bunkers, radar facilities, and missile batteries capable of firing the latest anti-ship and antiaircraft missiles.

In addition to the military presence on the islands, Beijing has also set up local fishing communities and sent citizens into the region. They have established administrative districts complete with governing branches, even opening the doors to research facilities. With these moves, China hopes to further legitimize and strengthen their claims of ownership.

Earlier this month, the Communist leadership ignited further fury by sealing off a section of the waterways to conduct naval drills. Ultimately, the region is an essential part of China's "Greater Bay Area economic development" plan, and since 2012 has been intent on populating a number of islands.

According to many analysts, China is looking to control all of the South China Sea, which puts it in conflict with the UN Convention on the Law of the Sea. That international agreement makes it clear that China only has limited rights to the maritime zones in the South China Sea.

However, with much of the world battling the SARCoV pandemic—which originated in the Chinese city of Wuhan—and the disruption of their economies, China's aggressive activities in the waterways have escalated in recent months.

The incidents include chasing Malaysian oil-exploration vessels out of their legitimate territories and sinking a Vietnamese fishing boat.

"China has steadily engaged in land reclamation and construction of military outposts throughout the South China Sea, even going so far as to install surface-to-air missiles, jamming equipment, and anti-ship missiles on some of these outposts," the spokesman continued. "China undertook these activities in violation of international law and in spite of a promise by Chinese President Hao Chenxu that he would not militarize the area."

What remains to be seen is just how far Washington is willing to go to curb China's "unlawful" maneuvers.

The US has deployed two aircraft carrier strike groups — the USS *Nimitz* and USS *Theodore Roosevelt* — for joint operations in the South China Sea. Moreover, there are P8-Poseidon Maritime Patrol Aircraft that traverse the sea, along with the US Air Force's B-52 strategic bomber — all while China was conducting its own training nearby. The US Navy is known to have undertaken at least six such Freedom of Navigation operations throughout the first half of 2020 alone.

Predictably, China has dismissed the harsh words issued by Washington. China's Foreign Affairs Minister, Liu Xiang, called the statements "irresponsible and a distortion of international law, calling out the United States for deliberately stoking tensions and undermining regional peace and stability.

In an earlier statement, state media tweeted that US aircraft carrier movement in the region is at the pleasure of the Chinese military. However, despite the increasing tensions and the speculation that a conflict could erupt at any moment, many experts assert that an all-out fight between the two superpowers is still far away.

At the moment, a war or other military conflicts appear unlikely. But, tensions will likely escalate as the US publicly challenges China's claims over the region and is ongoing aggressive stances threatening other countries.

* * * * * *

China could dump US Treasuries

September 4, 2020

(*Reuters*)—In view of the current escalating tensions between the US and China, experts warn that Beijing could cut its vast holdings of US Treasury bonds and notes.

With the relations between the two superpowers falling apart due to various issues such as the SARCoV pandemic, trade disagreements, and the tensions over actions in the South China Sea, global markets are shaky and becoming increasingly worried what might happen should the Chinese government sell the US debt it currently holds. China could use this threat as a weapon to counter rising US pressure.

"China will gradually decrease its holdings of US debt to about $800 billion under normal circumstances," a professor at the Shanghai University of Finance and Economics was quoted as saying, without giving a detailed timeframe. "But of course, China might sell all of its US bonds in an extreme case, like a military conflict."

China is the second largest non-US holder of

Treasuries, holding over $1 trillion. In recent months, they have steadily decreased their US bond holdings. However, some market watchers speculate that China may not be selling or buying directly, instead using third-party custodians to purchase the Treasuries.

If China opts to sell their current holdings and drop to $800 billion, that could trigger additional turmoil in global markets. This kind of disruption could send many countries spiraling into a depression.

This puts the United States into a position to become a potential default risk as the debt of the world's largest economy has increased sharply. It carries the potential to pass the internationally recognized 60% safety line.

* * * * * *

China fears financial restriction as US tensions rise

August 13, 2020

SHANGHAI/BEIJING (*Reuters*) — Tensions between the United States and China have escalated sharply over the past months, stoking fears in China that they could be shut out of the global dollar system. This action in the deepening of the financial war between the two superpowers may once have been considered far-fetched, but is now considered a possibility.

Chinese officials and economists have in recent months been unusually public in discussing worst-case scenarios under which China is blocked from dollar settlements, or Washington freezes or confiscates a portion of China's huge US debt holdings.

The threat of Sino-US financial "decoupling" is becoming "clear and present," said the head of Greater China economic research at Standard Chartered and a former economist at the People's Bank of China (PBOC).

Although a complete separation of the world's two largest economies is unlikely, the United States has been pushing for a partial decoupling in key areas related to trade, technology and financial activity.

Washington has unleashed a barrage of actions penalizing China, including proposals to bar US listings of Chinese companies that fail to meet US accounting standards and bans on the Chinese-owned TikTok and WeChat apps. Further tension is expected in the run-up to US elections.

"A broad financial war has already started…the most lethal tactics have yet to be used," an economist at the state-backed Chinese Academy of Social Sciences (CASS) who previously advised the PBOC, told Reuters.

The ultimate sanction would involve US seizures of China's US assets — Beijing holds over $1 trillion yuan in US government debt. Decoupling is not impossible and many warning China that they should make preparations for such an event.

The stakes are high. Any move by Washington to cut China off from the dollar system or retaliation by Beijing to sell a big chunk of US debt could roil financial markets and hurt the global economy.

Several have said that China is vulnerable to US sanctions and should make "early" and "real" preparations.

A former director of the international payments department of China's State Administration of Foreign Exchange and now chief global economist at BOC International (China) told Reuters, "We have to mentally prepare that the United States could expel China from the dollar settlement system."

After a five-year lull, Beijing is reviving its push to globalize the yuan.

The PBOC's Shanghai head office last month urged financial institutions to expand yuan trade and prioritize local currency use in direct investment.

Still, internationalization is hampered by China's own stringent capital controls. It could also face resistance from countries that have criticized China on matters ranging from the SARCoV to its clampdown on Hong Kong.

Beijing has no choice but to prepare for Washington's "nuclear option" of kicking China out of the dollar system. However, China cannot afford to be thrown into disarray when sanctions are indeed put into place.

* * * * * *

China is doubling down on its territorial claims

September 30, 2020

Beijing (CNN)—China's goal of becoming a global superpower has been cemented by Chinese president Hao Chenxu. Since coming into power in 2012, he has pushed China into taking a more aggressive stance on foreign policy, making bold moves across Asia.

This harder line has been observed in the South China Sea, where China is making territorial claims in hotly contested areas, and on the border with India where troops positioned on both sides of the border have frequently clashed. Doubling down on perceived challenges to its expansion, China is responding aggressively.

With the escalating disputes and increasing tensions with foreign powers, Hao has bulked up the military in addition to increasing the budget. The Chinese president has issued instructions along with the drastic improvement to resolutely safeguard national sovereignty, security, and development interests.

The South China Sea in particular has witnessed an increase in Chinese interests. Composed of small islands, reefs, and shoals, the waters host global shipping routes and are home to ongoing territorial disputes.

China has staked claims that it owns nearly all of the 1.3 million square miles of the South China Sea, disregarding the overlapping territorial claims by six other governments: the Philippines, Vietnam, Malaysia, Indonesia, Brunei, and Taiwan. Even though the United States doesn't hold any claims to the busy shipping routes, Washington has repeatedly challenged China's claims.

As part of their aggressive expansion, China has created numerous islands out from the reefs and sandbars that are hundreds of miles for its shoreline. They have turned these artificial islands into heavily fortified military bases complete with runways and various weapon systems. These actions have prompted outcries from the other governments, but the countries are too weak to force China from its positions.

The United States have conducted Freedom of Navigation operations to challenge China's claims, sailing warships through the South China Sea and close to the islands China is occupying. The purpose of these missions is to enforce the right of free passage in international waters. Beijing argues that that these patrols are violations of its sovereign lands.

Recently, the United States has increased the number of these operations and issued statements formally rejecting China's claims as illegal actions. In addition, Washington has sanctioned dozens of Chinese firms for constructing the man-made islands. Two US Navy carriers entered the South China Sea to conduct joint military exercises, demonstrating a strong show of force in the region. These moves have angered the Chinese government, sparking increased tensions. Responding to this show of force, China launched several ballistic missiles into the sea while stating that they do not fear a war.

Another hotspot for China is Taiwan, a self-governing democratic island with approximately 24 million people. The island split from mainland China at the end of a bloody civil war which saw the emergence of a Communist government ruling China. China claims that Taiwan is a sovereign part of China, even though the island has never been ruled by the current Communist party. For the past seventy years, the two sides have governed themselves.

China has attempted many measures to pull Taiwan into its grasp. Using diplomatic, trade, and military pressure, Beijing has tired to marginalize Taipei in the international community. China was successful in blocking Taiwan from joining various global agencies such as the World Health Organization.

The diplomatic pressure comes in the form of demanding that other foreign countries not recognize Taiwan as an independent nation. To date, they have largely been successful with this pressure with most countries abiding by the demand. However, many governments continue to maintain close unofficial ties with the island nation.

The warming of the relationship between the US and Taiwan has drawn China's ire. Military sales to bolster Taipei's military has forced China to respond with increased military drills near the island, including aircraft incursion in the waters and airspace near Taiwan.

Chinese officials warned in September that "China firmly opposes any form of official exchanges between the United States and Taiwan. There have been some hints from within the Chinese government of the threat of sanctions against US officials.

President Hao has been clear in his ambitions to "reunify" the island with the mainland, and has refused to rule out the use of force. Recent military drills were described in Chinese state media as a "rehearsal for a Taiwan takeover" and threats of invasion have increased sharply as tensions with the US rise.

* * * * * *

Chinese President tells troops to prepare for war

October 14, 2020

Hong Kong (CNN)—Visiting a military base in the southern province of Guangdong, Chinese President Hao Chenxu has called on troops to put all minds and energy on preparing for war.

During another inspection of the People's Liberation Army Marine Corps in Chaozhou City, Hao told the soldiers stationed there to maintain a state of high alert and called on them to be "absolutely loyal, absolutely pure, and absolutely reliable.

Mounting tensions between the United States and China remain high, with disagreements over Taiwan, the SARCoV pandemic, recent incidents in the South China Sea, and trade. The visits to the military installations come as sharp divisions between the two superpowers continue to mount.

Recently, the White House said that it was planning to move ahead with military sales to Taiwan, included the sale of three advanced weapon systems. Part of the sale is to include the advanced High Mobility Artillery Rocket System (HIMARS).

This drew a stern response from Beijing. China's Foreign Affairs Minister, Liu Xiang, called on the United States to immediately cancel any current or future arms sales to Taiwan and for Washington to cut all US-Taiwan military and diplomatic ties.

China has long claimed that Taiwan is an integral part of their territory, even though the democratic self-governing island has never been controlled by

China's ruling Communist Party. Hao has not ruled out the use of military force to bring the island back into Chinese control, capturing it if necessary.

Angering the Chinese government, relations between the United States and Taiwan have grown closer in recent years. In response, China has increasingly conducted military exercises around the renegade island. In one drill, nearly 40 Chinese military aircraft flew beyond the median line between the mainland and Taiwan.

In a speech, US Secretary of Defense Aaron MacCulloch said China "cannot match the United States" in terms of naval power and labeled Beijing a "malignant influence."

"China and Russia are using predatory economics, political subversion, and military force in an attempt to shift the balance of power in their favor, and often at the expense of others," he told the audience.

Chapter Four

Oval Office
Washington, DC
January 7, 2021

President Winslow eased down into the leather chair, thankful that he was still in office. The election had been a closely fought one, and the results hadn't been known for several days afterward. Those days waiting on the final results had taken their toll, and he'd needed the rest he was able to get over the holidays. Only partially refreshed, he knew he had to gather the energy from somewhere in order to push forward with the agenda he had started the prior year.

Looking into the rested eyes of his cabinet members, it was obvious they hadn't experienced the same tensions during the campaign. However, even though they all knew that they'd land somewhere if they'd lost, they were dedicated to their positions and cared about forwarding the plans and contingencies they'd all set. Of course, the chairman of the Joint Chiefs sitting in the room would have been the same regardless, even if Mickey Mouse had strolled into the room as the president-elect.

With a blustery day hammering bushes outside and rain loudly pelting the window panes, Frank leaned back and crossed his legs.

"Well, we narrowly survived, but we made it and are still here. We have another four years and the holidays are behind us, so it's time to get back to work. What do we have?" the president asked.

President Winslow knew the answer to that question, having spent time looking at the information contained in the folders before him during the holidays. Well, that and catching up on some much-needed rest. He didn't recognize the man in the mirror anymore. The reflection gazing back at him looked many years older than the vibrant middle-aged man who had first entered this office four years ago. Frank appeared to have aged ten times that.

"We have the affirmation we were looking for from Colonel Hayward and USAMRIID regarding SARCoV. SARCoV is definitely a manmade virus manufactured in the Wuhan facility," General Dawson answered.

"We have a resolution coming before the United Nations scheduled for February 12. We'll be asking for sanctions against China and for them to pay restitution for the economic damages sustained on account of the virus," Secretary of State Stevenson added.

"I thought we talked about sanctions until China begins dismantling the military infrastructure in the Spratly Islands, phasing those in until the islands are reduced to the shoals they once were. Has that changed?" President Winslow inquired.

"Oh, that's in there," Fred Stevenson hastily answered. "I was merely paraphrasing."

"I thought so. I just want to make sure we're heading into this on the same page. We're walking a tightrope here, and we need to make sure that all the pieces are in their proper places," President Winslow said.

"With the Chinese meeting our threats and upping the ante as well, I couldn't agree more. If they sell off their Treasury bonds, they could send our economy plummeting. That will inflict incredible harm on their system, too. We've heard these threats before. It's the same as us seizing their assets and cutting them off from the dollar. Their attempts to internationalize the yuan have largely been unsuccessful to this point, so we still have the upper hand there," the Treasury secretary stated. "None of those nuclear options on either side are in anyone's best interest."

"But, if we really start getting serious about restitution, then we need to have mechanisms in place to seize Chinese assets in this country and to identify assets purchased for them through third parties. This needs to be in place so all we have to do is pull the trigger," the CIA director responded.

President Winslow looked at the Treasury secretary.

"Hmm...well, yes. We can put those measures in place

without tipping our hand. While we're quite adept at identifying most of the third parties, um, we may need some assistance finding those deeply buried."

"Lucky for you, we have the tools necessary to dive into those transactions," CIA Director Collier quipped, casting a sidelong glance at Bill Reiser, the NSA director.

Their two agencies had conspired to find every last Chinese financial route of entry into the United States. They hadn't done anything about those vague third parties yet lest they give away their secrets. If they tipped their hand too soon, then China would find alternate methods of entry into America's financial market and the game would begin anew. It's better to deal with the devil you know than the one you don't.

President Winslow noted the split-second exchange, but didn't inquire further into its meaning. After four years, he knew there were some things better left unknown. What did they call it? Oh yeah, plausible deniability. He had authorized some pretty nefarious things during his previous term, and those were the very things his opponents used during the election campaign.

Frank was fairly certain activities had and were currently taking place that he didn't know about. Honestly, he didn't want to know about them. Still, the not-knowing sometimes worried him, as it would be his ass should those darkly closeted operations come to light. He trusted his two intelligence directors and felt that they wouldn't do anything that crossed that thick dark line that defined the gray areas they lived in. Well, at least without his approval. They knew they'd be crucified if caught with their hands in the wrong cookie jar. Nonetheless, shared looks like that made him nervous.

"Going back to the UN resolution, what do you think the chances are of it passing?" President Winslow asked.

"Same as usual when we put something like this forward against one of the big six. It won't pass, but at least we'll put the Chinese on notice that we and the rest of the world know where this came from. Now, they'll counter by saying that we made up the scientific information and it'll go down ally lines with regards to the poorer nations. But it should put several large corporations and some countries on notice that China may not be the ideal place to trade with these days," Secretary Stevenson answered.

"Okay, so we wait for the resolution and put mechanisms for asset-freezing in place. What if China increases their aggression in the South China Sea?"

Several in the room grew tense at the idea of a military confrontation between the two superpowers. That kind of scenario could lead to some scary places.

"We have several contingencies in place. It all depends on how they start it. As we all know, there are opportunities for intercepts to quickly escalate into a shooting war. We've taken every precaution we can think of to stop an incident from turning into something more. If one of their aircraft bumps into one of ours, our crews have been briefed to not react militarily. Instead, we'll take advantage of the situation and hand the ball back into your court," General Dawson commented, nodding to the secretary of state. "Now, if they go after one of our carrier strike groups, that's a different scenario, and we'll engage to defend ourselves while pulling out of the South China Sea before discussing further military moves."

"Good. We don't want things to deteriorate into a shooting match. It's important that we be able to control the tempo. We have too much to lose otherwise."

"I agree. We stand a good chance of not being able to fully support South Korea should we go to war with China, and you can bet that madman in the north will take advantage of the situation the moment the first shot is fired. You can equally bet that China will push him to invade. Odds are that China will also take advantage of the opportunity to invade Taiwan," General Dawson agreed.

"So, now we wait," President Winslow concluded.

As the room emptied, Frank paused to reflect on just how his cabinet seemed to be working together. It wasn't always so smooth, and it was good to see the usual cliques that formed around foreign policy discussions were missing. Perhaps it was that Americans were being held captive, or that they were all relieved to still have their jobs. However, that shared look between Bill and Tom sent shivers down Frank's back.

* * * * * *

United Nations Council Chambers, New York City
February 12, 2021

Elizabeth Hague organized the papers before her for the hundredth time. Looking up from her desk, she gazed across the chamber as other ambassadors began slowly filing in and taking their seats. Dark windows angled down from within a richly paneled curved wall encompassing the head of the chamber. Behind these windows were rooms designated for the many interpreters necessary for the main body to function.

Guest seats positioned around the edges of the curved head of the chamber were mostly empty with the exception of one woman dressed in the formal uniform of a United States Army colonel. Beside the woman was a man who looked to be Indian or Pakistani. Colonel Hayward from USAMRIID and Doctor Patel were chatting amiably as they also watched the chamber slowly fill.

Ambassador Hague stopped fiddling with her papers and composed herself for the upcoming presentation and vote on the resolution. She knew how this day would end but needed to put on the show regardless. That was the nature of diplomacy between superpowers these days. It was a stage for grandstanding and demonstrations, a way to deliver messages. It was also an attempt to sway other nations into following.

Elizabeth knew that being a woman was a disadvantage in some instances—or rather, with some countries—but she never let that affect her performance. She was good at her job, understood the ins and outs of the UN, knew how to arrange deals behind the scenes, and knew that she carried a reputation for steeliness that had earned the respect of many nations where women weren't treated as equals.

She surveyed the room. Normally, there would be the low murmur of conversation, but with the disparate languages present today, the chamber was filled only with the rustling of people getting settled into their chairs. Ambassadors put on headsets to make sure their systems were functioning correctly and their interpreters were online. When everyone was present amid the low hum of many people gathered, silence ensued as the secretary-general walked in and took his position at the head table. He called the assembly to order and read off a few notices. He then presented the resolution and gave Elizabeth the floor.

"Esteemed colleagues, I come to you with a matter of import that has affected all of us. It has spread to every corner of the world and destroyed years of growth for our nations, whether big or small. I am of course talking about the SARCoV-19 pandemic sweeping across the world. It has killed not only the old and infirm, but has taken our sons and daughters as well. Not only has it caused extended sicknesses but it has been shown to have lifelong health ramifications in the nature of permanent nerve damage and internal scarring."

Elizabeth paused for dramatic effect. Looking around the room, she caught the deep and penetrating gaze of the Chinese ambassador. That stare said that he knew where this was heading and that it wasn't going to be a fruitful endeavor. But he was searching for some hidden sign of the direction that the United States might take in other arenas, and for what the Americans knew. He had been in this business a long time and felt he knew what to watch for. However, Elizabeth had also been doing this for a long time and knew how to hide what she needed to, how to subtly divulge those secrets she wanted known.

"But I'm not saying anything that you don't already know. You have seen the human damage with your own eyes, have had to deal with torn families in your own countries. You have also watched your economies tumble into ruin. You have my sympathy for what you are going through, for this virus knows no boundaries, knows no religious or political beliefs. No matter our creeds, we all share in the consequences of this pandemic. For you, my heart grieves as I have seen the death and destruction close up.

"Although I hate to do this amid all this grief, I have to bring this matter to your attention. To do otherwise would be negligent. As much as I hate saying this, SARCoV-19 is not a naturally occurring virus, but is instead a manufactured one."

This created a murmur of conversation throughout the room. Elizabeth glanced over to the Chinese ambassador and the small delegation with him. The Asian man was now openly glaring at Hague, his glasses slightly reflecting the room's lighting. He didn't move a muscle, as if his gaze alone could destroy Elizabeth and halt her next words. In a way, it also felt as if he were daring her to voice them.

"Ladies and gentlemen, we have conducted lengthy scientific studies, submitting the results for peer reviews, and there is no doubt that SARCoV-19 was manufactured in the Wuhan Institute of Virology."

Elizabeth again paused as her statement took the assembly by storm, the low murmur of conversation suddenly rising in volume. Within seconds, the chamber turned into near bedlam as several ambassadors attempted to ask questions over each other. However, one voice in particular rose above the others, and the room became silent. The Chinse ambassador was speaking.

"Ambassador Hague, you and your nation are embarking down a dangerous path with these lies. This *science* you speak of is one obviously concocted by the United States specifically designed to discredit the People's Republic of China. This assembly is not a place for you to come seeking political gain. You embarrass yourself."

Ambassador Hague turned in her seat to stare directly at the Chinese ambassador.

"Mr. Ambassador, unlike your virus, the science is not manufactured, nor is it refutable. Any nation conducting their own studies will arrive at the same conclusion. If we are spreading disinformation as you claim, then that will come to light, won't it? But the fact remains that you," Elizabeth said sternly, pointing a finger at the Chinese ambassador, "manufactured SARCoV-19 and released it upon the world. You did this in an attempt to bolster your flagging economy. Shout, scream, glare, and deny all you want, but the science speaks for itself. It happened. You did it, and in doing so, you caused irretrievable harm to us all. Now we're asking for fair restitution for the damage you and your nation have caused to the rest of us."

Turning her attention back to the entire assembly, Elizabeth softened her tone and leaned forward, her hands open on the table.

"The resolution before you is lengthy and contains many scientific terms that may be difficult to follow, but I assure you that the information contained within and the conclusions reached are unfortunately correct. To say this in more understandable terms, I have invited Doctor Pate, director of the CDC, to walk us all through the science behind the findings."

Doctor Patel rose from his seat and strode to the raised desk where the secretary-general was seated. From there, he began to speak in a sure and confident tone. He presented the scientific findings, focusing on the step-by-step process conducted by the USAMRIID, without mentioning them by name. The director described the specific genetic sequence that pointed the finger at the Wuhan facility. Following his briefing, there were few questions.

Elizabeth sat silent for a moment as Doctor Patel departed the stage, looking around the room to gauge the reactions. She made eye contact with as many as she could. She saw a mix of emotions. Some of the ambassadors were angry at the news; others appeared confused as to whether they should believe what they were told. Still others seemed unconcerned. It was about what she expected, but the game had to be played out.

"This resolution calls for sanctions to be imposed against China until such a time that they make the forthcoming restitutions. We are asking each nation to pass this resolution and then submit their cases for restitution based on the loss of life and economic damages that came as a direct result of the pandemic. It also asks to curb other aggressions demonstrated by the People's Republic of China. Sanctions against China will hold until they dismantle the military bases and other structures on their manufactured islands in the Spratly and Paracel Islands. Sanctions will ease with each step taken by China, starting with the removal of military personnel and equipment," Ambassador Hague continued. "With this section of the resolution, we are only asking for this esteemed assembly to uphold the World Court's judgement that China doesn't hold any territorial rights extending from a manmade island."

For all of the ambassador's famed skill, the vote on the resolution to sanction China for the manufacture and dispersal of SARCoV-19 failed, just as Elizabeth and the administration she served suspected. Smaller countries who relied on China for a majority of their goods weren't about to nip at the hand that fed them, and the European Union wasn't ready to tackle anything so grand.

Ambassador Hague addressed the assembly following the vote.

"I'm sorry to see that this once esteemed body has become so politicized. This was not the intent when it was created, and it's a sad day for the entire world when we can't uphold a World Court decision. Today, I'm ashamed to be associated with such an organization."

She then neatly placed the resolution into the folder before her and stood. Colonel Hayward and Doctor Patel rose with her. With her chin held high, Elizabeth strode out of the assembly chamber, passing the Chinese ambassador on the way.

"This isn't over by a long shot," she spoke softly, staring the man in the eye.

"Is that a threat?" the Chinese ambassador replied, speaking perfect English.

Elizabeth smiled slightly, a softening of the lips. "Mr. Ambassador, I don't threaten. Consider it a warning."

Elizabeth then turned and continued toward the exit. The

show was over, including the interaction with the Chinese ambassador. Her performance was perfect. She'd served notice to everyone that this matter would be pursued. It also provided detailed evidence that the Chinese had attempted to conceal. Although the assembly failed to act, there would be actions taken outside of the chambers with regards to trade with China. No one had any doubt about it.

* * * * * *

South China Sea
Fiery Cross Island, Spratly Islands
7 May, 2021

General Tao hovered over the radar operator as he stared at the screen depicting the seas and air surrounding the base. Ever since his arrival on the island two weeks ago, he had been a terror to the soldiers and airmen stationed on the island. The days spent at the beaches and floating on the blue waters of the lagoon were at an end. When he arrived, the men and women stationed at the military installation were treating the assignment as a personal vacation. Well, that was over. Training sorties for the aircraft parked on the ramp and in bunkers had been increased. The ground soldiers placed for security ran endless drills against incursions. It was the same for the anti-air and anti-ship units protecting the islands. The general was there to make his mark, and the slackers among his troops weren't going to spoil that.

Blips shone brighter with each turn of the radar. Aircraft flew high overhead, many of them commercial jets coming out of Malaysia or the Philippines. A few American warplanes flew from their bases in Japan, but none of them came close to the twelve-mile territorial limit of the island. Out to sea, several smaller warships prowled. At the moment, two PLAN destroyers were shadowing two approaching American warships. It appeared that the Americans were about to make one of their freedom of navigation passes.

The thought of the Americans intruding into Chinese

territorial waters with impunity really angered General Tao. How long would his government allow for their legal national waters to be invaded at will by the Americans? It was an embarrassment. But he had his orders not to directly interfere. The best he could do would be to vigorously radio the Americans to leave, order the Chinese destroyers to close the distance, and direct his aircraft to conduct close overflights. What he'd like to do was to light up the American offenders and send them to the bottom of the ocean. That would teach them to interfere in Chinese waters. Instead, he watched as the two American destroyers continued to slowly close in on the island.

* * * * * *

South China Sea
Fiery Cross Island, Spratly Islands
7 May, 2021

"Okay, folks. Let's remember what happened to the *Howard* last year and stay sharp," Commander Simmons said.

The USS *Preble* was approaching the twelve-mile line at Fiery Cross Island on yet another FONOPS assignment. These missions had come more often since the beginning of the year. The pressure was being exerted on the Chinese, especially with the continued presence of two carriers operating in the South China Sea. This wasn't the *Preble's* first passage near one of the manmade Chinese islands, and it probably wouldn't be the last before they departed for their home port.

Commander Simmons stood looking at the plot. As usual, two Chinese destroyers were flanking the *Preble* and the *Pinckney* as they made their freedom of navigation passage.

"Crossing the line, sir," LCDR Wallins stated.

Commander Simmons nodded at the information. They had already gone to general quarters and there wasn't much more they could do. He looked at the plot, wondering why the two destroyers were maintaining their positions. Normally, one would break away as they approached the twelve-mile line and start to shadow them. It troubled Simmons when patterns changed.

"Perhaps they're pulling back because of what happened last year," Wallins said, reading Simmon's expression of concern.

"Yeah, maybe. I'll take an easy tour," Commander Simmons replied.

"You have that right, sir."

Nathan Simmons was ready to get back home. He should have been there already. The strike group put into Guam due to the SARCoV crisis sweeping through the *Roosevelt* and then having to quickly make ready for another deployment was just really bad timing. He was supposed to be back for the birth of his daughter, their second child. Instead, he was stuck in port while Anna Grace was brought into the world. The pictures he received did little to alleviate the sadness he felt at not being there. He couldn't wait to hold her.

"Aircraft approaching, bearing 135 degrees, speed five hundred knots," a sailor manning the radar plot called, pulling Commander Simmons back into the present.

The camera feeding one of the monitors swung out in that direction. Long swells rolled under a leaden sky, the gusty winds whipping spray from the top of the crests. The weather spoke of possible sleet later in the day and promised an uneasy night with increasing swells. Looking at the monitor, Commander Simmons could almost hear the wind howling around the ship. It was the time of year when it could be bitterly cold followed a day later by summer-like weather.

Two small dark spots appeared on the monitor, growing larger by the second. They were flying low, the radar confirming their height at three hundred feet. The two aircraft were coming in line abreast and aimed at the *Preble* like darts. Details materialized as the two attack fighters streaked across the water, missiles hanging on pylons mounted under the wings. Then, like a flash, the two aircraft with red stars on their wings and on each of their twin tails raced over the top of the *Preble*, a scant hundred meters above the masts. Even deep within the CIC, the roar of their passage could be felt and heard, causing some sailors to reactively duck.

Lieutenant Commander Wallins chuckled. "Sounds like they put it in afterburner."

"I guess they really want to make a show of it," Commander Simmons replied, smiling as the others within the combat center quietly laughed.

The radio started up and the game began.

* * * * * *

South China Sea
Fiery Cross Island, Spratly Islands
7 May, 2021

General Tao watched from within the island's combat control center as the American ship closed in on the territorial waters. He had sent a flight of Shenyang J-16 fighters aloft to conduct flybys should the Americans again invade sovereign waters.

"Sir, the captain of the *Changsha* is asking if he should break off and shadow the lead American vessel," a radio operator said.

"Tell him to hold position," General Tao impatiently replied.

The general knew that he would gain favor in Beijing if he could turn away one of the American missions. Besides, he despised the Americans. Their military power made China look second-rate. By inference, that made him appear inferior, and that wasn't something he could stomach. The way they acted with impunity raised his blood pressure every time he thought about it. So far, however, the Americans had steadfastly refused to back down regardless of the escalating measures he had taken. Well, that was fine. He had one more trick up his sleeve—one that would definitely anger the Americans and make them retreat if they knew what was good for them.

"The lead vessel crossed the twelve-mile territorial boundary."

Rigidly standing behind the radio operator with a grim expression, General Tao ordered, "Notify the flight to conduct a low pass and start the standard radio procedures."

The usual methods weren't deterring the Americans, as they hadn't each and every time. The problem, the general understood, was that the Americans were well aware they weren't going to be fired on or rammed. Therefore, they were content to shrug off the close calls and the warnings like water on a duck's back. They needed to be shocked into uncertainty and forced to pull away in order to reassess their situation. Even though they would protest loudly, it would still be a win for China and definitely a win for him, the general who caused the Americans to flinch.

General Tao walked over to the radio station and quickly wrote on a piece of paper. The radio operator paused in his repeated warnings. Reading the note, he looked up at the general questioningly. General Tao nodded and motioned in no uncertain terms that the note was to be read.

"American vessel. You have entered Chinese territorial waters. This constitutes an invasion. Leave now or you will be fired upon."

General Tao nodded and walked back to his previous position, waiting to see if the American vessel turned. Another couple of tense minutes passed with even the radio operator pausing to see what would happen. On came the vessel.

"Very well, then," General Tao whispered.

"Turn on our surface targeting radar and target the American vessel," General Tao ordered.

One could sense the secret gasps coming from the stationed personnel. They knew that the Americans would interpret the active targeting of one of their vessels as an act of war, as would any Chinese ship or aircraft. That was the line neither side ever crossed in this game the two countries played. The radar operator hesitated, looking back at the general as if he had misheard the order.

"You heard me. Target the American ship," General Tao repeated, his lips tightening.

The radar operator reached over and then turned the switch from "standby" to "on." He then selected the American vessel and the system chirped, notifying that it had a good target lock. It was then with some surprise that all within the room heard a faint whoosh from outside and noted the panels indicating that a missile had been fired. That was followed seconds later by several more. The entire contingent of anti-ship missile batteries fired their complements of missiles. It was then that the general realized that the system had been put into automatic rather than manual mode. He froze in horror as he watched his career, and possibly his life, come to an abrupt end.

But it was too late, the deed was done. Within seconds, fifteen YJ-62 subsonic anti-ship cruise missiles were on their way to a target only eight miles away. Flight time to target: One minute.

*   *   *   *   *   *

South China Sea
Fiery Cross Island, Spratly Islands
7 May, 2021

"We're being painted by a shore-based targeting system," a sailor shouted.

"Implement jamming and inform DESRON 23," Commander Simmons ordered.

"Missiles inbound from Fiery Cross, bearing 330," the same voice called. "That's nine...ten...twelve...fifteen inbound."

"Flank speed, full starboard rudder, come to heading 150. Unlock the SAMs and tell the *Pinckney* they're cleared to fire their Sea Sparrows," Commander Simmons commanded.

"What about deploying our decoys?" LCDR Wallins suggested.

"Standby with that."

"Aye-aye."

A rumble rolled through the ship as the single screw bit into the waters, the vessel surging forward as the speed increased. The deck heeled under the feet of those standing, the ship carving an elegant curve as it turned rapidly to the southeast. Water shot from the bow as the *Preble* cut into the swells, rising over wind-blown crests and descending into deepening troughs.

Commander Simmons thought about nestling the ship into a trough to present less of a picture for the missiles to home in on, but the swells weren't tall enough to hide much of the ship. Instead, he thought the changing picture of the ship up and down might fool the sea-skimming missiles. It wasn't much, but it was something, and in this situation, every little thing helped.

"Heading 150 degrees, speed 23 knots and increasing," the helmsman called.

On the fore and aft decks, medium-range anti-air missiles left their rails in a flurry of smoke. The high-speed darts rose quickly into the sky, found their targets, and dove toward them. The two 25mm Bushmaster chain guns and the 20mm Phalanx Close-In Weapons System (CWS) swiveled toward targets painted by the fire control radar.

"Nearest missile four miles and closing, thirty-two seconds to impact."

The central plot within the combat information center was filled with dozens of blips that weren't there half a minute ago. Fifteen anti-ship missiles fired from the Chinese island were heading toward the ship. Counter-battery fire from both the USS *Preble* and the USS *Pinckney* filled the skies with additional missiles as they sought to destroy the incoming threat.

"Let's get the drone aloft and make sure it's uplinked to the *Roosevelt*," Commander Simmons ordered. "And get me DESRON 23 on the line."

Three miles apart, the two American destroyers drove through the swells at high speed, their bows rising and plunging into the seas. Constant clouds of smoke engulfed the fore and aft decks, missiles arcing into the leaden skies. All the while, the crew of the two Chinese destroyers watched the show in both awe and shock.

Several miles behind the USS *Preble*, two small explosions flashed briefly just feet over the top of the crests. Two of the anti-air missiles from the *Pinckney* had found targets, the splashes of water quickly whisked away in the brisk gusts.

"Splash two," the radar operator called within the *Preble*'s CIC.

"Splash three," the operator called a second later.

"DESRON 23 on the line, sir."

Commander Simmons looked again at the board and decided he had a quick second or two to talk to the destroyer squadron commander.

"Sir, I assume you have our information. We're deploying defensive measures but still have twelve actives targeting us. I'm requesting permission to fire TLAMs at island targets," Commander Simmons asked.

"Negative, commander. This comes down from CSG 9. Do what you need to do to protect your vessel, but no offensive action is authorized at this time."

"Aye, aye, sir. *Preble* out."

And that was that. They were to fight their way out and hope the destroyers shadowing them or aircraft flying overhead didn't join the fight. The short conversation also told Commander Simmons that he wasn't going to get help from the carrier strike group. There wasn't much help they could offer, anyway. Any aircraft responding would arrive long after the show was over.

Commander Simmons watched the anti-air missiles take down the incoming Chinese projectiles. However, time was running short.

"Nine missiles, two miles out. Fifteen seconds until impact."

He watched the monitor depicting the outside of the ship; water boiled over the bow as the *Preble* dove into the trough.

"Standby on the chaff," Commander Simmons calmly ordered.

The bow of the ship pushed out of the water like some creature rising from the deep. It rose on the next wave, breaking free at the crest. The *Preble* then began to dive back down the backside of the swell.

"Deploy chaff," he ordered as the tail went over the crest.

Cannisters shot upward, angling away from the ship toward the rear. Those then broke open, deploying thousands of foil strips. Two of the Chinese missiles veered from their path and tore into the cloud of tinfoil. Thinking they were at their target, the missiles detonated. The explosions and the wind tore the thick clouds of chaff apart, but more were added in a continuous series.

Some of the remaining missiles were fooled by the countermeasures, but not for long. Breaking through the chaff, they found their target again. Six missiles out of the original fifteen still dove toward their moving target, acquiring it as it rose out of the troughs.

Aboard the *Preble*, buzzsaws sounded on the open decks as the Bushmaster chain guns and the Phalanx system opened up on the missiles as they came into range. Hundreds of rounds sped across the waters, tracers showing their path as they sought after missiles quickly closing in. In the space of ten seconds, three more missiles met their end as the large caliber rounds intersected and tore into the thin-skinned darts. One missile clipped the top of a wave and vanished in a massive spray of water.

Smaller splashes followed the remaining two missiles as they sped inbound, but they were too close. Had the *Preble* been a mile farther away when the missiles were fired, it might have had the time to finish the remaining two.

Maintaining position off the stern of the ship, the uplinked drone feeding the carrier strike group video of the action watched unemotionally as a missile streaked into view and slammed into the side of the USS *Preble*, cutting deep into the reinforced hull just below the CIC before exploding. The ship shuddered and smoke roiled out from the hole, pieces of the hull splashing into the surrounding waters. A second later, another missile streaked into view and rammed the ship just aft of where the first one hit. The USS *Preble* broke apart. Two halves of the ship bobbed a few times in the swells and then quickly vanished underwater, leaving behind an area of debris and slicks from the stored aviation fuel.

Of the 281 crew, only twelve made their way to the surface. They were quickly whisked aboard the Chinese vessel *Changsha*. The USS *Pinckney* turned to pick up survivors, launching their helos, but were turned away by the accompanying Chinese destroyer *Hohhot*.

"Chinese vessel, you have fired upon a United States naval vessel in international waters. We are heading in to pick up any survivors," the commander of the *Pinckney* radioed.

"Negative. We have already picked up any surviving prisoners. Leave or you will be targeted."

Prisoners? the *Pinckney* commander thought as he contacted the carrier strike group.

"Those aren't prisoners but survivors of an unprovoked attack."

"They were invading sovereign Chinese waters. They will be transported to the hospital located on Fiery Cross Island."

* * * * * *

South China Sea
7 May, 2021

"Launch the alert birds," Captain John Garner ordered upon hearing the news that the USS *Preble* was currently under attack. "And then get some tankers aloft. The patrols are going to start getting thirsty soon."

He then checked the plot. With the exception of a Russian and a Chinese trawler tailing the strike group, the seas were empty for a hundred miles around. Captain Garner glanced outside just in time to see an F/A-18E Super Hornet catapult off the deck with a roar, the afterburner turning the wet decks to steam. The aircraft climbed and quickly vanished into the low ceiling scudding briskly overhead. It was followed by another seconds later, the two aircraft joining up and proceeding to reinforce the fighters already patrolling the surrounding skies.

Satisfied that there weren't any immediate inbound threats, he turned to the DESRON 23 Commander.

"Are we prosecuting any submarine threats?"

"Negative, sir."

"Very well," Captain Garner replied, picking up a phone to the combat information center to relay the information.

*   *   *   *   *   *

Chomping on the end of a cigar, the admiral grumbled his reply into the phone, turning around to verify the information received on the CIC plot. He measured the attack currently underway against the *Preble* with everything else he was seeing. So far, it seemed to be isolated to the two destroyers. The Chinese seemed to be getting more forceful about preserving their illegal territorial rights around their manmade islands. The very thought that they'd fire on one of *his* ships pissed him off. Admiral Fablis would like nothing more than to shove a hundred cruise missiles up the Chinese bastard's ass, but his orders were very clear.

"Pull the *Lake Erie* in for defense," the carrier strike commander ordered.

With two of his destroyers off on the freedom of navigation operation and now fighting for their lives, his protective screen was severely limited. The addition of two littoral combat ships helped, but they didn't have the same capabilities as the Arleigh-Burke destroyers.

"Sir, the *Preble* is asking for weapons release to target Fiery Cross."

"Negative," Admiral Fablis replied. "They can do anything defensive in nature, but no offensive attacks are to be conducted at this time."

On a large monitor, a drone was relaying live video of the fight. Missiles were leaving the rails of the *Preble* as fast as they could be loaded, with more leaving the fore and aft modular cells.

"Get me Pearl," Admiral Fablis ordered.

Holding the phone to one ear, he watched water crash from the destroyer's bow as it plunged through the seas. In the background, he listened as his own operators called the number of missiles inbound to the *Preble*. Admiral Fablis pushed his will out to the destroyer and its crew, hoping to hear that the last missile had been sent into the sea.

"I have Admiral Blackwell on the line, sir."

"Put him through."

"Ed, I just received a report that the *Preble* is under attack. What's going on there?" asked Admiral Blackwell, the Third Fleet commander.

"Just that. They were conducting a FONOPS and the Chinese bastards fired fifteen missiles at them," Admiral Fablis answered.

The monitor then showed the first missile strike the side of the ship, followed quickly by the second. The ship came apart under the subsequent explosions, splitting in two and quickly sinking below the waves.

"Well, sir. They just sank the *Preble*. Permission to turn the island into a parking lot," Admiral Fablis said.

"I'm afraid this is going to go higher than either of us. This is in Washington's court now. Maintain your presence, but if it looks like the Chinese are going to launch attacks against you, then clear out to the Philippine Sea. I'm sending the *Nimitz* and Carrier Strike Group 11 to you. There will be a lot of fallout from this, so standby for further orders. You are cleared to enact a hundred-mile boundary," Admiral Blackwell stated.

"Aye, aye, sir. And if any Chinese naval vessel wanders inside the boundary?" Admiral Fablis inquired.

"Send them to hell."

"Will do, sir," Admiral Fablis responded, but the line had already gone dead.

"Sir, the Chinese aren't allowing the *Pinckney* to pick up any survivors. They're saying any survivors are prisoners and being taken to the island."

"Fucking hell!" Admiral Fablis sharply whispered. "Very well, recall the *Pinckney* and put this group under general quarters."

He continued to give orders, including a broadcast on emergency frequencies of the hundred-mile limit being imposed around the strike group. If any Chinese vessel came a foot inside the border, there would be a volley of missiles sent their way.

General Tao had achieved his purpose. He had turned away the American freedom of navigation sorties from the debated territorial waters. Anna Grace Simmons would grow up without ever getting to meet her dad.

Chapter Five

Beijing, China
7 May, 2021

"We've been trying to get the yuan to go international, but our progress is slow," briefed Lei Han, the Chinese finance minister. "Our problem is that many countries that had agreed to trade in the yuan are now hesitating due to the news of our involvement in the pandemic."

Lei himself hesitated mentioning anything regarding the Chinese manufacture of the SARCoV virus. That was a tender spot nowadays, and a subject better danced around. But the truth about why the economy was continuing to show declines and the yuan was falling in international markets needed to be known. All of their efforts to become the world's number one economy were slipping through their grasp since the American ambassador had announced that the virus was manufactured and intentionally released by China.

"We seem to be painted into a corner by the Americans," Paramount Leader Hao stated.

Lei nodded. "Agreed. We can't afford to back off from our position, and they aren't going to either. So, we either push forward and hope the other countries come around, or we come to an agreement with the Americans. At present, we're both in a position where the only moves are drastic ones. The Americans can seize our assets and we can sell off our investments. Either move will hurt both economies, so I doubt the Americans will be eager to continue."

Hao looked at his military commanders. He knew where they stood. If he left it to them, they'd launch attacks against the two American carriers currently patrolling the South China Sea. In the many talks they'd conducted, they were confident they could sink anything the Americans sent into their waters. They may not be wrong, but the strong military presence in Japan, particularly Okinawa, wasn't something he could dismiss. The Americans would have long supply lines, but Hao knew the

Chinese Navy wasn't a match for the American Navy in the long run. China's only strength was their massive number of aircraft and missiles. China may be able to box the Americans out of the inner seas, but America could box them inside the same area.

However, the situation could also be advantageous to China. They might be able to use the time to finally deal with the situation in Taiwan. They might even persuade the Philippines into allowing Chinese troops onto their soil. Hao would be willing to make concessions in the disputed Spratly Islands in exchange for that. If he could manage that feat, then China would control the inner islands and seas and gain significant control of the Philippine Sea. It was something to consider. The rewards would be great, but so were the risks.

First, they had to stabilize their market before they could start thinking of expanding territories. Perhaps for now, it was best to start backdoor negotiations with the Americans to alleviate the economic tensions between the two countries. Hao would accept a deal with them in the short term in order to expand China's realm of regional influence. In the longer term, any deal he reached with the Americans now would be negated once China firmly established themselves.

He said as much, the ministers around the table nodding at the wisdom of the priorities. Well, all except those with a hundred medals hanging from their uniforms.

The heavy knock at the entrance door startled President Hao from his thoughts. It was a rare thing indeed for these meetings to be intruded upon. Most matters could wait until they finished state planning, so it was with interest and not a little foreboding that Hao watched the doors swing open and one of the guards enter. Stiff-backed and eyes trained on nothing in particular, the guard crossed the room and placed a sheet of paper in front of Hao. He then stood at attention, waiting for any orders that might be given him.

Before pulling it closer, Hao stared at the paper laid carefully before him. For a moment, he wondered if the Americans had beaten him to the punch and frozen China's assets in the United States. But no, that wouldn't be reason enough for the meeting to be interrupted. Did Taiwan finally announce their independence following the arms sale from the Americans? That would definitely invite an intrusion. Perhaps an American and Chinese airplane collided in the South China Sea.

Reaching out, Hao grasped the paper and read through the contents, his fury rising with each word. The anger was quickly followed by a sinking feeling of dread. While there might be a backdoor meeting with the Americans, it wouldn't now be about their economic differences. Now it would be a discussion about averting a war.

Cell phones began going off around the room, the generals reaching for them. They looked to him with devices in hand. President Hao nodded his approval for them to answer as he was pretty sure what the conversations on the other end would be about. Hao was also pretty sure politics were at work here, making sure he was the first to get the news before the calls were made. He watched the surprise register on the faces of his top generals, which quickly changed to scheming and maneuvering thoughts, including political and military opportunities. Of course, heads could also roll over this. They all hung up and looked to him.

"Well, fuck! Someone explain to me why we've suddenly thrown away all leverage!" President Hao growled.

"We had a gung-ho general turn the targeting radar on an American vessel conducting one of their freedom of navigation operations. He did this without conducting the usual checks; the system was in automatic mode," one general explained.

Hao glowered. "This should never have happened in the first place. I want the general arrested and charged with treason. I'll have his head. We've now been put into a position where we either have to fight or accede our territorial claims on the islands. We can blame the general for a lack of control and make our apologies, but the Americans will press their advantage regardless."

Admiral Lin, commander of the South Sea fleet, saw his opportunity and took it. "This may look like a disadvantage, but we could use this to push our agenda. We can use this to finally clear the Americans out of the South China Sea and make valid our claims to the islands instead of losing them."

"I agree with Admiral Lin," National Defense Minister Zhou responded. "We have a chance here to continue our push for expansion. If we sink the two carriers, we'll not only send a message that China has emerged as a world military power, but we'll also convey our strength to other nations. That will make them more amenable to making the yuan an international currency as Finance Minister Lei has been trying to do."

"It is possible that we won't have to rely on the dollar for our transactions, thereby removing one threat the Americans hold over us," Lei excitedly stated, leaning forward.

Hao knew he needed to quickly take charge of this situation and not let his policies be usurped by those around the table who desired war. "I will think about this. Let's first discuss what route the Americans may take in response."

Those in the room sat in silence for a moment, their brows knitted with such intense concentration it appeared they were attempting to summon a demon from beyond. The foreign affairs minister, Liu Xiang, broke the silence.

"Seeing they didn't immediately attack the installation, my guess is that the Americans are going to use this to push their diplomatic agenda. I'm quite sure they'll again attempt to push the failed United Nations resolution of last February. That will assuredly include measures asking for the body to impose the World Court ruling and try to remove us from the islands."

"What are the chances of that happening?" Hao inquired.

"Well, better than they were an hour ago, but I still doubt it will pass. We can count on the countries we're about to sign a free-trade agreement with, and there are too many other countries who rely on us for their economies. The Americans won't try to push anything through the security council as we can too easily veto any move there. There is a chance that they'll petition the World Court with motions, widening the ruling already established and asking for restitution," Minister Liu answered. "They may also put in for the World Court to look at restitution for their economic downturns due to the pandemic."

National Defense Minister Zhou scoffed. "We'll just ignore those ridiculous rulings as we've done in the past."

"Of course. However, I will put it out there that too many actions against us will not only sway other countries to look elsewhere for their trade but will also give corporations pause before investing in China," Foreign Minister Liu commented.

"So, if the United Nation's route fails and we ignore any World Court ruling against us, what will the Americans do?" Hao asked.

"I can see them conducting even more of their freedom of navigation missions," Defense Minister Zhou replied.

"I'm asking specifically if the Americans will attack. And I'm speaking about the Spratly Islands," a frustrated Hao asserted.

"That certainly is a possibility. But I doubt they'll do anything until they've exhausted their diplomatic maneuvers. We can drag that out a year or more, and by then, today will be just a distant memory for the rest of the world," Foreign Minister Liu responded.

"Any attack will have consequences. Their carrier groups will have to enter into range of our aircraft and missiles. We have a number of nuclear submarines we can flood the area with, further negating their ability to operate. Their ability to sustain operations for an extended period of time will be hampered by the overwhelming numbers we can bring to bear. I'm saying that the Americans won't react right away, regardless of what they decide to do," National Defense Minister Zhou added.

Hao listened to his ministers. What they said sounded like good advice and mostly followed his own thoughts. However, the Americans had become more aggressive of late, and he was not sure that the pace of their little dance hadn't now changed. As much as the Americans held the diplomatic cards right now, that advantage would diminish over time. Hao envisioned the United States attacking the islands before their political clout began to dissipate, only holding back now because of the prisoners his sailors pulled from the sea.

"Are the prisoners still being held on Fiery Cross?" Hao asked.

Defense Minister Zhou nodded.

"Hold them there for now. They aren't to be harmed, and allow Red Cross visits. Keep them comfortable and fed, but secure. We'll use them along with our condemnations against the Americans for their continued intrusion on Chinese territorial waters. They're bargaining chips to be used down the road, limiting any American response. Keep them on the island, and the Americans won't attack as long as they're there.

"Make it known that they're on the island and will remain there. In order to forestall any of their special operation teams from conducting a rescue, we'll let it be known that any American soldiers coming on the islands will be considered an attack against China itself. Any American vessel penetrating Chinese territorial waters will be considered an attack, and they will be fired upon.

"So, for now, we'll issue a letter of condemnation for the Americans intruding upon Chinese territorial waters. In that condemnation, we'll say that we're sorry it came down to the sinking of the American vessel and subsequent loss of life, but that we cannot tolerate any intrusions into our territory. Issue that today before the Americans come around and issue theirs.

"Work on social sites to start turning public opinion in our direction. Make it look as if we were tolerant of the continued intrusions, but our patient talks with the Americans bore no fruit and we were left without a choice. We just won't tolerate this bully-like behavior anymore."

Hao paused before continuing in an icy tone. "And I want the man responsible for firing those missiles in prison by the end of the day."

* * * * * *

Washington, DC
White House Situation Room
8 May, 2021

The click of heels reverberating off the tiled floors matched the cold anger President Winslow felt. The sun hadn't yet risen and wouldn't for some time. He'd been woken and had been paying close attention to the transpiring events after initially confirming Admiral Crawford's decision to stand down and not initiate hostilities against the Chinese installation.

What angered President Winslow more than anything else was the lack of a telephone call from President Hao apologizing for the unprovoked attack. He would have accepted any lame excuse the Chinese president wanted to offer. However, instead of the expected call, the only thing coming out of China was a condemnation of repeated American intrusions into Chinese territorial waters, portraying the United States as a bully.

Walking down the brightly lit hallway with two Secret Service agents trailing behind, President Winslow's mind was busy poring through options. He had watched the video sent from the *Roosevelt* carrier group of the USS *Preble*'s valiant fight and subsequent sinking. Upon completing the viewing, he was more in line with Admiral Fablis's attitude to turn the island into a parking lot. Accompanying his anger was a feeling of helplessness. He couldn't just order an attack without pursuing more peaceful avenues first, and there were the twelve survivors being held hostage on the island to think about. During his walk to the situation room, there were moments he wished he could just vaporize the entire Chinese mainland. That would sure alleviate most of the headaches associated with his term in office.

The two Marines at the entry door came to attention. Reaching for the handle, one of the guards paused to wait for the president's okay. Winslow paused for a moment to collect himself, settling his turmoil and raging anger. His thoughts centered and he overrode his thirst for vengeance, exchanging them for more realistic and strategic actions. With a calm demeanor, he nodded for the Marine to open the door and then strode into the room.

"Ladies, gentlemen, please take your seats," he said, gesturing to those in the midst of standing for him.

A quiet rustle of movement intruded upon the somber mood prevailing in the room as chairs were moved and rearranged. The room was filled to near capacity with all of the department secretaries present.

"Okay, I'm assuming everyone viewed the video," President Winslow began.

Heads nodded around the room, including four admirals on a remote video cast on the large screen on the wall.

"Good. I don't want to have to watch that again," Winslow continued. "Let's go over what happened."

Secretary of Defense Aaron MacCulloch looked over to the secretary of the Navy, Jake Chamberlain.

"Mr. President, I'll let Admiral Crawford brief this one — Admiral?" Secretary Chamberlain commented.

The monitor screen filled with the Pacific Fleet commander.

"Aye, sir. At approximately 0100 Eastern Standard Time on 7 May, the USS *Preble* and the USS *Pinckney* were conducting a FONOPS mission off the shores of Fiery Cross Island in the Spratly Islands. FONOPS are the freedom of navigation operations we conduct in the area to negate the Chinese territorial claims of their manmade islands. If we did not conduct these operations, then China would be able to start making valid claims by default, and that can't be allowed to happen.

"These operations follow a pretty standard set of actions. We cross a twelve-mile line and the Chinese begin their radio broadcasts telling us to leave. This operation started off no differently."

President Winslow knew that the extended explanation was for the benefit of others who may not know what the FONOPS missions were about, chiefly the secretary of

Homeland Security. Joan Richardson was privy to much of the decision-making process, but not many defense-related matters.

"The USS *Preble* crossed twelve miles from the shores, and the radio back and forth began with the ship iterating they were operating in international waters and conducting themselves accordingly. Again, this was nothing new or different. At that time, two Chinese fighter attack aircraft conducted a low pass over the ship. The USS *Pinckney* was in a trailing position three miles behind.

"At eight miles, a Chinese targeting radar came online and targeted the destroyer, firing fifteen missiles from shore-based anti-ship batteries. Both the USS *Preble* and the USS *Pinckney* engaged the missiles with their defenses, shooting down thirteen of the missiles. Unfortunately, two missiles made it through the defenses and hit the *Preble*. It sank almost immediately, taking most of its crew.

"The USS *Pinckney* attempted to close in to pick up survivors but were stymied by two Chinese destroyers. They were told that the crew were being picked up and transported to the island as prisoners. It's believed that there were twelve survivors pulled from the sea who are still being held on Fiery Cross," Admiral Crawford briefed.

"Are there any questions for the admiral?" President Winslow inquired.

No one spoke.

"Thank you, Admiral," President Winslow responded. "Okay, we need to discuss where we go from here. As much as we all want to strike militarily, we have to pursue diplomatic options first. After all, we can't allow ourselves to fit into the bullying theme the Chinese are taking. So, let's start there. Fred, what do we have?"

The secretary of state cleared his throat and attempted to smooth down his wiry hair, which seemed more unkempt than usual.

"I started talks with Sweden about opening backdoor negotiations with China regarding the survivors. At a minimum, we may be able to find the bargaining chip they're going to use them for. We'll be pressing hard on the world stage for the immediate release of the sailors, portraying them as victims rather than the prisoners China is claiming them to be. It'll be a game that neither of us will back away from, but one that must be played out for the world's populace.

"We'll go back to the United Nations with our resolution, this time with the message, 'See, this is what happens when you stall and give an aggressive nation an indication that they can do as they please.' Like the last one, it probably won't pass, but it will give more nations pause when they contemplate dealing with the Chinese.

"I plan on filing two cases with the World Court. Both will be seeking restitution. One for the SARCoV-19 impact on our economy and the second one for the unprovoked attack on the USS *Preble*. Even if they're awarded, the Chinese are likely to ignore the rulings. However, this will again give nations and corporate entities pause when contemplating new dealings with China. The goal here is to hedge them in with all manner of negative actions against them. Enough of it, and we may see the release of the sailors without them being used as bargaining chips.

"Now, I want to bring to light the upcoming free-trade agreement in the works with fifteen eastern Asian and Pacific nations. This includes the Philippines. It appears that China and the Philippines are drawing closer together even though they still have issues surrounding disputed regions and resources."

"We have to keep China out of the Philippines," CIA director Tom Collier interjected. "If they're allowed to station troops or aircraft there, then we'll have lost the inner and outer island rings. That means we can be kicked out of the South China Sea *and* the Philippine Sea with ease."

"Tom, I'm aware of the ramifications. But you're right, we can't allow China into the island nation. Fred?" President Winslow asked.

"I'll speak with President Ramos, but I'm not sure that it will do any good. Maybe this incident will prove to him of China's aggressive nature, as if he doesn't already know," the secretary of state answered.

"Offer them our assistance in dealing with China's aggression in their fishing and oil-producing territories. We can sell them more frigates at bargain prices so they can better compete with any interfering Chinese naval vessels," President Winslow offered.

"As I said, I can try, but I'm not sure how much weight we carry with President Ramos anymore," Secretary Stevenson concluded. "The Chinese are offering him the moon."

"And if that fails?" Director Collier inquired.

President Winslow knew exactly where his CIA director was headed, and noted the NSA director's head perk up a notch.

"You know we can't condone state-sponsored hits, assuming that's where that question is leading," President Winslow stated.

"Now, I wouldn't suggest you condone any such thing," Director Collier replied. "But, I am suggesting that you allow us to work a little more closely with the various rebel groups camped in the highlands."

"Let's discuss that should we need to. I am authorizing you to look into the matter and put together some contingency planning," President Winslow responded.

Nothing further was said regarding the matter. There were messages to be read between the lines, the meanings of which were perhaps differently interpreted depending on your position within the cabinet.

"Is there anything else we're pursuing in the diplomatic arena?" President Winslow asked.

The secretary of state shook his head in the negative.

"Do we have the mechanisms in place for freezing Chinese assets?"

"We have identified as many assets as we're going to," the Treasury secretary said. "Just give the word and we'll have all of them frozen inside of fifteen minutes."

"Good, keep your phone handy and make sure you're in a coverage area. So, here's the deal. I want our people out of there. The Chinese aren't going to get away with this. They may attempt to stall our response in the hopes that this incident will fade into the background as far as the rest of the world is concerned. We're not going to let that happen. I want us to be ready to roll back to the tariffs we had in place before the trade agreement and additional sanctions placed on Chinese electronics. As I said, I want our people out of there."

"Shall I summon the Chinese ambassador for a dressing down?" Secretary of State Stevenson inquired.

"Absolutely not! We're not going to give them the satisfaction. They can fret and stew over what we're going to do."

"I assume that's the same for initiating any contact with President Hao."

"If he wanted to talk, he had a chance before issuing their condemnation. A call now would be seen as weakness. If he wants to chat, he knows where I can be found."

The secretary of state nodded.

"At this point, we've covered our diplomatic moves and we'll be moving into military matters," President Winslow stated.

The room came alive with shuffling as those who knew they weren't a part of the next proceedings gathered their belongings and departed.

"Now, we've covered our diplomacy. I want military options as well. What will a rescue mission look like? What will an operation against the island involve? I want to know the ramifications and how we can prepare without tipping our hats," the president questioned.

"Let me start off by saying that Britain and Australia have both offered their support and assistance. Britain is offering to take over 100 percent of the Hormuz operations. That will free up two destroyers and a cruiser we have stationed in the straits," Secretary of Defense MacCulloch stated. "Australia is offering to augment one of our carrier strike groups with two destroyers."

"I would suggest taking them up on their offers. With the

Australians as part of the group, the Chinese may think twice about attacking a multinational task force. Plus, it will look more like a multinational endeavor rather than just an American one," Secretary Stevenson advocated.

"Okay, let's accept those offers," Winslow said. "So, military options?"

The Chairman of the Joint Chiefs glanced up, his inquiring demeanor asking if he should provide the answer. Defense Secretary MacCulloch nodded.

"Mr. President. If we focus on a strictly rescue operation, we'll utilize one or two SEAL platoons infiltrating the island via a SEAL delivery vehicle embarked on one of our LA-class submarines. We'll have the survivor location pinned down and then the SEAL team will go in and rescue them. One or two Ospreys will stage out of Okinawa or on a carrier and wait offshore under the radar, sweeping in to pick up the survivors and SEAL team or teams.

"This option will minimize our military presence, therefore not giving the Chinese much to complain about. The world will see it as a hostage rescue. I don't see the Chinese reacting to this scenario militarily. SEAL Team Seven has been put on standby for two platoons and they're already poring over maps of the island. I've also taken the liberty of alerting the SEAL Delivery Vehicle Team One out at Pearl. The USS *Santa Fe* is in port at Pearl and they've been put on alert for a mission," General Dawson briefed.

"Continue with that contingency planning. What time frame are we looking at should I give the okay?"

"We can have the delivery vehicle and SEAL team briefed prior. We should have a definitive location with the next satellite pass over the island. That's scheduled in a little over two hours from now. We can have all pieces together in twelve hours, but I ask for two to three days for the teams to run practice drills. Then a day of travel for the *Santa Fe* to arrive in its mission area, so four days. If you give the go-ahead in three days, then we can move within twenty-four hours," General Dawson answered.

"Do what you need to move to a point of deployment. With all we're going to be doing on the diplomatic front, you'll easily have your three days. I wouldn't anticipate giving the go-ahead for at least a week or two," President Winslow responded.

"Sir, if I may add. If we wait until we exhaust diplomatic measures, then the Chinese will know we have no further option but this one and will be waiting for us to try it," General Dawson added.

"Duly noted. Just put this together and I'll keep what you said in mind. Now, does anyone see any other ramifications than the Chinese throwing a temper tantrum?"

"They'll try to push harder to bring the Pacific nations to their side and may start building more manmade islands, but I don't see them reacting militarily," Secretary Stevenson replied.

"Very well. I want us to look at a larger operation, rescuing the hostages and then punishing the island," President Winslow said.

"Are you talking about leveling the island or just delivering a couple of cruise missiles?" Secretary MacCulloch inquired.

"Leveling it," Winslow stated.

"Sir, that will involve a few more assets, but it won't be much more than what we discussed. The rescue will have to occur first and the hostages pulled back to a safe distance, there to hunker down while the actual strike is taking place. Another SEAL team will have to be involved to take down the installation radar system if we're to deliver an effective strike. That will have to be timed so that the incoming missiles aren't detected, but not early enough that they'll be able to get their aircraft aloft. So, that will likely mean sub-launched cruise missiles with air-launched missiles fired from our B-2s as a follow-up volley.

"The hostages and SEAL teams can be picked up during the confusion when the missiles are hitting or afterward. Those will still be Ospreys waiting out of the radar picture."

General Dawson paused. "You know, the rescue birds

can start moving in once the radar is taken out. Keep in mind, sir, this is just a quick contingency planning that we did when we received the news."

"Okay, so I have it straight. The hostage rescue scenario stays the same regardless of which route we take. In the larger action plan, the rescue comes first. Then the radar is taken down once the hostages have been rescued, and that is timed with submarine and aircraft missile launches," President Winslow clarified.

"That's about it in a nutshell," Secretary MacCulloch stated.

"I can think of about a hundred ramifications stemming from destroying the island, but I want to hear it from you. Fred, let's start off with those of a diplomatic nature."

"Well, the immediate one is that we'll lose our sympathy card. It will be viewed as a tit for tat and the world will continue on as it did. Nothing will be gained on the diplomatic front, and we'll lose any advantage we seek to profit from. They hit us, we hit them back—done. We'll scream about the sinking and they'll scream just as loudly about their island being attacked.

"They'll likely start rebuilding immediately, even if we contemplate hitting the island so hard that it reverts back to the shoals it once was. There won't be much we can do to stop them," Secretary Stevenson said.

"That is, unless we state that we'll keep hitting the island if they attempt to rebuild. We can make statements that any rebuilding will destabilize the region," Secretary MacCulloch added.

"That won't do diddly-squat. We've said the same thing for years and it hasn't done any good," Secretary Stevenson retorted.

"Unless we truly do keep hitting any attempts they make to rebuild."

"That will eventually be taken as an act of war."

"And hitting the island won't?"

Secretary of State Stevenson paused and then said, "Okay, good point."

"Gentlemen," President Winslow interjected. "We're on the same side here. So, on the diplomatic front, they'll holler just like we're about to do. But in the end, the status quo will be maintained. Is that what you're saying, Fred?"

"Pretty much."

"So, now let's look to the military reaction."

"Now, this is where it could get interesting," Defense Secretary MacCulloch responded, leaning forward. "And by interesting, I mean dangerous. They could just focus on their economy, content to rebuild the island and call the entire thing a draw. They could up the ante and go after our carriers in the South China Sea, bringing enough firepower to bear to wink them both. They'll pay dearly in terms of equipment lost, but stand the chance of losing two carriers. Not only that, but we'll also become viewed as a beatable foe.

"As it stands, the world is afraid of the firepower we can bring to bear anywhere in the world in a short period of time. The sinking of two carriers will diminish that fear in a hurry, especially in Iran and North Korea. In short, we can't allow that to happen, but neither can we be viewed as being easily chased out of the area. That will invite other nations to think we can be pushed around. The way I see it, we'll have one chance at a first strike at anything in the region, but then we'll have to retire outside of their range, moving in for short strikes. Their navy is no match for us, but we can't ignore their submarines, which can fan out over the seas and fire on us from just about anywhere.

"That's one avenue. They can also retaliate against a like target, like Guam. Remember, we pulled the bombers out because of just such a scenario. I see this as the most likely avenue for them to take. Attacking our carriers will involve a much larger retaliation from us, and we'll likely end up in a no-holds-barred war with China. That's something neither of us wants."

"Excuse me, sir, but I'm not convinced that we'll end up in a larger war if we're attacked or they escalate matters," chief of naval operations Admiral Durant interjected. "If we don't attack their mainland, they won't attack ours. If we keep hostilities to just armed forces in and around the eastern Asian seas, I believe that will be the extent of operations on both sides. We attack their subs, airborne aircraft, and surface vessels out of port, they'll do the same. They believe they can keep us out with their sheer numbers, and we believe we can beat them with our superior technology."

"I see what you're saying, Admiral. But, can we keep it limited like that, and won't we be tying our hands?" President Winslow asked.

"I do believe we can limit the nature of engagements. Sure, we can't hit their land-based bombers on their airfields, but we can certainly hit them once they're inbound. We take out their subs with our own, thereby opening up the sea and making it safer for us to travel through. Well, the Philippine Sea for sure, but that's all we'll need. Then we strike out against any surface fleet ships that are away from their ports. This will hopefully lure their bombers out, and we eliminate them in a series of engagements. In this scenario, it's important that we remain out of range of their cruise missiles so the Chinese aren't able to launch over their own territory. Our worry will be how they view Okinawa and Guam and whether those constitute American homeland bases and are thus off-limits. I just want to note that this will take time and that there isn't a short-term solution regardless of what direction we decide to take."

"Very well, those are definitely things to keep in mind. What else?"

"Well, sir. We need to keep Taiwan and South Korea in mind. If things do escalate, then we'll be hard-pressed to protect South Korea as the Chinese will be able to easily intercept any reinforcements we may need there. That little bastard to the north won't need much persuasion to march south. And I seriously doubt the Chinese will waste an opportunity like this to strike across the strait to Taiwan. So, we run the risk of losing both should this come down to a shooting war, limited or not," General Dawson commented.

"All good points. What reinforcements can we put in

place now?"

"We can alert the various Marine expeditionary units we have stationed across the Pacific, putting them on a seventy-two-hour notice," Marine Commandant Calloway stated.

"Very well. Do that and continue along with the SEAL team contingency we discussed earlier. We'll put out our own condemnation letter within the hour, and I'll want a presidential address to the nation scheduled for nine P.M. Eastern time. I think that's all for now."

*   *   *   *   *   *

After poring over the video taken by the drone hovering near the USS *Preble*, the Pentagon released it to the major media outlets. It quickly circulated, and by noon, it was viral worldwide. The condemnations were quick among the world's populace, but there was also the usual rhetoric that America was reaping what it had sown. And thus went the social media platforms; outrage and cheering.

The United States issued a strongly worded condemnation of China's unprovoked attack against an American naval vessel traveling in international waters. It spoke of China's unchecked aggression in the region, defying a World Court ruling against their manmade islands. The United States hinted at sanctions and a reinstatement of tariffs should the Chinese government not provide restitution for the sinking of the vessel and the subsequent loss of life. There were calls to release the twelve sailors being held hostage.

At 9 P.M. Eastern Standard Time, the outlets halted their programming to cut over to a scheduled presidential address. One by one, television screens switched over and were filled by the presidential seal.

"Ladies and Gentlemen, the president of the United States," a narrator stated.

The TV sets then changed to show a somber President Winslow sitting at his desk in the Oval Office.

"My fellow Americans, I come to you this evening with

grievous news. Less than twenty-four hours ago, an American naval vessel was attacked by Chinese missiles while sailing in international waters. My heart goes out to the 201 families who lost loved ones ... to the families broken by this unprovoked attack. Out of respect for the families, I will not be showing the video now circulating across the internet.

"Not only has China attacked one of our vessels, but they are also holding the twelve survivors hostage. President Hao, release these captives so that they may rejoin their families. With this, there will be no negotiation. Return the hostages.

"I'm here to tell you that the increased aggression displayed by the Chinese government will no longer go unchecked. Too long have we stood by and allowed China to bully their neighbors and defy the World Court. We attempted to reason with China, but it has now become apparent that they intend to illegally expand their borders.

"We ask that the Chinese government show a measure of remorse and provide restitution for their reckless actions. This won't bring our loved ones back, but it will provide some relief for the grieving families. And as a measure to protect against this kind of tragedy occurring again, China must dismantle their illegal manmade islands.

"I have placed our military forces under an increased alert. However, at this time, I have not ordered any form of retaliatory attack. We are not the Chinese who resort to force as a first form of negotiation, but instead seek peaceful resolutions. However, I will see our sailors being held in captivity freed from their bonds.

"As a final note, I want to emphasize that we Americans will not tolerate this kind of naked aggression, and that this direct action against the United States of America carries consequences."

Television sets across the world flashed again to the presidential seal and then resumed their normally scheduled programming.

Chapter Six

United Nations Council Chambers, New York City
10 May, 2021

All eyes followed Ambassador Elizabeth Hague as she strolled down the center aisle of the UN council chambers. They knew what the emergency meeting was about and what would follow, but all were eager for the drama about to unfold. Many wondered if the United States would make a direct attack against China or be content with merely trying to push the resolution before each of them. The call for action wasn't much different than the failed one proposed back in February of this year, so it had many wondering what else the United States had in store.

Ambassador Hague didn't make any eye contact as she strode down to her seat and settled in, arranging papers in front of her. Once she was seated, the secretary-general called the assembly to order and gave Elizabeth the floor.

"Esteemed ambassadors," she began, "I came to you in February, warning of the consequences if China's aggression was allowed to continue unchecked. Well, we now know where that decision led. The question in front of us today is if we're going to let this continue. For if we fail to act now, China will view its actions as being condoned by this legislative body. So, I ask each of you, what will happen should we fail to act? Will they then invade the Philippines? Vietnam? Australia? Anyone else they have disputes with?

"This body was created at the end of an era of devastation in order to provide for a more peaceful world for us and our children to live in—a place to negotiate peaceful resolutions without engaging in wars and, if necessary, to step in with soldiers to create boundaries to enforce the peace or sanction nations should they overstep the boundaries put in place by this august governing body.

"The United States condemns the actions taken by China in the sinking of a vessel sailing peacefully in international waters. We ask that this body take up the outrage of those families needlessly torn apart by China's unchecked aggression. And along with that condemnation, I come before you again asking for sanctions to be enacted against China until such time as they prove to be curbing their aggressive and illegal attempts at expansion.

"I came to you a month ago pleading for action, but we failed to prevent this tragic loss of life. Do not make the same mistake this time around."

A hush settled over the assembly as she leaned back in her chair. Many within the assembly turned their gaze toward the Chinese ambassador once the translations were made.

"China is the one who has shown patience as the United States repeatedly intruded upon Chinese sovereign territory," the Chinese ambassador began. "The so-called aggression is on the part of the United States, not China. These constant invasions of our territory amount to acts of war, but it is we who have shown restraint. The action against the American warship sailing on a mission of harassment was because we were left with no choice. We have pled with the American government time and time again to-"

Ambassador Hague jerked upright in her chair.

"Mr. Ambassador, you know as well as everyone else here that you have no territorial rights to the illegally made islands, as has been proved by a World Court ruling. You opting to ignore the ruling against you only proves your aggressive intentions, so please don't insult this assembly with your ramblings. You attacked a foreign vessel peacefully sailing in international waters, and nothing you can say will change that fact," Elizabeth scolded in a stern voice. "We are not children to listen to your fairy tales. There will be payment for your uncontrolled aggression, and holding our citizens hostage will not go unanswered."

As with the prior resolution, this one failed to pass, the votes going along nearly the same lines as before. However, there were additional countries willing to put their name to a motion condemning China's actions. Even though the motion didn't carry any teeth, this again was something to walk out of the assembly with.

Elizabeth gathered her materials and strode silently back up the aisle without so much as a glance for anyone within the assembly. Her stiff back and pursed lips spoke volumes more than any words she could have uttered. The large doors swung closed behind her as she exited. Withdrawing her phone, she dialed the number she had been given.

"Ambassador Hague," President Winslow answered.

"Mr. President," she replied, "the resolution failed as anticipated. We were able to gather a number of signatures condemning China's actions, but that's the best we're going to get along this avenue."

"Thank you, Elizabeth. We gave it our best effort."

"I'd like to slap that smug smile off the Chinese ambassador."

President Winslow chuckled. "I'm sure you'll be given the chance to see it vanish, but we'll have to be patient."

"I could wait three lifetimes to see that, Mr. President," Elizabeth responded.

"Hopefully you won't have to wait that long."

With that, the line went dead. One part of the required diplomatic maneuvering had been completed.

* * * * * *

Hickam Field, Hawaii
10 May, 2021

The ocean to the west shimmered under the glow of late evening sun, the shadows of the KC-135 refueling aircraft stretching long across the ramp. Glints of sunlight sparked off the tinted windshields as the van made its way around the large four-engine airplanes. Petty Officer David Hawser squinted as the sunlight played games with his tired eyes.

He'd received the recall notice late the day before while visiting his family in Seattle, Washington. His brother had just shown up, and David felt bad about only being able to visit with him for a short time. The two were close, and it was seldom that David was able to get away. But, he'd signed up for this gig, and when duty called, you didn't bitch and moan about it. Well, not much, anyway. Since then, he'd spent his time scrambling to find a ride back, hoping there was a Space A flight heading out. Luckily, he was able to catch a flight out of McChord and had just made it in time to find the van parked and waiting for him on the tarmac.

He had an idea for the reasoning behind the recall — the sinking and hostage situation had been all over the news for the past couple of days. In light of the recent news articles and his sudden recall, his family also had an idea where he was heading. David's father had pulled him aside and the two shared a moment together, with his father finally saying, "Give 'em hell, son. Watch your back and make sure you come home." David's father had been in Desert Storm, and his grandfather in Vietnam.

The two hugged fiercely. "I will, Dad."

"You just make sure you do," his dad said as they broke apart. The older man turned quickly and walked back into the house without looking back.

The ride with his mom and brother to the gates of McChord had almost been worse, but here he was now, and that was behind him. Something big was in the wind and he needed to be mentally and physically ready. There was never enough time to rest while on mission.

The van wove its way and stopped in front of two gigantic hangars. There, another van had just pulled up and was in the process of disgorging the rest of his squad. It was almost as if it had been planned. David stepped out of the van, the evening warmth soothing after the chill of the Seattle weather and the cold plane ride over. He grabbed his duffel bag out of the vehicle and hefted it over his shoulder.

"Well, look what the cat dragged in," a voice rang out.

"Yeah, well, I'll look better after a good night's rest. Unfortunately for you, Crimson, the case of uglies you inherited is forever," David replied, recognizing the voice of the team medic.

Low chuckles echoed off the tall hangar doors as the team extracted their bags and waited as the vans pulled away. One of the hangars had Marine guards posted at the entrance doors built into the giant sliding ones. Red tape marked the ground along with red ropes marking off the entrance, indicating that only those authorized to pass could do so. The Marines wouldn't hesitate to shoot anyone not authorized to cross those lines.

"I guess that's for us," Petty Officer Ken Bollinger said, pointing at the entrance.

"I suppose so," David replied and started for the door.

Outside of the taped-off area, David called out to the Marines, "SEAL Dive Team One, Alpha Platoon."

A guard waved him forward and held a hand out for David's ID. He checked it against a held clipboard and waved him through after handing back the card. David walked through the door and paused to adjust to the different lighting as the rest of his six-man team were checked one by one.

To one side of the vast interior was an area concealed by draped tarps. Behind the enclosure came the sounds of construction. Against the back wall, a briefing area of sorts was set up, with chairs lined in front of several screens and television monitors. On the opposite side of the construction was a large table covered in cloth. To David, this was nothing out of the ordinary, although this setup was a little larger than he was used to. He knew that the coverings weren't meant to keep things hidden from him or his team but were in fact meant to deter prying eyes. They'd be removed once the construction was complete and the workers left.

The fact that a SEAL dive team platoon was involved spoke of a shore landing, and there was only one that was currently making the news. He was 90 percent sure they were going after the twelve sailors being held hostage on the Chinese island.

"It's about time you got here, Sunshine. I hope you enjoyed your beauty rest," a voice called from the briefing area.

First squad turned in David's direction, all adding their two cents about second squad's late arrival.

"Well, sir, someone has to be able to go out in the world without frightening children," David replied. "The lot of you live under a bridge and scare travelers trying to cross."

"Get the man a mic. It's apparently comedy hour," someone in first squad replied.

"The only thing funny in here is your sister's persistence in sending nudes."

"Fucking take her...please. Her husband is such an asshole."

The two squads merged with handshakes, backslapping, and laughs.

"Good to see you, David," Lieutenant JG James Baldwin said.

"Likewise, sir. It would have been nice to get some sleep, but there's the big one at the end to look forward to," David replied.

The lieutenant ran the platoon when both squads were in the field together. If they split apart, then he was in charge of first squad while David was second squad's leader. First squad carried the name Gold Team whereas second squad was Blue Team.

"What's the skinny?" David asked.

LTJG Baldwin shrugged his shoulders. "Your guess is as good as mine, but it probably has to do with retrieving those poor bastards being held on Fiery Cross."

"Yeah, probably so."

"Attention on deck," one of the Marine guards called, his voice echoing in the cavernous space.

The members faced the front and came to attention. From a side room came a Navy commander wearing the trident of a SEAL, along with Lieutenant Newsome and Chief Petty Officer Fields, the platoon leaders.

"As you were, gentlemen," Commander McIntyre stated as he came to rest at the front.

"This won't be your briefing," Commander McIntyre

continued once the shuffling subsided. "That will be later. I just dropped by to welcome you to your new quarters for the foreseeable future. Amenities will be arriving throughout the rest of the day and night. You'll sleep and train here with your meals brought to you. Once per day, you'll be driven in to clean up, and god knows you animals need it. Construction will be complete by morning, when our real work will begin. For tonight, I've ordered pizza to be brought in. You can make your selections after I leave. And seeing how most of you can't be trusted with pointy objects — or crayons, for that matter — I've asked Chief Petty Officer Fields to take your orders."

"Wait, sir, are we talking about the same CPO Fields? I wasn't aware that he learned to spell! I believe congratulations are in order," David commented.

"How about I rest my boot in your ass, Hawser?" CPO Fields replied.

"Gentlemen," Commander McIntyre continued as if he hadn't been interrupted, "in all seriousness, this operation will be followed at the very top. Let's show them what sets us apart from everyone else, and remind them why we get the big bucks. That will be all."

The group broke apart with CPO Fields becoming the center of attention as orders were placed. That night, the entire platoon ate far too much and spent the next few hours watching movies. Behind them continued the relentless noise of construction.

* * * * * *

Hickam Field, Hawaii
11 May, 2021

The next morning saw major changes to the interior. The tarps were withdrawn from the construction on one side of the room, revealing a series of plywood buildings with cutouts for windows and doors. The large table on the other side of the room had its covering removed and held a scale layout of an island, complete with buildings. A long runway near a manmade lagoon occupied half of the island. A placard on one side of the mockup listed the location as Fiery Cross Reef, Spratly Islands, along with coordinates. The entire layout looked similar to a model train enthusiast's layout.

In addition to the living quarters, the briefing area included standing easels and additional electronic equipment that had been wheeled in during the night. The hangar seemed much larger without construction crews and the noise that had echoed throughout. With the exception of the platoon, the giant hangar was empty of people. The sunlight filtering through the translucent windows set high was a reminder of the nice day outdoors while they were trapped in the hangar. Not all of the space was reserved for work activities: a recreational section had been carved out complete with foosball, ping pong, pool, air hockey tables, and a basketball hoop.

However, those areas were quiet as the platoon members gathered in the briefing area. The banter and discussion quieted as a lieutenant crossed the hangar and strode to the monitors. Two easels had been covered with cloth.

"How are you today, gentlemen?" Lieutenant Daniels asked.

"Good, ma'am," David answered, with the others giving varying greetings.

"That's probably going to change," she said, removing the coverings from the easels.

One held a large satellite photo of an obvious military installation; the second showed a wider overhead view of the same location situated on an island.

"As you know," Lieutenant Daniels continued, "the Chinese fired upon and sank the USS *Preble*, an Arleigh-Burke destroyer conducting a FONOP mission. There were twelve survivors picked up by the Chinese who are currently being held hostage on Fiery Cross Island."

An aerial view of the South China Sea came into view on one of the monitors.

"The island is part of the Spratly Island chain located here," Lieutenant Daniels stated, pointing to an area between the Philippines and Vietnam.

"Your mission is the rescue of the hostages. As of now, delivery vehicles are being loaded onto the USS *Santa Fe* and the USS *Tucson*. These will be your primary means of ingress. As you can see in the photos, the western side of the island houses a single runway for almost its entire length. There is little else on that side except for missile batteries and two bunkers on the southwestern end with another set of bunkers near midfield. The rest of the western side is bare shoreline, but to access the rest of the installation, you'd have to cross the runway, lone taxiway, and tarmacs. This area is overwatched by the control tower. Needless to say, exposure would be great.

"The northern end of the island is taken up primarily by the manmade lagoon capable of holding multiple warships of all types. The lagoon is accessed by a deep-water channel carved out of the reef. This is patrolled by a either a frigate or corvette stationed at the island. Structures and additional missile batteries occupy the northern section of land adjacent the runway and a section on the northern end of a spit on the eastern shore of the lagoon. The antenna farm situated nearby indicates that these buildings house a communications center and more than likely a combat control center. This is also likely to house the radar facility.

"The eastern side holds administration buildings, along with the fresh water and fuel storage facilities. It is in one of these buildings near the airport that we believe our sailors are being held. The Chinese are allowing Red Cross visits; we'll be able to follow these via satellite to get a firmer picture of where they're being held. We'll also monitor if and where guards are posted and if food is being brought to any particular building.

"The Chinese have upped their alert levels, conducting an increased number of active patrols. We also have some indication that they're mining the narrow beaches around the island. The exception to that seems to be the interior beaches of the lagoon. So, we're looking at two options for ingress. One is through the channel. If that is chosen as the best possible landing site, then you'll make your way to the beach near where the spit of land connects with the main island. That will mean having to avoid the maritime patrols.

"The second option is to come in on the southern point near the end of the runway. From there, you'll head inland toward the hostage location or make your way along the beaches before heading inland. The major obstacle here is the tower situated on the southern end, which can keep nearly the entire southern portion of the island under observation.

"The plan at the moment calls for two Ospreys to be positioned offshore under the radar where they'll wait for your signal. When the hostages are in your possession, you'll rendezvous at an exfil location that's yet to be determined. Following the rescue, you'll then egress via the delivery vehicle and return to the *Santa Fe* and *Tucson*. So, in a nutshell: infil, rescue the hostages, exfil them via the Ospreys, and then return to the sub.

"Now, at this time, the mission is a rescue operation, but the mission planning must remain flexible enough to widen those parameters to include taking out the radar installation. The radars are located on the northern part of the island. If the mission expands, then two teams will infil. One team will be responsible for the hostages while the second one takes out the radar. This will all be firmed up soon. Are there any questions at this point?" Lieutenant Daniels asked.

"What will be the rules of engagement?" Lieutenant JG Baldwin inquired.

"You will be guns free, but use them with discretion. We don't want to leave behind a trail of bodies or a reason for the Chinese to strike back. If they lose a couple of guards, they'll bitch and moan, but it won't be enough to warrant a retaliatory strike," Lieutenant Daniels answered.

"Do you think they will anyway?" David questioned.

"What? Retaliate?"

"Yes, ma'am."

"That's a discussion for those with a much higher paygrade than mine or yours."

"When are we slated to go in?" Lieutenant Newsome

asked.

"No date has been set as yet, but there were whispers of an early June date. Anything else?"

Heads shook as each team member's thoughts crowded with the upcoming mission parameters. There wasn't a whole lot to go on, but they knew that details would be coming soon and the plan firmed up. With the briefing over, they began discussing methods for infiltrating the island, studying the provided satellite photos, and running through training exercises on the mockups. With each additional detail, they alter their plans.

* * * * * *

South China Sea
11 May, 2021

The creak of the blacked-out boat rising and falling on the dark waves seemed to carry for miles across the endless expanse of water. The faintest shred of illumination peeked out from a crewman hovering over a map spread across a rickety table, shielding the beam of his red-lensed flashlight with his body.

It was just after midnight, and Felipe Mendoza was crouched by the gunwales of the wooden boat, searching the inky void of the moonless night for any sign of his rendezvous. In these waters, they were just as likely to run into a Chinese patrol harassing Philippine fishermen.

It had been a tortuous past twenty-four hours getting to this desolate spot in the middle of the vast sea. The long flight into Singapore had only been the beginning. From there, it had been a series of boats like this current one, hopping from island to island. Only late yesterday afternoon had he departed a remote shoreline along Palawan's north coast, venturing out to meet his next ride, which would land him on Philippine shores. But Felipe was used to these long infiltrations, having done them for much of his fifteen years as an agent of the Central Intelligence Agency.

He checked his watch again, starting to get a little nervous about the situation. His next pickup was thirty-four minutes late, and he should have been out of here fourteen minutes ago. That was his usual allotment for past-due meetings. Anything longer usually meant bad times for those who hung around. It could mean a double-cross or that his contacts were found out by other intelligence officers. Turning toward the captain of the vessel, Felipe asked for the third time if he was sure they were in the correct location.

"The GPS was calibrated before we left. We are in the right place," the captain answered, his voice strained. He too was nervous about the late rendezvous.

Felipe was about to order them out when a flash of light broke out of the darkness. It was quickly followed by two more, and then another series of two. Felipe sighed, the tension leaving with the exhale. All was again right in the world. Had there been a different number of flashes in the final series, he'd have known something was amiss. How he would escape would have been a different matter. He brought the flashlight gripped in his palm over the edge and signaled back.

Before long, another wooden fishing vessel emerged out of the darkness and came alongside. The two boats rubbed against each other, the creaks intertwining with the splash of the waves as Felipe clambered over to the other vessel. He nodded at the new captain as the boat pulled away, leaving the first one to bob in the waves, quickly vanishing in the dark.

"Sorry for the lateness," the new captain said in halting English. "Chinese frigate."

Felipe quickly searched the surrounding waters for any sign of running lights, but the seas were blacker than the starlit skies above. Unless the naval ship was running dark, they were alone.

"No worry, my friend," the captain said, noticing Felipe's searching gaze. "My radar better than theirs."

The captain moved to the side, lifting the cover of a heavy tarp to reveal a screen of green with a sweeping hand. Several lighter blips appeared, but most were near the edges of the screen. The only near one was the vessel he had just departed from.

Felipe nodded and settled in, staring ahead into the darkness. Eighty miles ahead was the main Philippine island of Luzon, his landing point. That was at least five hours away. Knowing that he'd get little rest once he went ashore, Felipe dozed to the rocking of the boat as it rode the swells of the South China Sea.

*   *   *   *   *   *

Batangas, Philippines
11 May, 2021

A change in the waves woke Felipe. It was still dark, but he was able to make out two dark land masses in the distance, one to each side of the boat. A larger one loomed off the bow with lights dotting the far end of a large bay they were about to enter. Felipe instantly knew they were about to enter Batangas Bay, the last stage of his arduous journey.

Bracing himself against the swells, he yawned and stretched. Dawn was still a couple of hours away, and he looked forward to being able to sleep on a real bed. How long that would last would depend upon factors over which he had no control. He had his assignment and he would receive the go/no-go message soon. If his mission was a go, then life was about to become very busy. If not, then he'd remain in the Philippines for a while longer and shop the open markets. He might even visit some of his extended family, although he wasn't sure he wanted to put up with *that* chaos.

The boat slowly chugged across the bay; a few headlights could be seen tracing their way around the curve of the shoreline. The lights of the main city grew more distinct as they edged closer. The hum and the vibration of the motor were a part of his world. Water splashed from the bow as the lone propeller pushed the boat through the waves. Overhead, a few clouds began to blot out some of the twinkling stars as a front tried to push in.

Very few boats were prowling the bay; there was one ferry pulling away from the terminals. Others were docked with lights blazing, even now with a line of cars slowly working their way onboard. The captain worked toward the Calumpang River flowing out of the jungled highlands, passing a moored tanker parked at an offshore pumping depot. The waters were tricky with shallow sandbars forming outside of the two main channels. Fields surrounded the river at the entrance point, and the lights of the city glowed into the night sky.

Felipe thought again about his family, many of them living not many miles away. But the truth of the matter was that he was a man best left on his own. He'd had many opportunities to visit in the past, but always came up with one excuse or another to put that off for another time. If he were honest with himself, he'd admit that he didn't see them because he was afraid that he'd start longing for the close bond of a family. That's the kind of distraction he just didn't need in his current occupation, where he was either one hundred percent in or not in at all.

The horizon lightened as the boat chugged up the river, passing under the Calumpang Bridge. A concrete pier hugged the shoreline; the captain put his boat in alongside. Felipe hopped out just prior to contact and ran into the fields. He heard the boat's engines rev up as the captain pulled away and started making his way back downstream.

Felipe slowed and walked toward a small motorbike that was parked in a dirt lot. Reaching under the gas tank, he pulled the keys from the tape and was soon motoring down a dirt road until it intersected with a paved one. The bike was more noise and smoke than power, but he soon found himself pulling into the Hotel Ginazel. He parked just as the first rays of the sun crested the horizon, spilling light across the land. Checking in, Felipe found an old but intact backpack lying on the bed. Pulling out a satphone, he checked in and then took off his boots. With a tired sigh, he stretched out across the bedspread. Contented at finally being able to lie on a soft bed, he fell asleep looking forward to ordering a shit ton of good food when he woke.

* * * * * *

Ninoy Aquino International Airport
Manila, Philippines
12 May, 2021

The Gulfstream IV, bearing no identification other than a tail number, descended over Bacoor Bay. Secretary of State Fred Stevenson looked out at the clouds whisking past the windows. Off to the side, the lights of Manila glowed through the overcast skies. As the business jet broke through the low cloud layer, the expanse of lights coming from the Philippine capital city spread out like multicolored jewels.

The approach lights to the runway flashed underneath as the Gulfstream probed downward to touch the earth once again. The white runway lights marked the edges of the paved surface while airliners waited at the hold line with their red rotating beacons and flashing anti-collision lights, their interiors partially filled with early-morning travelers. The main gear touched down with a slight screech of heated rubber and a small patch of smoke. The nose lowered and the reversers kicked in, their roar mixing with the noise of jet engines.

Fred Stevenson had just touched down for his private meeting with Philippine president Ramos. This was to be yet another attempt to bring the Philippine president around to the United States. The rumors were that the Chinese were going to land troops and aircraft in the Philippines, and that wasn't something the United States was comfortable with. A move like that would certainly deny them free passage in the Philippine and South China Seas at China's discretion. Those areas, through which a vast amount of shipping traffic passed, would essentially come under Chinese control, and there wouldn't be much the United States could do about it outside of an all-out war. At the very least, Stevenson hoped that they could keep President Ramos neutral.

The aircraft taxied clear of the active runway and parked

on the small air base ramp. After descending the stairs, Fred was escorted to a waiting limo and whisked away. Very few saw what had occurred, and even fewer would recognize it for what it was. The limo departed the airport and sped up the Manila Metro Skyway, eventually arriving at Malacañan Palace, which served as both residence and presidential office.

Greeted at the doorway, Fred was ushered into a private office by President Ramos. There, the two men shared a drink and small talk before getting down to the reason for the secretary's clandestine and spur of the moment meeting. Secretary Stevenson again showed China's involvement in the SARCoV pandemic, along with their increased aggression in the South China Sea.

"We can offer our assistance in the future for your fishing and resource claims in the South China Sea. We can also assist with your World Court claim against the Chinese militarizing the Spratly Islands," Fred offered.

"What can the United States do? You are so far away and cannot fight the Chinese so close to their shores," President Ramos countered. "If I were to side with you or even take a neutral stance, then I would be putting myself in jeopardy. That's not something I can afford in today's times. My economy would be in ruins."

"I wouldn't be so hasty as to dismiss our capabilities out this far. Remember we have bases in Okinawa, Guam, Japan, and South Korea that essentially hem the Chinese in. In addition, we can offer some of our frigates as gifts, perhaps even have our Coast Guard patrol your fishing grounds," Secretary Stevenson added. "I believe we can work out some favorable trade deals that would be at least comparable to what the Chinese are offering."

"I'm sorry you traveled so far, but my hands are tied. Perhaps if you thought me and my country were so important, your President Winslow would have visited in person. I cannot help you," President Ramos stated.

"He would have been here if he could, but with the increasing crisis with China and our people being held hostage, he isn't able to leave Washington at this time. He holds the highest regards for you and your country. I hope you can understand and take his situation into consideration. We have a lot to offer that wouldn't require putting our troops or equipment ashore."

"I wish I could help you, but I must live with China in my backyard, and they're offering more than I can afford to turn down."

There were messages there that went unsaid, but Fred heard them loudly. The secretary of state had no doubt that subtle threats had been directed against the Philippines that Ramos wouldn't admit to. To go against China would put him and his country at greater risk.

The conversation continued for some time, but the Philippine president didn't budge from his position. The more that was said, the more Fred Stevenson gained the idea that a vast fortune was about to change hands, and President Ramos was to be the primary recipient. Of course, he couldn't prove it, nor was he about to offer his own bribe other than the assistance he already had. The outcome wasn't surprising. Nevertheless, it was with a heavy heart that he left the presidential palace and returned to the airport.

* * * * * *

NSA Headquarters
Fort Meade, Maryland
12 February, 2021

Allison Townsend yawned as she plopped down, her chair squeaking as she settled into the seat that had conformed to her shape over the years. As an NSA analyst, one of her early morning duties was to pore over recent satellite photos of the world's hotspots. Lately, she had been assigned to the far eastern theaters, or more specifically, China.

She set her refreshed coffee cup down, wincing as some of the hot beverage splashed over the rim, adding yet another spill to the stained desk. Every drop of caffeine was needed these days as her tired eyes took in the seemingly endless torrent of pictures that crossed her desk. Allison paused only long enough to ensure that the new spill wouldn't soak into the scattered papers and then pulled up the latest images.

The fourth photo caused her eyes to open more than the several cups of the thick, black coffee. She knew the Zhanjiang port without even having to look at the annotations, but she checked just to make sure. She scanned the previous photos to find the landing ships docked in their usual locations. However, this new one showed equipment lining the docks and the roads leading to the concrete piers. Tanks and personnel carriers mixed with a variety of other gear crated for loading. There was no doubt that equipment was being loaded onto the Type 072 landing ships. The helicopter decks were still clear, but those craft wouldn't be flown aboard until the ships were already at sea.

Quickly pulling up recent photos of other ports that were home to the PLAN South China Sea Fleet, she found the same activities for other landing ships and a few of the amphibious transport docks. It was apparent that a landing force had been put together and was in the process of boarding. Allison knew from experience that the process would take approximately seventy-two hours. It looked like the Chinese planned to put troops and hardware ashore, somewhere, in three days.

From scanning photos of naval air bases, it didn't appear that they were preparing for a major operation. That probably ruled out Taiwan as a target, but not completely. She dialed up her counterpart over at the CIA. The phone rang twice before it was answered.

"Hey, Tom. I have something interesting here. Have the Chinese announced any major exercises in the near future?" Allison inquired.

"Not that I'm aware of, Allison. Why? What's up?"

"I'm going to send you a few photos. Let me know what you think," Allison said.

She waited for a moment and knew the moment Tom saw the satellite pictures.

"Woah! When did these come in?"

"I just started sifting through today's download. Those are only hours old at the latest," she answered.

"Looks like they're planning something biggish. That's probably a reinforced regiment's worth of equipment we're looking at. We need to get this started up the chain immediately."

"You start on yours and I'll get mine cranking," Allison responded.

"Sounds good. Don't we have two carriers in the South China Sea at the moment?"

"Last I checked," Allision replied.

"That's what I thought. Okay, I'm going to hand-carry this upward. Good find."

* * * * * *

Ninoy Aquino International Airport
Manila, Philippines
12 May, 2021

Secretary of State Stevenson stood on the tarmac with phone in hand. The Gulfstream's aircraft power unit whined in the background, the lights glowing from the windows illuminating the wings and pavement. Members of the Secret Service stood at the top and bottom of the ramp, those at the top silhouetted by the aircraft's open door.

The warm night air surrounded him like a blanket. However, he paid no attention to it as he focused on the meeting with President Ramos. It had gone about as well as Fred expected, but it still angered him to be lied to. Of course, he knew he also lied to others, but it still irked him to be on the receiving end. In his opinion, President Ramos was about to snuggle up closer to the Chinese, and that didn't bode well for America's ability to project power in this part of the world.

Might as well get this over with, he thought, dialing the phone.

He was immediately put through to the president but

was a little surprised to hear that Bill and Tom, the NSA and CIA directors, were also part of the call. The line clicked as Phil Dawson, the chairman of the joint chiefs, also came online. Fred came to the conclusion that his information was deemed more important than it really was or that something had occurred while he was in his meeting.

It couldn't be that important or I would have been notified on the way to the airport.

"Fred, what do you have for us?" President Winslow inquired.

"About as expected. President Ramos isn't interested in solidifying our relationship and seems to be firmly in bed with the Chinese. I get the impression that it's a lot more than the upcoming trade agreement," Stevenson answered.

"We just received word that the Chinese are loading up military equipment on their landing craft. Our analysts say that a reinforced battalion of troops may be heading to the Philippines," NSA director Bill Reiser replied.

"His resistance to negotiate now makes a lot more sense," Fred responded. "I knew he was lying, but I couldn't figure out just why he was being so adamant."

"I bet there's a substantial cash exchange about to occur as well," CIA director Tom Collier stated.

"That was my thought, too. So, we've about exhausted our diplomatic avenues with regards to the South China Sea incident, and the Chinese know it. They don't think there's a thing we can do to stop them from closing down the South China Sea and serving notice to any who travel through the Philippine Sea as well," Fred said.

"They're not far from wrong. We can't put our carriers in the way without having freedom of navigation thrown back in our faces," General Dawson stated.

"You know, President Ramos could have an accident," Director Collier commented.

"As much as that would ease our problems, I can't condone any action like that," President Winslow said.

"Plausible deniability," Director Collier muttered to

himself.

"Of course not, sir. I wouldn't recommend that to you in any case. We may have to get used to a new world," Director Collier said, louder.

"I hope it doesn't come down to that," President Winslow responded. "We still hold the *Preble* card."

"Well, we all heard Fred say that we've about expended our diplomatic options. The World Court may come out in our favor, but that decision will come after the world has moved on from the sinking," Collier said. "Are we then looking at military options?"

"I think we should table that until Fred returns. We'll reconvene then and work through our options," President Winslow stated.

One by one, the goodbyes were said and lines disconnected.

Fred Stevenson pocketed his phone and strode up the stairs. Soon, he was swirling a whiskey on the rocks as he readied himself for a long plane ride back to Washington, DC.

Tom Collier, the CIA director, hung up and immediately dialed another number. He was on that call for exactly five seconds with even fewer words spoken.

* * * * * *

Hotel Ginazel
Batangas, Philippines
13 May, 2021

Felipe Mendoza set the tray of food off to the side and wiped his mouth. Taking a drink of water, he then picked up the satphone, which buzzed on the bed next to him. He listened to a set of random spoken phonetic alphabet letters and replied to the code with the appropriate ones on his end.

He then heard the sentence," Operation Hidden Tiger is a go. Repeat, Operation Hidden Tiger is a go. Acknowledge."

"Acknowledged. Hidden Tiger is operational," Felipe answered, hanging up.

Taking another satphone from his pack, he dialed a number and went through a similar verification process before informing the agent on the other line that Operation Hidden Tiger was now live. Arrangements were made and Felipe hung up, returning to finish his meal.

* * * * * *

Hotel Ginazel
Batangas, Philippines
14 May, 2021

Stuffing the ragged-looking backpack, Felipe ensured the satphones were placed in compartments hidden inside. It would pass a quick muster, but obviously not a thorough search. His clothing matched his pack—worn and patched. When he arrived outside of the city, he'd smear his face with a tinge of dirt. Coupled with the motorbike, he'd present a picture that would not merit a second glance, let alone arouse suspicion.

The low moisture-laden clouds that had rolled in had moved on. With the sun just clearing the mountainous terrain to the east, Felipe cranked his motorbike and began his journey out of town. Heading north to Manila, he'd then turn to the east and start a slower trek into the highlands along the eastern coastline of the Philippines.

* * * * * *

The paved highways gave way to deeply rutted dirt roads as Felipe made his way higher into the jungled mountainous terrain. The cities turned to small towns, which then became villages of aluminum-sided shacks leaning under the shade of palm trees. Beyond, the hills continued to rise into dense jungle. Underneath the solid green canopy lay his immediate goal: meeting with the commander of one of the larger rebel forces hidden under the thick canopies.

His motorcycle left a thin trail of whitish-gray smoke as Felipe bounced over and through ruts in a section of the road.

Ahead was one of the last villages before he truly began his trek into what could be considered the highlands.

Rounding a corner, he released the throttle and slowed the bike as he came face to face with a roadblock. Two Jeeps and a Humvee-like vehicle were parked to one side with bored-looking soldiers leaning against them and smoking cigarettes. One of the men dressed in green fatigues pushed away as Felipe came to a stop. Several of the soldiers also came alive, turning toward the stopped bike and holding their weapons in a more threatening manner.

The sergeant swaggered over. "Papers."

Felipe slowly dug into his pocket and handed his identification over to the burly man. Below his ID was a neatly folded wad of cash. The sergeant took the ID and gave it a perfunctory glance before flipping through the bills. Nodding, he took another look at the identification while pocketing the cash, and then returned the card to Felipe. Turning back to the roadblock, the sergeant motioned for the barricade to be opened. Two soldiers hefted the barricade arm, lowering it after Felipe passed. They then returned to smoking cigarettes and being bored, but a little more excited for their shift to end — the sergeant was known for taking his troops out for drinks if the take was large enough.

Continuing through the village, Felipe looked at several men squatting near one of the dilapidated buildings. They eyed him closely as he passed, and Felipe knew one or more of them were sentries for the rebel group hiding in the mountains. Once he vanished beyond, one of the men would disappear into the shack to make a phone call. Hopefully the right contacts would be made by other parties inside the country once he gave the mission signal, or he wouldn't have to worry about making it back through the checkpoint. His body would join hundreds of others hidden in the jungle, probably never found.

Not far up the road, he found a roadblock of a different nature. The men here wore a mishmash of military clothing and were most definitely not bored as they leaned against the battered pickups. They were alert and spread across the road, their automatic weapons trained on Felipe as he bounced along the ruts. He pulled to a stop and showed his hands as one figure stepped out from the line to move forward.

"The fox jumped over the sleeping dog," the man said with only a trace of an accent.

"People who pick their teeth with their elbow are annoying," Felipe responded.

He mentally shook his head, wondering whose full-time job it was to come up with pass phrases. That's a job he'd like to move into when his current occupation wasn't viable any longer. The man nodded and told Felipe to shut off his bike. Guns were lowered and several men stepped forward to assist with lifting the motorbike into the bed of one of the pickups. Felipe climbed up after it along with some of the men, and the small convoy of old but reliable pickups started down the road, their engines straining as they climbed some of the steeper sections of the road.

The road narrowed and the ruts deepened the higher they climbed, but they eventually arrived at a compound surrounded by log walls. The canopy high overhead hid the encampment from any prying eyes in the skies above, although Felipe wondered how they managed to remain invisible to thermal cameras. But that was a question for later, perhaps.

As they drove to a central building, Felipe noticed several Americans in the same mismatched gear as the rebels. He knew Green Berets when he saw them, and he wondered how long the four he clocked had been with this group. Perhaps they were backups in case his mission went awry, but they looked like they'd been here for a long while, so he wasn't sure that was the case. For sure there would be a contingency plan in case he failed, but he doubted it would come from these men.

Felipe hopped from the back when the truck came to a halt. As soon as his feet hit the ground, a large man emerged from the main building. Grinning and wearing a set of stars on the lapel of a green military fatigue shirt, the man came down a series of steps and thrust his hand toward Felipe.

"To what do I owe this pleasure?" the rebel general said.

"I think perhaps we should speak of that in private," Felipe countered, shaking the general's hand.

"Of course, of course. Come right this way," the general replied.

They entered the building and Felipe followed as the general led him into a room sectioned off from the rest. The general gestured Felipe into a seat and sat on the edge of his desk. His demeanor shifted from a jovial general among his troops to a more serious mien.

"This is a hastily arranged meeting. In my opinion, missions quickly planned don't often go well," the general cautioned. "But, as long as we're only used for information, then I guess it's none of my business beyond that."

"General Gonzales, it's not my wish to put you or your troops in any danger. As you mentioned, I only require information," Felipe stated.

"I will do what I can. What is it you need?" General Gonzales inquired.

"I need to know the president's schedule, or be directed to someone who does. I'm told that you're the man to talk to about that."

General Gonzales pursed his lips, obviously not comfortable with the conclusions that he was arriving at. He had fought against the president's policies for years, but conducting an assassination was coloring outside of the lines. The unwanted attention that would bring would demolish all of the progress he had worked for.

Felipe saw the tense expression and correctly guessed its meaning. "General, none of this will find its way back to you. I can promise you that."

"I can't say that I'm as happy to see you as when you first arrived, but I keep my promises. I will direct you to someone who will know the information you seek."

Felipe knew that the CIA was funding the general and had agreements in place for assistance. But he also knew that General Gonzales truly believed in his cause and wouldn't threaten it for any reason, even if it meant going against a request from the CIA. The general knew that the CIA needed him as much as he needed them, so he had a little leeway in what he would process.

"Thank you, general," Felipe replied.

General Gonzales nodded. "You will remain here tonight and my men will return you in the morning. You won't make it through the checkpoint today in any case."

The general then walked behind his desk and hastily scribbled something onto a piece of paper, tucking it into a manila envelope.

"Your information is in here," he said, handing the package to Felipe.

* * * * * *

Manila, Philippines
16 May, 2021

Felipe met — or rather talked with — the man indicated on the piece of paper General Gonzales had given him. The person on the other end of the phone had his voice disguised, placing the informant as someone on President Ramos's staff or a higher-ranking member of the military. Regardless, Felipe found that President Ramos was to give a speech in his hometown and thus he found himself there.

A platform was being erected in the soccer stadium, and military police were blocking anyone venturing that way. After finding a hotel with a room overlooking the construction, Felipe ensured the line of sight between his room and the platform where the president would be was adequate. It would be a long shot, but at least there weren't any cross streets with tall buildings. That diminished the possibility of swirling winds.

Satisfied with the location, he ventured down to an open café where he met with another agent, Andreas Cruz, who settled into a seat opposite Felipe and ordered a plate of chicken inasal.

"How goes it with our patsy?" Felipe asked in a low voice once the waiter withdrew.

"He's ready," Andreas answered.

"And what if he gets cold feet?"

"He won't. He's still grieving pretty heavily over the death of his son. He'll be there," Andreas said.

Felipe nodded. In this business, you had to have blind trust in some instances, and paranoia in others. This was someone he had to trust. The patsy, as he called it, was an older Filipino man whose son had been murdered by the death squads that roamed the cities and countryside alike. They hunted down suspected criminals and drug addicts, murdering them without trial. That was President Ramos's system for reducing crime. To be fair, it proved effective—the crime rate had dropped significantly since the program was implemented and there were those who greatly appreciated the measures. However, it also brought the ire of some families who were too poor to do anything about what had happened to their loved ones. Andreas had befriended the man in question, who was only too happy for the opportunity to do something about those who had taken his son. He was willing—nervous, but eager.

"You do have the weapon to give him?" Felipe inquired.

"Yes, yes. All is in order. We'll be ready, just don't miss," Andreas said, then went quiet as the waiter approached with a basket of bread.

Felipe scoffed at the notion. The weapon he spoke of was a handgun with special modifications made to its internals.

"Very well, until tomorrow. Enjoy your chicken," Felipe said, pushing away from the table.

Felipe spent the rest of the day strolling through one of the open markets near the square, eyeing food and also analyzing exits in case his primary one became blocked. The difference between this time and the others he had spent in similar markets were the masks everyone was wearing. At one stall, he watched out of the corner of his eye as a motorcade came into view, the others in the market with him turning as the flashing blue lights of police cars and waving flags of the president's limo caught their attention.

Shortly after, Felipe strolled back to his room with a

packaged to-go meal in hand. He immediately knew that someone had been in his room, but it was expected and he wasn't too worried about it. Setting his food on the bed, he reached underneath it and extracted a long, wrapped package. Inside was a QBU-88, one of China's marksman rifles. It chambered a 5.8mm round and was fixed with a 12× scope, a nonstandard issue but one Felipe had insisted on. He looked over the rifle to make sure it hadn't been messed with, wishing he was in the hills so he could make sure the sight was still accurate.

Well, I guess I'll find out tomorrow, he thought, hating to carry that variable into tomorrow's mission.

Normally, he wouldn't take the chance; he would find a way to test the accuracy. But there wasn't enough time to locate a suitable location and he didn't want to risk jeopardizing the mission. Besides, he had centered it before departing and he doubted much had occurred to change the settings. That was one thing the agency was very careful with. No one wanted a botched mission. With so many military personnel about, there was just no way he could depart and return with the rifle without raising an eyebrow or two. Setting the rifle back under the bed, he switched on a television show and settled back to enjoy his meal.

* * * * * *

Zhanjiang Port, China
17 May, 2021

Commander Ackland rubbed his eyes as he made his way into the control center, gladly accepting a cup of coffee that was waiting for him.

"Looks like we have a surge underway, captain," the XO stated.

The USS *Texas*, a Virginia-class attack submarine, rested near the bottom just outside of the Zhanjiang port quietly motoring only enough to maintain its position in the currents. Four days ago, they had been ordered to shift their patrol area in order to monitor the entrance, and now Commander Ackland understood the reasoning. Sonar was picking up a surge of traffic above and beyond what they usually encountered. The many screw noises underway made it difficult to pick out individual ships, but there was no mistaking the active pinging from several Luyang III-class destroyers.

"Sonar, Conn," Ackland called. "Are they going to be able to find us?"

"It's doubtful with our positioning, sir."

"Are you able to ascertain ship types?"

"It looks like we have three destroyers, contacts Alpha one, two, and three, bearing 334, 332, and 330 degrees, speed fifteen knots. Behind them are two to three Jiangkai frigates, contacts Bravo one, two, and three, bearing 325 degrees, also fifteen knots," sonar replied. "All contacts appear to have a baseline heading of one one zero degrees and are actively pinging."

"Oh, hang on, we have some big boys coming out. I count three Type 072 landing ships and two Yuzhao-class amphibious transport docks. Someone wants to put a lot of troops ashore somewhere," sonar added.

"Okay, let's keep count and get that info into a flash message. Once we're clear, launch the buoy with a thirty-minute delay."

"Escorts are spreading out, sir. It looks like they're taking up screening positions for the bigger boys. Base heading remains one one zero degrees," sonar said.

"Very well. XO, fortune has favored us with positioning. Set a course to follow and keep us inside their screen," Commander Ackland ordered.

"Aye, aye, captain."

* * * * * *

NSA Headquarters
Fort Meade, Maryland
17 May, 2021

Allison Townsend walked briskly to the watch commander's desk, carrying the latest satellite photos from Zhanjiang Port in hand. Slapping them down on the surface, she immediately drew her supervisor's attention.

"The Chinese have sortied," Allison stated.

The supervisor looked through the photos and lifted the handset, punching in an extension.

"James here, sir. Yes, sir, we have photographic evidence to back up the priority flash traffic we picked up from a station keeper that was parked off the entrance."

The supervisor listened for a moment, placed the call on speakerphone, and then lifted his head. "Allison, how many ships are we talking about?"

"Three Type 072 landing ships, two of their amphibious docks, and six escorts ... three destroyers and three frigates," she answered.

"Destination?"

"It looks like their course is toward the Philippines. They could swing south and head for the Spratly Islands, knowing that we may try something there. But, with the far east trade agreement looming, I don't doubt that the Philippines is their destination. I believe they're going to land troops there as support to President Ramos. I have other photos of Chinese troops gathering at one of their naval air bases. I would guess these ships will land and then they'll airlift the rest," Allison replied.

"James, CIA agrees with your analysis. I'm authorizing a retasking of satellite coverage so we know the moment the bastards change course," the man on the other end of the line said. "This has already been elevated up the chain, but those pictures will help. Make sure to also send those naval airbase photos along."

The line then clicked as the other end hung up.

* * * * * *

Manila, Philippines

17 May, 2021

Felipe snugged the QBU-88 marksman rifle to his shoulder and settled his head onto the cheek rest. The crosshairs centered on the podium erected at the soccer stadium. From his room high up in the Taft Hotel, he had a direct view into the stadium approximately two city blocks away. The curtains next to the open window hung motionless, which made Felipe's job much easier. The tricky part would be making sure the bullet didn't hit the tangled mess of electrical lines that were a prominent part of every Philippine telephone pole.

The extended bipod was set on a table in the middle of the room with the lights out. Even if he was glassed from security personnel, they'd have a difficult time seeing inside the room, and an open window wasn't anything out of the ordinary in the Philippines, where air conditioning was rare. That was one of the reasons Felipe chose this location. It was damn near ideal except for those damned power lines, but he'd have to contend with them anywhere he went.

President Ramos walked onto the erected stage, surrounded by his personal security teams. Those in attendance cheered the waving figure as he approached the podium, security fanning out in front. Felipe didn't have the clearest shot given those standing in front of the president.

"We're in place," a voice sounded in his earpiece.

* * * * * *

Andreas guided the old man into the crowd without being overly conspicuous. He cheered along with the others as President Ramos emerged and walked across the stage. The security poised in front of him and along the edges had constantly roving eyes, searching for the slightest sign of danger. At his side, the old man nervously licked his lips, not clapping or cheering. He looked out of place. Giving half a nudge, Andreas nodded toward the old man who then participated in a half-hearted manner.

Andreas hoped the man's nervousness wouldn't give

them away or draw unwanted attention. He just had to maintain for another few minutes at best. Looking at the elderly man, Andreas imagined that he could see the man's heart nearly thumping out of his chest. Catching the man's attention, Andreas handed him a handgun, which he shakily took hold of and quickly stuck in the seat of his pants. Normally, this exchange would have been done beforehand, but Andreas didn't trust that the old man could get past the security at the entrance.

God, I hope this goes right, Andreas thought, bringing his sleeve to his face in a motion to wipe his nose.

"We're in place," he softly radioed.

"Copy. I'm ready," came the reply.

Andreas then guided the man further near the front and leaned in. "Okay, we're not going to get closer. It's time."

Andreas then stepped away as the old man reached for the gun at his belt and pulled it out. His hand shook as he raised the sidearm and pointed it toward the podium. The gun shook so badly in the old man's hand that Andreas knew that there was no way he would hit the president. The sight of a gun created a disturbance and the crowd suddenly parted, wanting to get away from the scared-looking man with the handgun. Someone yelled, and then another.

The eyes of the security at the podium were drawn by the disturbance and noticed the old man and the weapon. They burst into motion, weapons coming clear and launching themselves toward the threat. The old man lost his nerve and dropped his arm. Andreas had his hand in his pocket, fingering a device. With a quick motion, he moved a switch and clicked a button. The gun in the man's hand fired. Security fired a second later, their bullets tearing into the frail chest, splattering those nearby with droplets of blood. The old man was thrown backward, the gun in his hand flying through the air.

*   *   *   *   *   *

Felipe watched through his scope. He saw the security

team move toward the crowd, the path to the president clearing. Some were heading toward the president, so this timing was going to be tricky. At the edge of his vision, he saw the smoke from the patsy's gun. With the crosshairs centered on the Philippine president's chest, Felipe pulled the trigger.

The 5.8mm round tightly spiraled from the barrel and streaked out the window. It raced downward, somehow finding a hole through the mess of wiring. It passed over the crowd verging on panic. Blood flowered on the white shirt of President Ramos as the slug slammed into his chest. He staggered backward, his hands coming up to clutch at the wound.

Another loud retort sounded from somewhere in the crowd as Andreas remotely set off another round. Felipe heard Andreas say "now" in his earpiece and he fired again. A second bullet forcefully hit the president in the chest again, driving him to his knees. He collapsed to the side and was dead before he hit the stage.

Andreas retrieved the sidearm and fled with the now panicked crowd. The security in place attempted to stem the tide of frightened people, but they were unable to control the mass exodus. He quickly took the gun apart and dropped pieces in various waste bins, saving the modifications, which he would destroy later.

Felipe broke down the rifle and stuffed it in his ragged backpack. Making sure to collect the spent shell casings, he exited the room and then calmy but quickly worked his way down to the ground floor. Sirens were erupting in the streets outside with people gathering near the windows to see what was going on. Felipe went into the parking garage and started up his dilapidated motorbike. Using alleyways, he worked his way clear of the immediate area.

In no time, he was pulling up to the dock area of the Pasig River, less than a mile from the hotel. Parking his motorcycle and with the sound of sirens drifting across the city, Felipe walked across an old barge and onto a tugboat. In minutes, the boat cast off and sailed out into Manila Bay.

Felipe powered up the satphone and dialed a number.

The other side answered and Felipe said, "Operation Hidden Tiger completed."

He hung up, turned off the phone, and tossed it overboard, along with the parts of the rifle. An hour later, with Corregidor Island off to the side and with the towering Mount Mariveles behind it, the tugboat departed the bay and sailed into the open waters of the South China Sea. Another hour and Felipe was in international waters, being transferred to a fishing boat. He thus began his long journey back home.

* * * * * *

Malacañan Palace
Manila, Philippines
18 May, 2021

Dressed as a Filipino colonel, Andreas Cruz presented his identification at the entrance to the presidential palace, the early morning sun warming the new day. Andreas noted that the guards were alert and actively patrolling the grounds. The entire city was on lockdown following the tragic assassination of President Ramos at the hands of a grieving father whose son had been supposedly murdered by the government's death squads.

In the interim, the head of the military, General Aquino, had taken charge of the government, locking down the city to prevent any potential rioting and looting. His address to the nation the previous evening told of his temporarily taking the presidential office until proper elections could be held.

Andreas was admitted onto the palace grounds; he drove up to the residence and presidential palace. Yesterday had been quite eventful, and he regretted having to use the old man like he had, but it had been all for the greater good … right? There were some missions that he was sure would haunt him in his later years when he had more time to think about them, but for now, his role wasn't over.

Yesterday, he had escaped with the rest of the panicked mob fleeing the stadium. Once clear of the immediate area, he phoned completion of phase one. He then found an open rickshaw and was taken to his hotel. There, he waited for news that the Philippine police had discovered that it wasn't a grieving old man who had shot the president, but that the bullets had come from somewhere else. Nowhere did any news of that kind materialize. The authorities were evidently convinced that they had their shooter and weren't looking elsewhere. Of course, that could still happen, or it could be being talked about behind closed doors. Today, he'd find out if that were the case.

Andreas worked his way past additional checkpoints and made his way into the interior. A colonel demanded respect, but wasn't someone who would draw undue attention. No one questioned why he was there, only that the ID matched the person holding it.

The click of his polished boots on the tile floor echoed slightly in the wide hallway. Coming out of another hallway, Andreas spotted General Aquino, the former head of the armed forces and now interim president. He was surrounded by several armed guards. Andreas turned toward the general and his entourage as they began marching toward the apparent Philippine colonel.

As they neared each other, the general's eyes didn't turn in Andreas's direction until they were close. Then, General Aquino halted as he focused on the man in front of him. Sensing some confusion on the part of their leader, two of the guards came forward and stood between the colonel and the general, their weapons held ready to use in a moment's notice.

"You shouldn't be in this section of the building, uh, Colonel Vasquez," General Aquino stated, eyeing Andreas's nametag.

With the guards screening the colonel off, General Aquino continued on, his attention shifting from the errant colonel to more pressing matters of state.

"A mutual friend from the District of Columbia sends their regards and congratulations on your recent promotion," Andreas commented, talking over the heads of the guards.

General Aquino continued walking, barely paying attention to what the colonel said, but he did wonder why Colombia would concern themselves with the interim president of the Philippines. He then stopped dead in his tracks as the words penetrated the crowded space of his mind.

Turning, the general addressed Andreas. "What did you say, colonel?"

"A friend wishes you a heartfelt congratulation," Andreas repeated, eyeing the guards warily to let the general know that there were things that shouldn't be stated in the open.

"Let him through," General Aquino ordered. "And you are dismissed. Colonel … Vasquez, come with me."

The two walked in silence as the general led them to a private room.

"Okay, you have my attention. I assume you have a message to deliver," General Aquino opened as if he'd been expecting a contact.

"Yes, sir. The acquaintance I'm speaking of is in Washington, DC. Other than congratulating you, I am here to offer you the friendship of the United States. I believe we have the mutual goal of an independent Philippine nation. I'm authorized to tell you that we can assist with natural resource protection and asserting your lawful rights. Along with that, there is the matter of firming up the legitimate claim to the presidency," Andreas responds.

"Did you assassinate President Ramos?" General Aquino inquired.

"I can only go by what the news media are reporting about a grieving elderly man gunning the president down. We are as shocked and heartsick as you over the tragedy. But, this unfortunate set of circumstances can also bring our two nations closer," Andreas answered.

"If I do decide to be more than the interim president, I will not be anyone's puppet. I need that understood from the outset, and this feels like the beginning of a one-sided relationship," General Aquino replied. "It took us a long time to gain our independence from your nation and I have no desire to go back."

"Let me ask you this question, Mr. President," Andreas said, deliberately addressing the man as the president instead of general. "Do you think that China is seeking to be a puppet master of a Philippine vassal state? Are they not planning to put their soldiers and other military equipment on your island? Isn't that the kind of status you shed when the treaty with America expired?"

The general's eyes narrowed as Andreas's question hit the mark.

"What do you know about this?"

"It's kind of hard to miss a fleet like that sailing from their ports and not guess their intentions," Andreas replied. "Once they come ashore, you know that they will never leave, and your ability to make your own decisions will erode. We do not seek to use your nation as a military base to conduct operations from. You are a valued friend, not a goal to be accomplished. At least, we'd like to work toward that. A partnership rather than a hierarchical relationship. You have a lot to offer, as do we."

Andreas was careful not to use terms like the United States or America, which would suggest power being exerted on the general. It was "we" and "us" — as he said, a partnership.

"So, we tell the Chinese to back off and you legitimize my presidency, is that what you're saying?" General Aquino questioned.

"In a nutshell, yes."

"Know that I will sign the free trade agreement with China regardless of what transpires between our two nations."

"We wouldn't think of telling you what to do with this nation of yours. We only ask that you not allow the Chinese military on your shores," Andreas said.

General Aquino paused for a long moment, pondering the ramifications of what was in front of him. If he continued with the current Chinese relationship, there was a chance that he would have to step down in favor of someone more reliable to Chinese interests. General Aquino had spoken against the increasing Chinese pressures exerted on his country several times, along with the many incursions into their fishing grounds. The Chinese knew that, and the general was worried about a Chinese bullet with his name on it. If he changed paths and accepted America's offer of friendship, then he could be protected and move forward with his own ideas for his country.

However, there was the fact that the Philippines were a close neighbor of China and he could count them increasing the pressures currently being exerted. Chinese warships would force fishing vessels from the fishing grounds and push for expanded oil drilling in Philippine exclusion zones. They could even blockade imports to a certain degree.

"There will need to be a public announcement of friendship and support. I'd want assurances in writing before moving forward on this path you describe."

"Of course. That can be arranged. You'll hear of our public support within forty-eight hours. But, sir, we'll also need assurances regarding the Chinese, and seeing they're currently heading this way, that will have to be immediate," Andreas stated.

With a heavy sigh, General Aquino walked over and picked up a landline phone, dialing a number.

"Get me the Chinese ambassador...Yes, now...No, I want to see him personally. Ask him to come to the presidential palace. I'll be in my office," the general said.

Leaving the room immediately afterward, they adjourned to the presidential office to await the Chinese ambassador's arrival. It took nearly an hour, but the man and several of his entourage eventually appeared.

"Mr. Ambassador, as the interim president, I am informing you of my intent to keep our free trade agreement."

"That is good news. I am sure President Hao will be pleased to hear that," the Chinese ambassador responded.

"I am also informing you that is the only agreement I intend to keep at the moment. As of now, I am calling off any agreement we had in place to put your soldiers and equipment ashore. We can still be friends, but I won't allow foreign troops on our soil. If I were to do that, my current position would not last long."

The Chinese ambassador cleared his throat to catch his thoughts. "You know, general, we can ensure your position, especially if you had the backing of, well, additional troops to support your cause."

"I have made my position clear. Call your ships back."

"I wish I could do that, but I'm afraid that I will not be able to get a message in time to do anything about that. Please accept my apologies, but I'm afraid it is too late."

"It's never too late, Mr. Ambassador, so do not think to dictate my decisions. If they come inside our territorial waters, we will fire upon them," General Aquino stated.

"I will relay your message, general, but I cannot promise anything."

With that, the Chinese ambassador departed.

"And now, how will you keep me from being assassinated? I'm sure that just became an option for them," General Aquino said.

"We can assign professionals for a short time if you would like," Andreas offered.

The general hesitated and then nodded. "For a short time — until your announcement is made, and then I want them gone. I also want the advisors you have in the mountains gone."

"Done," Andreas replied.

"Okay, is that proof enough?"

"There is one other matter," Andreas said.

"Of course there is. What is it?"

"It's nothing much. General Gonzales should become your next head of the armed forces."

"That rebel scumbag. No way!" General Aquino stated.

"I believe you'll find that you both have mutual goals, and that will also be one less pain for you to deal with as you move forward with running your nation."

"Fine, but again, I will not have American troops or equipment using our islands. So barring that, what else will our new friends require?"

"Nothing. You'll hear an announcement shortly. And you'll receive a deal for additional warships to assist with your resource claims. Again, congratulations," Andreas said and then departed.

With those words, General Aquino became President Aquino.

Chapter Seven

Oval Office
Washington, DC
19 May, 2021

Tom Collier, the CIA director, resumed his seat on one of the couches in the Oval Office. The president walked over to his chair and sat down, placing a steaming mug of coffee on the table.

"Okay, gentlemen, we all heard the news about President Ramos. Before I go any further, I want to know if we had anything to do with this," President Winslow asked.

Around the room, heads shook in the negative.

"Are you sure about this? I don't want to enact a policy only to find out that it was based on something flimsy down the road. Tom? I'm mostly directing this toward you. Did you have anything to do with this?"

"No, sir," the CIA director answered. "You were explicit that we weren't to do anything along those lines. However, I will say I jumped on the opportunity when I saw it. I authorized contact with General Aquino. I did that so that we could be there before anyone else leapt aboard, specifically the Chinese."

"In person or phone contact?" President Winslow inquired.

"In person, sir."

"That seems...convenient...to have people there almost before the body cooled."

"You know we have people everywhere, sir. I merely had our embassy send someone over to reach out...to grease the skids, as it were," Tom responded.

"Okay, just so we're sure. So, the question before us is whether we support General Aquino. As you all now know, he was the head of the Philippine Armed Forces and took command when the late President Ramos was killed. Tom here says that the general is amenable to opening dialogues between us and is leaning toward us over the Chinese."

"That's correct," Tom interjected. "I'm told he informed the Chinese ambassador to turn around the ships that are still heading their way. The ambassador responded by saying it may be too late. General Aquino was informed that we would decide one way or the other within forty-eight hours."

"Mr. President," JCS general Dawson cut in. "I just want to say that, as of an hour ago, the Chinese task force—filled with a reinforced regiment's worth of equipment—is still heading toward Philippine shores. We have one Virginia-class attack submarine shadowing the group with two other LA-class subs waiting in their path. If we want, we could halt them. I just wanted that on the table for consideration in case no one thought about it."

Tom Collier inwardly sighed. The conversation had now drifted past whether or not the United States was involved. He had the embassy in Manilla in his pocket, but he really detested having to lie in these meetings. He had caught the quick sidelong look from Bill Reiser, the NSA director. The man hadn't been fooled in the least. Hell, he had probably watched the entire thing go down. Who knew exactly what Bill did or didn't do, knew or didn't know these days. It was safer just to assume the man knew everything.

It was a combination of efforts between the two agencies that had discovered the passage of funds to the late President Ramos's monitored offshore accounts. The recent deposit was from an entity known to be a front for the Chinese government. The knowledge that the Philippines were about to become more deeply imbedded with China spurred the administration into action, chiefly Tom and the CIA.

At any rate, the heat was off him for the time being. Tom had retired from naval intelligence, having spent over twenty years there analyzing enemy intentions. That served him well in his current position; indeed, it was the reason he had been selected. He didn't exactly color within the lines. Operation Hidden Tiger had been on the books for years, but using the old man and the death squads that were a product of President Ramos himself was Tom's little addition to the scheme.

Tom knew that with all that was happening, Winslow wanted the headache of the Philippines gone. It was Tom's job to quietly take care of certain things so there could be plausible deniability around the table. And judging from the ships heading toward the island nation, he had activated the Hidden Tiger operation not a moment too soon. If the Chinese had been allowed to land, the United States might as well have given up the far eastern seas, including Taiwan. Tom was sure they were next on the list. Now, if they gave their support to the general, they'd still have access to the South China and Philippine Seas.

"If I may, sir. Who here thinks it's a bad idea to support the new *interim* president if he's willing to be friendly? Or if not friendly, then at least neutral. I feel to do otherwise would allow the Chinese full access to block off far east Asia should they desire," Bill commented.

No one had anything to say.

"So, it's decided then. We support General Aquino until elections are held?" President Winslow questioned.

"And hold those off for as long as possible," Tom mentioned.

"Let's see how this *friendship* transpires first," President Winslow replied. "So, now, how do we turn those ships around?"

"Sir, we have two carriers in the South China Sea. I suggest we move them into blocking positions without actually impeding. With the news of our support for the general and the threat implied by our strike groups, I'm sure the Chinese will get the message," General Dawson answered.

"Very well, let's move them into position. But, and this is important, I don't want anything that could escalate to an unintended confrontation. We have other things in the works that could get fouled up. I'll have an announcement of our support drafted up and released today, along with our condolences for the tragic death of President Ramos."

The president left the office feeling much better than he had the day before.

White House Briefing Room
Washington, DC
19 May, 2021

"President Winslow will not be taking questions following his briefing, so I expect you to respect this request," the press secretary stated. "Ladies and gentlemen, the president of the United States."

Flashes illuminated as President Winslow walked out of the entry door and strode across the small stage, coming to stand behind a podium with the presidential seal emblazoned on the front. Entering behind him were the secretary of state and the secretary of defense, the latter an odd addition. However, foreign nations would recognize the implication of his presence. Shuffling a few papers, he began the hastily organized press meeting.

"Thank you for coming on short notice. I first want to express my personal condolences to the family of President Ramos, who was struck down by an assassin's bullet. The grieving family has the sympathy of the United States. These are tragic days indeed when leaders are murdered in the normal course of their lives, when people feel they can strike out at will against those conducting peaceful actions," President Winslow started.

The press corps and subsequent news stories would catch the perhaps not so subtle inference to the *Preble* incident.

"General Aquino has dutifully stepped into the presidential office as the interim Philippine president. As the current president of the Philippines, I am sure he will do an admirable job in that position and has the full support of the United States. It is our hope that the strained relations we have experienced in the past will be put to rest and the relationship between our two nations become normalized again.

"As an offering of goodwill between our nations, we are gifting two frigates that we have removed from our inventory but which will enhance the good nation of the Philippines in their long-standing attempts to protect their resources in territorial waters. That's all I have to say at this time. Thank you."

President Winslow and the secretaries then walked off stage to a hundred shouted questions and the flash of cameras. When the press secretary also departed, the reporters rushed out of the room to write and file their stories, each having their own interpretation of what was presented.

Walking down the long hall to his office, President Winslow sighed. Amid all of the chaos and the increasing pressures due to the sweeping pandemic, at least one thing had gone well. There wouldn't be any Chinese troops in the Philippines. Or so he hoped.

*   *   *   *   *   *

South China Sea
19 May, 2021

"You've all read the operation orders," Admiral Fablis stated. "We're moving into a blocking position ahead of the Chinese task force as a show of strength. We are not, I repeat, we are not to engage any Chinese vessel or aircraft or get into a situation of escalation. I'll have anyone's ass who manages to place his aircraft in the same time and space as a Chinese one. In case I need to spell it out, that means a collision."

The commander of Carrier Strike Group 9 looked around the room and to Admiral Prescott, the CSG 11 commander who was on one of the monitors. Admiral Fablis was in overall command of the two carrier strike groups ever since they joined together into a single task force.

"Sir, what if the Chinese task force calls our bluff and pushes onward?" the *Roosevelt* captain inquired.

"Then we'll do as ordered. If we have to, we'll stand aside. We'll be in position early tomorrow and we'll immediately start putting on a show of the power we can project. Currently, the Chinese have a force of eight J-11 fighters patrolling over their task force, the cover having tanker support and being relieved with an additional eight fighters stationed on the Spratly island of Fiery Cross. Is that correct?" Admiral

Fablis asked of the *Roosevelt*'s carrier air group commander.

"Aye, sir," the CAG commander answered. "That is the current information."

"Very well. In three hours, we'll go to general quarters. At that time, I want shipborne radars to go dark and the task force covered with E-2 Hawkeyes. CAG, I want a nonstandard pattern so the Chinese can't quickly locate us based on where the Hawkeyes are positioned," Admiral Fablis ordered.

"Aye, sir."

"All right, gentlemen, let's remind these bastards why they should fear a naval strike group. *Roosevelt*, you'll have the strike packages and the *Nimitz* will provide covering patrols."

* * * * * *

South China Sea
20 May, 2021

"Tiger flight, come right to zero niner five, descend to angels niner. Bogeys will be at your twelve o'clock, five miles at angels eleven, heading zero niner five," Raven One instructed.

The radio call came from an EA2-Hawkeye patrolling a hundred miles to the east and controlling the movement of fighters. Lieutenant Blaine clicked his transmit button twice to acknowledge the call and rolled his F-35C to the right, his wingman following behind in trail position. The other two Lightnings of his flight were spread a mile to his left in a tactical formation. They also turned with the lead element, rolling out on an identical heading, this time a mile to the right of Lieutenant Blaine.

Ahead, Kyle Blaine could see several black dots a couple thousand feet above his altitude. The flight was now directly behind and hidden by the tail end of the enemy target ahead. The "angels" altitude for the strike package that took off from the *Roosevelt* was set at twenty-seven thousand feet. All altitudes given were broadcast with this baseline to confuse anyone listening in. Radar could tell, but that's why they also employed EA-18G Growler electronic warfare aircraft to jam those signals.

The weather was mostly clear with a few scattered clouds ten thousand feet below the flight of the F-35Cs. Looking down, Lieutenant Blaine saw many thin trails of white marring an otherwise blue sea. He was eyeing the ships of the Chinese task force they were ordered to intercept.

Every time he saw the wake of ships, he thought of the contrails he used to see in the sky as a kid. In this case, the world was turned upside down and the contrails were forming on the surface of the sea. One entire section of the South China Sea glimmered yellow from the sun hanging in its midmorning position.

Kyle advanced the throttles and closed in on the twin-tailed Chinese fighters weaving in giant S-shaped turns over the task force sailing seven miles below. Across the skies, other F-35 formations were rolling in behind the Chinese J-16 fighters riding protection over the fleet. The dots took on definition, and he could see the missiles slung on hardpoints under the wings of the opposing fighters, the exhaust pouring out of their engines turning white several feet behind.

He thought about how any American flight wouldn't be caught flying about in a contrail-forming range.

Talk about a huge giveaway, he thought, continuing to close in. *We must have flown into amateur hour.*

Part of the mission briefing included at what altitudes contrails would likely form and directions to minimize time spent in that zone. The radio was alive with additional instructions to the other flights closing in on the fighter patrol.

"Raven One to all flights, light 'em up."

Across the thirty-two F-35C aircraft now positioned behind eight Chinese J-16 fighters, search radar selector switches rotated from standby to on. The targeting radars were left on standby. In most situations, targeting a foe in peacetime could be considered a hostile act that would invite retaliatory measures.

The slow, lazy S-turns became more radical maneuvers as the Chinese pilots sought to find the aircraft associated with the sudden appearance of thirty-plus airborne search radars situated at their six o'clock position. The Chinese pilots wondered where their warning was, not realizing that several EA-18 Growler aircraft were jamming their radio frequencies.

With the Chinese fighters frantically turning and changing altitudes, the F-35C aircraft peeled off and set headings for the *Roosevelt* steaming three hundred miles away. They had shown that the covering fighters didn't stand a chance against the United States Navy and had immediately flown away before accidents could occur.

Ten minutes later, the EA-18 aircraft turned off their jammers, and the radios in the J-16s came alive with warnings and instructions. Eight additional J-16s had departed their base at Fiery Cross Island and were en route, but they were too late to have been effective in an actual attack.

Sequenced for landing, Lieutenant Blaine led his flight up initial. The four aircraft in a right echelon formation raced up behind the carrier at twelve hundred feet. At middeck, he cleared his side for other aircraft and then then rolled the F-35C hard to the left, breaking away from the other three Lightning IIs tucked in on his right wing.

Pulling nearly six Gs, he chopped his throttle back to idle, slowing the aircraft rapidly. Rolling out in the opposite direction, Kyle lowered his gear. Below him, the carrier steamed away at twenty knots with a cruiser tucked in as close escort. When the carrier, its deck covered in aircraft and the crews landing more, was at a forty-five-degree angle behind him, Kyle lowered the nose and rolled into a descending turn that would bring him directly behind the ship.

"Tiger One, call the ball," a voice intoned in his helmet.

"Tiger One has the ball," Kyle replied.

"The ball" was an optical landing system using lights that stabilize a glide path down to the deck, rolling to maintain a constant angle to compensate for the deck rolling and pitching. Kyle steadied his glide path, focusing on the two lines of green side lights and the center light rather than the moving deck. If the center light remained positioned directly between the green on the sides, then the aircraft was on the correct path.

The ball slipped below the green lines and Kyle added a touch of power, easing the nose of the fighter up a touch until the center light was again lined up. Blue water slid beneath, the wake of the carrier a long line cutting through the swells and vanishing underneath the nose of the approaching F-35C.

Swooping over the curved fantail of the deck, Kyle again chopped his power. The aircraft dropped and slammed onto the decking. Kyle ran the throttle forward, the afterburner igniting in case he missed the wire. Lieutenant Blaine jolted in his seat and was thrown forward, pulling the aircraft out of afterburner as the hook captured the number three wire and the fighter rapidly slowed. He then taxied clear and shutdown as instructed by the deck crews.

*   *   *   *   *   *

Ocean swells glimmering in the sun filled one side of the canopy as Lieutenant Thompson rolled the F/A-18F Super Hornet into a tight turn. He had to watch the Gs as two Harpoon anti-ship missiles were tucked under the wings and the large weapons wouldn't stand the high-G maneuvering the aircraft was truly capable of. The sidewinder out on the wingtip hardpoint rode a scant eighty feet over the sea's surface as the Hornet rolled to a new heading as given by Raven One. This would put Thompson and the rest of his flight following on their final attack heading.

Raven One downloaded the position information of the large vessels in the center of the Chinese task force heading for the Philippines. Chris Thompson had been assigned one of the large Type 071 amphibious transport docks carrying four hovercraft, several transport helicopters, and anywhere from six to eight hundred troops.

"I have the package," his backseat electronic warfare officer stated. "Target info loaded into the Harpoons. Ready to fire."

"Copy," Lieutenant Thompson said as he rolled out on

the new heading.

The swells of the South China Sea rolled gently underneath the Super Hornet as Chris threaded the aircraft between two Chinese destroyers that were serving as the outer pickets for the convoy.

Being so low, he couldn't see the vessels, but the information downloaded from the Hawkeye showed on his screen. The last thing they needed was to actually surprise the Chinese fleet into thinking it was an actual attack on their ships. It was a risk, but the admiral wanted to demonstrate the power of an American carrier strike group, plus it afforded a great opportunity to run a scenario against a Chinese task force. It wasn't often they came out of port in such numbers other than to conduct annual exercises. Those were great for subs to conduct mock-firing exercises, but the surface fleet stayed away.

"Coming up on the release point, all checks complete," the EWO commented.

"Copy," Chris replied.

The Super Hornet raced over the top of the waves at five hundred and forty knots. Behind Chris, the rest of his flight followed, with other flights conducting similar approaches to either side. The attack was being flown to come in from all sides, launching a total of sixty-four Harpoon anti-ship missiles intended to saturate the defenses. The idea was that when the Chinese radars managed to break through the jamming, the automatic defense systems would be overwhelmed and unable to cope with all of the inbound missiles coming at them from all sides.

Chris simulated firing his two Harpoon missiles, notifying Raven One that they had fired. The radios came alive with the calls from the other flights as they also notified of their simulated shootings.

"All Amber flights, break off and RTB," Raven One called, giving flights altitudes and headings so the aircraft didn't run into each other. The carrier approach control would handle the sequencing once the aircraft flew closer. "Growler One and Two, cease jamming efforts. Growler One, turn left heading zero eight zero, climb and maintain angels three. Growler T, turn left heading zero eight five, climb and maintain angels five."

The two EA-18 aircraft turned off their radar and radio jamming and turned toward the carrier three hundred miles away. The F/A-18s that had run simulation against the ships put their aircraft into mil power and climbed away from the fleet, all heading for the circling tankers. The overall plan had been to engage the Chinese fighter protection while the F/A-18s snuck in and fired their Harpoons.

When the jamming ceased, the screens of the Chinese escorts came alive with sixty-four bogey aircraft departing the area at high speed. Radio messages that had been frantic now made their way to the intended recipients, but all involved knew how the day would have unfolded had this been an actual attack.

The Chinese ran through their tapes to search for ways to counter what the Americans had thrown at them while the United States sought to improve on what they had conducted. All computer simulations of the strike had shown an overwhelming win with all five of the landing ships damaged or sunk without a single American aircraft lost.

*   *   *   *   *   *

Three hours following the simulated attack, the roar of heavy turbo-props thundered across the island. One by one, two KJ-500 aircraft lumbered down the runway in ungainly fashion and reluctantly lifted into the air. Making a wide swing to the south, the two Chinese airborne warning and control aircraft began a long climb into the nearly cloudless skies.

As the two aircraft were becoming black dots in the sky, activity around the airbase increased. One after another, Xian H-6 bombers left their revetments to taxi to the single runway. Again, the base rumbled as the jet engines were spooled up and the bombers departed. Slung under the hardpoints on their wings were YJ-12 supersonic anti-ship missiles. It took just over thirty minutes for the thirty-six laden bombers to claw for altitude over the South China Sea.

* * * * * *

"Two bogeys. Contact Alpha One bearing one niner five, three hundred ten miles, level at two five zero, speed five hundred knots. Contact Alpha Two bearing two zero five, three hundred twenty miles, level at flight level two five zero, speed five hundred," the radar operator called.

The combat information officer aboard Raven Two, an E-2 Hawkeye monitoring the southwestern sector of the task force, acknowledged the call. The information was automatically downloaded to the radar plots of the airborne aircraft and the ships rolling through light swells. Positioned to each side were two F-35C aircraft providing protection.

"There it is," the RO commented. "We're being jammed. It looks like they're conducting standoff jamming. Contacts Alpha One and Two are now classified as two probable Chinese KJ-500 AWAC aircraft. There's most likely a strike package hidden in the clutter."

"Pilot, come to heading one niner zero and inform the task force that we're repositioning in an attempt to burn through the jamming," the combat information officer ordered. Turning to the aircraft control officer, she asked, "Has Tiger flight finished refueling?"

"Aye, ma'am," the ACO answered.

"Very well. Have them run low under the two contacts and have them light up their radar. And let's get two Growlers in their direction to return the favor. Make sure they have protection."

"Tiger flight, Raven Two. Turn left heading one niner five, descend and maintain three hundred. Increase speed to one point five. Growler One, turn left heading two one zero, descend and maintain angels minus two. Eagle flight, turn right heading zero two zero, descend and maintain angels minus four. This will be vectors for intercept with Growler One," the

ACO radioed.

In short, he sent one flight of four F-35Cs on a heading toward the Chinese jamming aircraft, having them head down to the deck at two thousand feet. They were then to race toward their target at Mach 1.5. The purpose was to get them under the radar coverage of the inbound Chinese aircraft and then have them fire up their radars quickly so they could downlink any information they could get regarding additional aircraft, specifically an inbound strike package. That would quickly burn Tiger's fuel, but the ACO sent two additional flights in the wake of the EA-18 jammers so they could tackle whatever Tiger flight found without being located.

He sent the EA-18 Growlers closer to the KJ-500s to start their own jamming, giving them Eagle flight, another four F-35Cs, as escort. The key was to identify an enemy strike package and get intercepts out to them before they were able to identify the ships of the task force and get into launch range. It was a game played both above and below the ocean's surface. This had to be done quickly as the known Chinese anti-ship missiles that could be fired from aircraft had a range of approximately two hundred miles. They probably wouldn't fire, but they might.

The USS *Nimitz* launched its alert aircraft and readied more for flight. Those on patrol ensured they were heading to tankers so they could begin any upcoming engagement with a full load of fuel. After the attack and sinking of the *Preble*, the Chinese were capable of anything, and each inbound flight of Chinese aircraft was treated as an actual attack. That was always the case, the game played on both sides. However, they were taken more seriously these days. Even the cat and mouse game played by the anti-submarine forces took on a deadlier tone.

*   *   *   *   *   *

The waves were a blur under the streaking fighter as Lieutenant Blaine drove his F-35C over the top of the crests at nine hundred miles per hour. Hanging nearby was his wingman, with the rest of his four-ship flight spread a mile to the right. The fuel burn at that speed and altitude was ridiculous, but he understood what Raven Two needed. When notified, he would zoom his aircraft and energize his search radar. Hopefully, he would be able to burn through the jamming being conducted against the task force and find what the Chinese were trying to hide.

He would turn it off just as quickly, but the strike package they sought would hopefully be found and downloaded to the rest of the fleet. Then, other aircraft could be vectored in, achieving their own burn through and engaging the Chinese bombers at a long enough range that they couldn't launch their missiles. His second element of two F-35Cs would be kept in the dark in case a second radar reading was required. They would then turn tail and run for the protection of the task force and tanker.

Twenty minutes after beginning their run into the target, Raven Two called, "Tiger flight, begin your climb. Energize your radar passing through angels minus seven."

"Copy, climbing," Lieutenant Blaine replied.

He then started a zooming climb with his wingman in tow. The other two in the flight remained low but began to let their speed bleed off so they wouldn't consume as much fuel and also wouldn't be far from their leader in case the missiles stowed underneath were needed.

The altimeter wound up rapidly as Kyle climbed. There could be no doubt he'd be picked up on radar, but the plan was for him to be out of there before any fighters in the area could vector in on him. By the time they arrived, he'd be heading home and lost in the ground clutter.

The needle raced through twenty thousand feet. "Tiger flight, energizing."

Kyle reached over and turned on his search radar. Instantly, his screen was littered with aircraft. It showed the two AWAC planes twenty miles apart and heading toward the task force. In the time it had taken him to fly three hundred miles, the two Chinese airplanes had flown a hundred and sixty miles closer. The two leading were now a hundred and sixty miles from the carriers.

Ninety miles behind were fifty-two other aircraft. Thirty-six were at flight level two five zero, or twenty-five thousand feet, while the remaining sixteen were at flight level three five zero. The lower ones were most likely inbound bombers flying in groups of three while the higher ones were their fighter escort. If this were a real war, Kyle would target and destroy the closer KJ-500 aircraft, thus eliminating the electronic protection the inbound aircraft enjoyed. He and his flight would then fire their AIM-120D AMRAAM missiles at the incoming bombers. As it currently stood, all they could do was to report a simulated firing and return.

Lieutenant Blane then rolled his aircraft over and dove for the surface with Chinese fighters vectoring toward him. Pulling high Gs, he leveled out a scant two hundred feet over the sea's surface, heading toward the tanker support waiting for him and his flight.

Raven Two accepted the downlink from Tiger Flight, getting a clear picture of the inbound bombers. Fighters were vectored into their targets and simulated firing their missiles. However, enough were kept back in case this was an actual attack. When the bombers reached a hundred and fifty miles, they turned away from the task force to return to their bases. The only weapons exchanged were simulations.

The computer analysis that followed showed one carrier heavily damaged with a loss of twenty-eight Chinese bombers. However, there was still a real Chinese task force inbound to the Philippines.

*   *   *   *   *   *

Chinese bombers simulate an attack on a US Navy aircraft carrier in the South China Sea

Chinese bombers recently simulated an attack on a US Navy aircraft carrier in the South China Sea, a US defense official said Friday.

The Navy's *Theodore Roosevelt* carrier strike group is currently operating in the South China Sea alongside the USS *Nimitz*. The Chinese military sent H-6K bombers, J-16 fighter jets, and aircraft flying past Taiwan and into the contested waterway.

The next day, an unidentified mainland military analyst told China's state-affiliated *Global Times* that the Chinese move may have been a training exercise intended to "boost the PLA's combat capability against US aircraft carriers," as the bombers could practice launching a saturation attack against the US ships.

The *Financial Times*, citing persons familiar with the US and allied intelligence, reported Friday that the Chinese bombers and fighters simulated an attack on the *Theodore Roosevelt* carrier strike group. The Chinese bomber pilots were also reportedly overheard confirming naval strike orders and simulating the firing of anti-ship missiles.

A US Indo-Pacific Command spokesperson said that "the *Theodore Roosevelt* Carrier Strike Group closely monitored all People's Liberation Army Navy (PLAN) and Air Force (PLAAF) activity, and at no time did they pose a threat to US Navy ships, aircraft, or sailors."

A defense official said that the Chinese aircraft did not come within 250 nautical miles of the US Navy vessels, putting them well outside the maximum estimated range of the YJ-12 anti-ship cruise missiles the H-6K bombers can carry. There was a simulated attack run though, the official said.

Sources told Reuters the Chinese bombers were simulating a combat operation against a US flattop, with one saying that "they purposely conducted the drills when the US carrier was passing through the Bashi Channel."

The People's Liberation Army Navy (PLAN) activities are the latest in a string of aggressive and destabilizing actions.

The spokesman said that "these actions reflect a continued PLA attempt to use its military as a tool to intimidate or coerce those operating in international waters and airspace, to include their neighbors and those with competing territorial claims," adding that the "United States will continue to fly, sail and operate wherever international law allows, demonstrating resolve through our operational presence throughout the region."

The US Navy said in a statement last Sunday that the *Theodore Roosevelt* carrier strike group is on a routine deployment to the US 7th Fleet area of responsibility to conduct maritime security operations.

China objects to the regular presence of the US military in the South China Sea, even though it has operated in the area for decades.

"It does no good to regional peace and stability for the United States to frequently send military vessels and aircraft to the South China Sea to show off its muscles," China's Foreign Affairs Minister, Liu Xiang, said during a press briefing Monday.

The latest developments in the South China Sea highlight the challenges the United States will face as it deals with Beijing and China's growing military power.

* * * * * *

Beijing, China
20 May, 2021

Paramount Leader Hao Chenxu was barely listening to the reports of his ministers, wondering where the plan went wrong. Sure, the Americans were bound to see the ships being loaded, but by then, it was supposed to be too late for them to do anything about it. The toehold they'd hoped to gain in the Philippines evaporated like mist in the morning sun. There wasn't any doubt in his mind that the assassination of President Ramos had been conducted by the Americans, but how did they get assets in place so quickly? Well, it had been a gamble anyway, and one they'd lost for the moment.

The ministers were conducting the blame game, saying it would have been different if their ministry had been allowed to do this or that. Hao knew that competition between ministers kept them sharp, but this was not the time for division between them. Too much was at stake.

"We pushed too early and the Americans reacted, that is all," Hao interrupted one argument. "This opportunity is lost, but we have other avenues we're pursuing. This is no one's fault but my own, so we will push past this and decide on our next course. But first, where do we currently stand?"

Defense Minister Zhou knew what the paramount leader was referring to. "Our ships are still underway. The Americans have run simulated attacks against the fleet, as we have against their two carriers. The results show that we would have lost half of our task force with a loss of both of their carriers."

Judging from the brief expression of confusion from his southern fleet commander, Hao had an idea that the actual results weren't quite as his defense minister described. He could see for himself how it would have ended.

"The interim Philippine president was adamant with our ambassador about landing troops. I believe you are correct in assessing that this opportunity has been lost," Foreign Affairs Minister Liu added. "We should indeed focus on other endeavors."

"I see nothing to gain by continuing this. Send the order to turn our ships around. We will continue working on Malaysia, Borneo, and other Indonesian nations to see if we can get the same agreement we have with Cambodia. If we can dock our ships in their ports, then we'll be able to exert a greater influence. It won't be quite what we would have had with the Philippines, but it's still something.

"Now, with this regional trade agreement, we will slowly get the far east economies reliant on our exports. Then we can use that influence to bargain for the use of ports, airfields, and bases. No country would go into economic ruin over sharing resources like that," Hao stated.

"I would like to suggest another action plan," the defense minister said. "I firmly believe that a war with America is inevitable, limited or not. I think we should strike while we have two of their carriers in range. If we sink both of them, that's 40 percent of their naval power gone. The UN will be quick to intervene lest the conflict escalate. We'll accept the cease-fire and have gained control of the South China Sea."

"I still hope to avert an armed conflict. There are too many variables involved. For one, we can't accurately predict how far it might escalate. And once we start down that path, we can't be the ones who pull back," Hao replied. "If we can get Malaysia, Indonesia, talk North Korea into invading the south, and pull Taiwan back into our fold, we'll threaten the American bases at Guam, Okinawa, and Japan. Couple that with our bases in the Spratly Islands, and we can exert enough pressure to force the Americans from the South China Sea. We then move onto establishing friendly terms with Iran and other Arab nations, thereby extending our influence into the Gulf. You see the natural progression of that. A war with the United States will set our timetable back years."

"Only if we lose," Defense Minister Zhou commented.

"True. Only if we lose. We will fight if we have to. Prepare your plans for such an inevitability, both as a first strike and defensive action, but hold off on any action for now. And issue the order to turn around within the hour," Hao ordered. "Now, I hear news that a Swedish delegation has asked to mediate for the release of the American prisoners. Accept their offer, but delay talks for as long as you can. We may still use them for negotiation purposes."

* * * * * *

South China Sea
21 May, 2021
The surface was leaden gray under high overcast skies. Lieutenant Thompson looked down at the thin white trails marring the surface. They were straight lines leading to a hook shape as the ships of the Chinese task force turned around at the very edge of the Philippine territorial waters. It appeared as though the Chinese armada was finally turning back to port.

"I wasn't sure they'd actually do it," LTJG Enquist stated.

Chris Thomson looked back to the two Harpoons slung under his wings. "Yeah, glad we didn't actually have to use those."

"Do you think we'll actually get into a shooting war with them?"

"It depends on who you listen to. Most of the betting pools aboard ship say so," Thompson responded.

"I, for one, think it'll be a messy affair if we do. I mean, we can take care of their navy, but they had a shit ton of missiles that have a pretty long reach. I just hope that someone with sense gets us the fuck out of Dodge before we get a close-up view of how many," Enquist commented.

"Yeah. The sea has the potential to get very crowded in a very short period of time," Chris replied.

"Eagle flight, turn left heading three five five, descend and maintain angels minus three. Looks like they're going home," Raven Two radioed.

"Copy. Left to three five five. Out of angels six for angels minus three."

* * * * * *

Hickam Field, Hawaii
24 May, 2021

The general chatter and laughter died away as Lieutenant Newsome entered the hangar's briefing area and came to stand in front of the two teams. A large-scale satellite photo of Fiery Cross Island was situated on an easel.

"Okay, ladies, we've been training for the past two weeks, so you're well acquainted with what's expected. The hostages are located here in this building about midpoint on the island near the airfield. The latest information shows that we have twelve hostages, all ambulatory. So, that will make our job a little easier.

"If we are conducting a rescue only mission, then Gold and Blue teams will park their delivery vehicles on the southeastern point where the approach lights to runway 5 extend into the water. The likelihood of them mining their own approach lights is minimal, so it should be a clean infil. Adjacent to the landing beach is a container farm. Satellite footage hasn't shown it to be guarded, although roving patrols do pass through the area. On the other side is an empty field on the southern point of the island. That area is codenamed 'Kitchen' and will serve as the exfil point for the hostages once they're secured.

"Gold Team, codenamed 'Mother Hen,' will proceed to the hostages while Blue Team, 'Chicken Little,' sets up a perimeter at Kitchen."

"Who thought up those names, sir?" Petty Officer Hawser asked.

"I did, Hawser. Why, do you have a problem with them?" Lieutenant Newsome asked, insinuating that no problem should be found.

"Uh, no sir. But, perhaps we could hire out that part of the planning next time. That's just a suggestion, sir," PO Hawser commented.

"Duly noted. Can we move on, or would you like to talk yourself into latrine duty?"

"I'm good, sir…thank you."

"Okay, that's what I thought. Now, once Gold Team procures the hostages, they'll broadcast their success and proceed to Kitchen. Ospreys will be circling offshore under the radar and move in to pick up the packages. Once that's accomplished, move to the delivery vehicles and depart.

"Weather is expected to be clear with scattered clouds moving through the area. We'll update that once we arrive. The new moon will be on the tenth of June, so we'll be shooting for that date if word comes down soon enough from upstairs. We'll arrive on station on the eighth, so we can get a good idea of their sea patrols. But, be ready to go any time after the eighth."

Lieutenant Newsome paused to see if there were any questions. Satisfied that there weren't any, he plowed ahead.

"If we get word that the larger-scale action is going to be implemented, Gold Team's infil, mission, and exfil remains the same. They're to focus on retrieving the hostages. Blue Team will motor through the dredged channel leading into the manmade bay, parking on the northern shore just inside the entrance. They have small patrol boats motoring inside and out, so you'll have to keep an eye out for those.

"From there, make your way to the radome farm they have on the northern tip of the island. That is both guarded and patrolled with the command center only a hundred yards away. The cables are buried and believed to be armored, so be prepared to cut your way through. Luckily, it seems that all of the radar cables are in a single conduit, so again, that makes it a bit easier. The pathways are marked on your maps. Now, these were annotated when the Chinese were building the facilities and we were watching, so there's a chance that they're different now.

"Once Gold Team calls en route to Kitchen and the ospreys are inbound, you'll blow the cables and take out their central radar. That will force them to light up their mobile units, which will then be dispatched by aircraft from the carriers. From that point, it will become a fleet action and our job will be complete. It's important that we take out all of their main radars in order to allow the aircraft and cruise missiles to close in on the island undetected. They have some nasty anti-air capabilities and we need to blind them. Questions?"

"We talked about taking out their power generators along with the radars during one training exercise. Is that still on the table? And if not, why?" PO Hawser inquired.

"As you'll recall, the main generators are just too far from the radar farm, and each building has its own emergency generator. It won't be feasible to plant explosives at each one. The risk is too great. Their security measures have increased since the *Preble* sinking. Clearly, they're anticipating a rescue mission," Lt. Newsome answered.

"Yeah, I remember. I just keep thinking that they'll have those mobile units up and running almost immediately. What about identifying them and placing charges? We could set ashore earlier than ol' Mother Hen and start our work. If it becomes too risky, then we'll abort. I believe it's worth it."

"Let's just stick with our plan. The air jockeys have their plan for taking those out, or so they say. We'll just have to trust they know what they're doing."

"College kids playing video games. But, we'll stick with the original."

"That would be appreciated. So, defenses. We have satellite information that the east and west beaches are mined. There used to be water activity from the stationed soldiers, but that has stopped completely. As I mentioned earlier, it's believed that the areas we plan to infiltrate are clear. There are active foot and motorized patrols along the perimeter and on the airfield tarmac night and day. The airfield is especially patrolled due to the bombers and fighter aircraft, so avoid that if at all possible."

He paused, looking over the men seated before him. He tried to match the faces returning his gaze with the men who would go undetected into an enemy base and spirit away twelve sailors who were being held hostage. The eyes betrayed both warmth and coldness, and he knew he wouldn't want to be on the receiving end of what these men brought with them. However, it was still difficult to fit those in front of him with the reputations that SEALs carried. SEALs weren't human. They were made mostly of myth and legend. He took a deep breath and fell back into his role.

"There are tall observation towers at both ends of the eastern spit of land. There's also one on the northern section of the lagoon. Two more are on the southern end, one of which has the potential of overlooking Kitchen. Be wary of lines of sight. Atop each one is a radome. We're not sure of the capabilities there, but it may be that they're looking along the shores for anything approaching low. That would be us, ladies, so make sure you don't broach the surface close in. Finally, the western beaches all have bunkers guarding them at intervals, so be aware of those.

"We are weapons free for this operation, regardless of which mission is given the green light. If someone gets in the way, they're to be taken care of. Gold Team will be traveling on the *Tucson* and Blue Team on the *Santa Fe*. The delivery vehicles have been loaded and we depart tonight, so rest up. Food will be courtesy of Outback. Menus will be distributed here in a minute, so make sure you get your order placed. Good luck, gentlemen, and we'll see you back here in a month. Drinks will be on me."

* * * * * *

The ocean waters past the entrance to Pearl Harbor

glistened under the rays of the nearly full moon. The lights of Honolulu to the east and those of the base behind glowed in the night sky. Just east was the roar of departing civilian airlines and military transports, their red flashing navigation beacons showing their various flight paths. A C-17 crossed low over the harbor entrance, its gear down and locked, flaps drooping aft of the wings. Powerful beams of light thrust forward, seeking the safety of a landing surface. Further out, other landing lights showed aircraft spaced for landing, their long flights nearly at an end.

Contrary to the hustle and bustle of the island night life, two dark objects slithered low in the water, motoring slowly for the open sea. Once clear, two LA-class fast attack boats settled quietly beneath the waves, becoming ghosts of the deep.

*   *   *   *   *   *

White House Situation Room
Washington, DC
28 May, 2021

"Are you sure about this?" President Winslow asked, feeling his anger rise.

Ever since the Chinese had denied American access to the twelve hostages without a hint of their release, he'd sat through meetings and attended functions with building frustration. Some parties were calling for direct action, and there were mutterings that the wrong person had been elected. It was wrong, the entire world knew it, yet there was nothing he or anyone could do short of starting a shooting war. If that happened, then the sailors' chances of making it back would significantly drop.

"As sure as I can be, Mr. President," the secretary of state answered. "The Swedish delegation is stating that the Chinese are deliberately slowing the discussions relating to the hostages, yet engaging just enough so they can say they are negotiating."

President Winslow looked around at his cabinet members. The time for political niceties had run its course.

"Well, okay then. I, for one, am tired of this shit. We need to take action to make them move. I want their assets frozen. Make waves that we're contemplating blocking the yuan from the dollar. Let's see how well they can trade given that!"

"You understand that action will hurt our own recovering economy," the Treasury secretary cautioned.

"Will it hurt them worse?"

"More than likely. How much more would be pure speculation. If we do block the yuan, then all economies are going to be hit pretty hard. We could be looking at a worldwide downturn. That won't make us any friends."

"I doubt it will be long before those bastards come around. We're being forced into taking this drastic measure to show them we're serious about getting our people back," President Winslow stated.

Sensing the president's frustration, Secretary Stevenson explained, "I know it seems like nothing is happening, but we all understand that any movement on the diplomatic front is a slow process. Believe it or not, we are making headway and will start to see things moving."

"Be that as it may, I think it's time we started discussing military plans should things begin slipping and we find ourselves enmeshed in a war," President Winslow countered. "General?"

"Well, sir, there are three different avenues that would be most likely to occur. First, there is South Korea to think about. Should we engage in a shooting war in the South China Sea, then you can place money that China will push North Korea toward a reunification effort. We'll likely see a call-up of reserves massing along the DMZ within the first couple of weeks. North Korea currently has nearly 7.7 million soldiers. As a comparison, South Korea has 3.7 million, and we have twenty-nine thousand.

"We can easily put an additional three divisions and several regiments in place, which would add another forty-five thousand. Their equipment is already in place, so we can conduct a massive airlift, but I would suggest doing this prior to any shooting war, as we'd be hard-pressed covering such an effort that close to Chinese shores.

"Our suggestion is to push an additional four divisions from the United States: the First Marine division out of Pendleton, the First Calvary division from Fort Hood, the Seventh Infantry division from Lewis-McChord, the Fourth Infantry division from Fort Carson, and the Second Armored division out of Fort Bliss. We can issue a recall and have them boarding ships within seventy-two hours. If you think we're close, I say we announce a large exercise with South Korea. Once the shooting begins, we'll have a difficult time getting reinforcements ashore if we have to force a passage, especially during the early stages of any engagement.

"As you suggested during one of our meetings, the Marine expeditionary units were placed on a seventy-two-hour notice. It's my opinion that we should immediately begin to stage them on Okinawa," General Dawson suggested. "Doing so now will gain us time."

"Will that be enough to stop the North Koreans?" President Winslow inquired.

"No, sir. But it will slow them down enough that we may not immediately lose the peninsula. Once we take care of the Chinese submarine threat, then we may be able to open a corridor for additional reinforcements into South Korea. However, for the initial time period, those forces will be on their own. There's just too much firepower China can bring so close to their own shores, and we'll need time to diminish those threats.

"Now, with that said, we're deploying our three Ohio-class cruise missile nuclear submarines into the area, along with Task Force Seventy-Four. That force comprises four Los Angeles-class fast attack submarines, which will be stationed around them for protection. Once we find the North Koreans massing for an attack, the plan calls for a preemptive strike and to place four hundred and fifty Tomahawk cruise missiles in their lap. That will slow their initial onslaught," General Dawson answered.

"And if we can't hold them back?"

"Then we retake it once a cease-fire with the Chinese takes effect. We just have to make sure that the Korean peninsula isn't included in any agreement."

"So, that's one prong. What's the second one?"

"There's a chance that we may lose Taiwan at the outset. China has been slavering over that unification forever; I don't see them passing up an opportunity to invade. We'll initially be denied access to the South and East China Seas and unable to assist if we wanted to. We could place a few Virginia-class attack boats in the Taiwan Strait, but those are shallow waters and will more than likely be teeming with anti-submarine forces. If Taiwan is lost, we wouldn't be able to take it back like South Korea without incurring a larger-scale war with China. If I correctly understand your directives, we don't want a land war with China and seek to limit any fight to the oceans," General Dawson responded.

"Is there no solution to avoid that?" President Winslow asked.

"Well, we could recognize them as a nation, sign a mutual defense agreement, immediately sell them a ton of equipment, and place troops ashore," Secretary of State Stevenson suggested.

"That'll really piss off the Chinese," CIA director Collier chuckled. "You want some angry Chinese, that's how you get angry Chinese."

"And they might attack anyway. As a matter of fact, that move might even prompt them to attack more quickly," NSA director Reiser interjected.

"That's true. But, it might be enough to give them pause," General Dawson commented. "They might view it as an escalation into the realm of a land war, much like we would if they invaded Guam or Okinawa. We might be able to buy some time while we prosecute the main focus of any engagement in the region. But, in all likelihood, the odds are that we lose Taiwan while forcing the Chinese to relinquish their territorial claims on the Spratly Islands."

"Okay, let me think on that one. I'd like contingency plans incorporating both sides," President Winslow said. "Now, I'm assuming the third line would be, how did you put it, the main focus?"

"Yes, sir. So, without talking of any escalations that would have to occur to bring us into a shooting war, I'll discuss our current main contingency. Again, we pulled our bombers out of Guam so that they wouldn't be such a lucrative target. The British took over the escort duties in the Straits of Hormuz, thus freeing up our ships. We may be able to get one large strike in before we have to pull our surface vessels from the South China Sea.

"We'll have reinforced South Korea and have our Marine expeditionary units staging in Japan and Okinawa. That will give us the ability to place land forces should we need them. If a war becomes inevitable, we'll replace the littoral combat ships currently with the task force in the South China Sea with destroyers and pull those LCSs back to patrol the waters around Pearl, Japan, Okinawa, and the west coast along with P-8 ASW forces. If we confine our attacks to only Chinese forces away from their homeland, then we can hope they'll do the same.

"The Chinese will deploy their nuclear and diesel-electric subs en masse. That and the number of bombers/missiles they have available is the reason why we'll have to pull our carriers back. Instead, we send in our attack boats and whittle down their submarine forces, if not eliminate them. That will take time."

"How long?" President Winslow interrupted.

"We currently calculate two weeks, but some of our models run that out to three weeks, so that's what we're basing our plans on," General Dawson answered.

"So, the forces in Korea will have to last at least that long?"

"Correct, sir."

"And you think they can do that?"

"With help from a substantial number of sea-launched cruise missiles, I hope so."

"What's your level of confidence?"

"There's a 65 to 70 percent chance of our forces holding out long enough. Now, that's barring the use of nuclear weapons on either side. Those would substantially change the game," General Dawson replied.

"Okay, thank you. Carry on."

"Once we have dealt with their submarine forces, then we have to do the same with their bombers. That means we'll have to lure them out and destroy them in large numbers. There are several contingency plans to do just that depending on where we are three weeks in. Their surface vessels are large in number but behind in technology. But remember, they have a lot of missiles that we simply can't ignore. If they decide to deploy their fleet, then we'll be able to deal with it, but that will take time.

"There's a chance that they may just opt to park their carriers in port and let their submarines fight. They have to know that their naval fleet is no match for ours, so they'll think twice about deploying them against us. They'll seek to avoid losses, especially when they're in the midst of attempting to build a blue-water navy."

"I'm afraid that I must insist on keeping the war confined to the water and stay away from striking at bases on their homeland. I know that will make matters more difficult, but that's something I have to insist on. Otherwise, any war will escalate into something none of us want," President Winslow iterated.

"Yes, sir. That was clear, but it does make it more difficult. We'll have terribly long support lines, whereas China will be fighting in their own backyard. As I mentioned, our biggest problem will come from their Shang-class nuclear fast attack submarines. They'll be able to flood the Philippine Sea with them and use their diesel-electric boats to canvass the East and South China Seas. They can easily lay low and guard the entrances without fear from airborne ASW forces. They'll be difficult to ferret out and destroy, but I believe we'll be able to do it.

"Another problem is their extensive number of hypersonic anti-ship missiles. Their range is small, but they have a variety of delivery systems. What I'm saying is that it won't be a walk in the park, and it will take time before we can venture again into the South China Sea. The opposing Chinese forces are numerous and they'll be operating on their own turf," General Dawson briefed.

"I think we need to keep in mind that the United Nations will be screaming for a cease-fire. That inevitability will need to be handled with care, making sure that we actually come out with favorable conditions," Secretary of State Stevenson inserted.

"Agreed," President Winslow affirmed. "Okay, so move ahead with any troop movements you determine to be necessary. If this gets ugly, I want us to be ready and not having to react. How are the hostage rescue plans coming along?"

"The SEAL Dive Team departed on the twenty-fourth so they could be on station for the new moon on the tenth of June. The conditions will be ideal for the raid, so I'd like for us to keep that date in mind when making decisions. Now, the teams are ready for either mission, the rescue or the larger-scale attack with stand-off weaponry. The Red Cross has been to the island a number of times, and we have a good idea of where the captives are being held. The SEALs will be in position on the eighth of June and ready to go on your signal, but again, keep in mind, sir, the ideal window of June tenth," General Dawson responded.

"Okay, thank you, gentlemen," President Winslow said, effectively ending the meeting.

The room came alive with the shuffling of papers and the squeaking of chairs. The president waved the secretary of state and the Treasury secretary back to their seats.

"There are a few other items I'd like to discuss," President Winslow said once the room had cleared.

*   *   *   *   *   *

Bangor Naval Base, Washington
31 May, 2021

The dark outline of the Olympic Mountains rose abruptly above the glimmering salt waters of Hood Canal, the rays of a nearly full moon riding low above the jagged mountain crests frosting the distant trees that hugged the slopes. Silver-lined clouds scudded across a star-studded sky, periodically dimming the bright night. Slowly, the moon sank below the hills, leaving behind mountains darkly silhouetted against the backdrop of the heavens.

As the moon departed for another night, thick, heavy ropes were cast from a long cigar-shaped vessel that seemed blacker than the night enveloping her. Tugs pulled the large nuclear submarine from the docks of the Delta Pier, water churning from the rear as the boat came under its own power.

The dark shape sank below the cold waters, following the two patrol craft ensuring the passageway was clear of fishing vessels. Slowly, the sub emerged into the larger channel of the Strait of Juan de Fuca. Ahead lay the deep waters of the Pacific Ocean. Thirty minutes after the departure of the USS *Ohio*, the USS *Michigan* followed.

In addition to the mighty nuclear boats, the three Seawolf-class fast attack submarines assigned to the development squadron were being readied to get underway. Across the west coast, Guam, and Pearl Harbor, LA- and Virginia-class fast attack submarines departed their bases and steamed west. Slowly, America's underwater naval power moved toward the far eastern waters.

*   *   *   *   *   *

Worst Single-Day Drop Since 2008

1 June, 2021

New York, New York (*NYTimes*) — The news that the United States froze Chinese assets and threatened to block the yuan from the dollar sent shockwaves through the financial world. Monday looked ugly from the opening bell, losing over a trillion dollars by the time the bell was again struck.

In Beijing, the Chinese market took an even larger hit, losing 11% of its valuation before being shutdown ahead of the close of business. It was the start of a general market sell-off that was felt in all market economies.

The action taken by the Winslow administration was a result of a rapidly deteriorating trade war with China and the twelve American sailors being held hostage by China. "Those men and women are being illegally detained," said Fred Stevenson, the secretary of state. "We want to see them freed unharmed and returned to their families."

In addition, a bipartisan bill was introduced into Congress that would essentially dissolve the $1.1 trillion of Chinese debt as restitution for the economic damages encountered as a result of SARCoV...

Chapter Eight

Geneva, Switzerland
3 June, 2021

Fred Stevenson sighed heavily as he listened to his Chinese counterpart, Foreign Minister Liu. It had been much the same all day with little sign of a breakthrough. Fred knew the Chinese wanted to exchange the American hostages in return for a release of China's frozen assets, and they were again making that demand. However, the good thing was that freezing their assets and threatening to block them from trading in US dollars quickly brought them to the table.

"Those men aren't hostages," Minister Liu stated. "They are prisoners taken while invading the territorial waters of China. It is America who is conducting illegal activities by locking our legitimate interests. However, in the sake of peace, we are willing to return the prisoners unharmed. In return, China wants their legitimate assets unfrozen and returned."

"Minister Liu, you know as well as I that the ship you fired upon and sank was operating in international waters. Therefore, your actions were illegal, and those sailors held against their will are then hostages by definition. You will return them immediately, and then we can possibly discuss further matters," Fred insisted.

"Those were Chinese territorial waters," Minister Liu countered.

"Not according to the World Court Ruling."

"A ruling we don't acknowledge. The prisoners in exchange for the return of our legal assets," he again asserted.

"As I've said countless times today, the United States doesn't negotiate for the release of hostages."

"Prisoners."

"Hostages," Fred said, standing to depart. The others who were part of the US delegation also stood with the secretary. "We're retiring for the day. Perhaps you'll use the time wisely to think on what we've said, and there can be headway tomorrow. Good night to you, minister."

Back in his room, Secretary Stevenson called President Winslow on a secure line.

"It's much the same, Mr. President. They aren't budging from their position that the sailors are prisoners of war and therefore legitimate bargaining chips in their eyes," Fred said once the call was answered and patched through.

"Keep at it, Fred. I know it's frustrating, but I'm green-lighting the rescue mission and okaying the full strike package. We need to make it seem like this negotiation is the avenue we're going to take to get the hostages back. Sell it, Fred. We don't want them to get the idea we may be considering alternative measures."

"Will do. I'm going to need an entire bottle of aspirin if I have to listen to that man say the same thing for another eight hours tomorrow. Maybe I'll drink heavily before going in. But, at least the catered meals are worth it," Fred commented.

"Stay with it, Fred. It'll be over in a week."

With that, the line clicked dead. Fred tossed back a neat whiskey he had filled prior to the conversation, considering another before heading out to dinner with his delegation.

* * * * * *

President Winslow lifted the handset and placed it back into the cradle.

"Well, you heard me. We're going with the larger-scale operation. I'm sick of the shit they keep pulling. I want them to understand that we mean business and to send them a strong message letting them know. I want that island leveled...sunk, if that's possible. If we merely go in and rescue the hostages, then we'll just be back where we started and have lost any political advantage we still have. The Chinese will have gotten away with sinking a naval destroyer of ours in open waters. No, I want to send them a signal that they can't fuck with us like that and that their free ride of expansion is over. If we're going to do this, then we're going to do it right."

"Just so you understand, they'll want to save face, so there's a good chance that the Chinese will retaliate in kind," CIA director Collier mentioned.

"I know that. If they want to keep losing ground, let them. We can continue to fight them financially, but the pain we cause them is also felt by us. If they want to keep pushing along a military line, then we'll have a greater advantage in that arena—or so our defense spending says. I'm tired of playing nice and reacting. Freezing their assets was a beginning. We'll erase our debt to them and hit that island like it's a bug."

"Sir, may I assume that we can plan this for the night of June tenth, Tokyo time?" General Dawson inquired.

President Winslow nodded.

"Very well, sir. I'll send the signal to the units involved that Operation Blue Thunder is a go."

*   *   *   *   *   *

Four hours later, a single-word message was received aboard the USS *Tucson* and *Santa Fe*—"Blanket." Two SEAL teams reordered and focused their thoughts. The two teams would be going ashore separately, one for the hostages and the other to take down the main radars covering the islands and their vicinity.

"It's about fucking time we're doing something about this," Admiral Fablis muttered as he read through the operations order.

The task force comprising the two carrier strike groups centered around the USS *Theodore Roosevelt* and the USS *Nimitz* found themselves conducting business with renewed energy and focus. The littoral ships that were part of the outer screen performing anti-submarine warfare turned about and plotted courses back to differing ports. Their positions were taken by arriving destroyers dispatched from Pearl Harbor, with the USS *Chafee* replacing the lost USS *Preble*.

In the depths of the Pacific, the USS *Ohio*, one of the three SSGN submarines that departed the Bangor Naval Base in

Washington, diverted from a course that would have taken them into the East China Sea. The new plot showed them heading further south, ending up with a new temporary station located in the South China Sea. The seven-blade screw increased revolutions as the cruise missile boat picked up speed.

* * * * * *

South China Sea
9 June, 2021

"Sir, the Chinese satellite just set."

"Thank you," Admiral Fablis said, replacing the handset in its cradle.

A minute later, the ships of the task force turned to a southwesterly heading and increased their speed to thirty knots. Any submarine that was able to avoid the ASW screens would be forced to match speed in order to keep up and would therefore be easy to find. Two hours later, the satellite again set. With an all-clear from the ASW screens, the two carrier strike groups turned south toward the Spratly Islands. They'd use the two-hour window until the next enemy satellite arrived overhead to close within strike distance of Fiery Cross Island.

* * * * * *

South China Sea
10 June, 2021

The faint sound of waves crashing against the outer reefs drifted across the darkened island. A constant surge of rollers flowed across the shoals to hiss gently on the manmade shores, slowly retreating only to be pushed back ashore by those following.

The stillness was abruptly broken by the roar of a jet engine, with others following. Taxi and runway lights flared into existence, punching their way into the inky night. Bright lights stabbed along paved surfaces as the four fighter jets taxied to the runway, the whining roar of their engines indicating their barely contained power.

Without pause, the lead aircraft turned onto the runway. Flames leapt from twin tailpipes as the Chinese pilot applied thrust. The aircraft leapt forward as if unchained. Like a ferocious beast, it roared down the runway and climbed steeply into the night sky. The flames were quenched and the jet fighter was lost in the darkness. One after the other, three more followed.

The roaring quickly faded; the lights of the airport environment turned off as suddenly as they'd appeared. The faint sound of crashing waves slowly again washed across the base as the stillness returned. Unknown to the pilots embarking on their patrol, six pairs of eyes watched their departure through masks half-submerged in the rolling surf. With darkness returning, six black shapes rose from the waves and flowed ashore.

* * * * * *

Water ran down the glass like raindrops against a window pane as LTJG Baldwin eased above the surf. Barely visible under the starlit skies, waves gently rolled onto the beach. The hiss of the receding water sounded like the caress of fine silk, while from further offshore came the faint roar of swells curling over the outer reef.

The SEAL team leader bobbed in the rollers, splashing against one of the metal pylons that were part of the runway approach lighting that extended into the water. The roar of jet engines rose above the natural sounds, and only a moment later, bright beams stabbed from the runway environment. Looking around, James Baldwin saw — only because he knew where they were and what to look for — small black shapes near other pylons, each one another member of his team.

The lights glared brightly as the jet turned. James watched silently as each aircraft took off with a roar, spouting a tail of flame. They rose into the sky like dragons, swallowed quickly by the void of night. Darkness and silence returned to the island. The jets had been ill-timed, but the angle of the bright lights was such that there was little chance of a reflection off the face masks. As one, the six SEALs rose from the shallows, their weapons trained on the nearby beach and eyes searching for sign of any patrols. Before leaving the *Tucson*, the team had learned that an additional company of Chinese soldiers had offloaded onto the island.

"That's going to make for one crowded place," Petty Officer Collins had commented.

LTJG Baldwin knew that was an understatement, but wasn't overly concerned about the infil to the building where the hostages were being held. It was the chance of the rescue being discovered by some nosy guard checking on their prisoners and finding them missing that concerned him. They had to hold at Kitchen for several minutes before the Ospreys would show up to carry the hostages away. If the Chinese decided to turn the lights on and play "find the SEALs," things could get a touch dicey.

Before hitting the beach, they turned and traversed the shoreline, always remaining in the water so the waves would hide their tracks. The beach ended at a breakwater of rocks near the stacked containers. Without a word, they again paused, this time to remove their scuba gear. Donning other gear from their packs, the team changed from aquatic creatures to ones of land. NVGs with thermal overlays were checked, bolts peeled back to ensure live rounds were chambered.

Petty Officer Bill Collins whispered into his radio, giving the code that Gold Team was ashore. All they had to do now was to traverse half the island through mostly open fields, working their way past a fifty-foot observation tower overlooking that part of the island, maneuver up to the building holding hostages, take out any guards, rescue the sailors, then turn around and do it all again with twelve additional personnel in tow. The fact that the island was observing blackout procedures would help some, but who knew what lay in those towers with the radomes on top.

Huddled among the large rocks of the breakwater,

Collins withdrew a tablet from his pack and quickly assembled a tiny drone. Checking that the connection was good, he tossed the drone out over the water where it climbed and hovered. Faint green illuminated his face as he looked at the screen, scanning what the onboard camera showed. The immediate area was clear, so he directed the quiet drone inland.

In the empty lot next to the containers, he paused the drone and gathered Baldwin's attention. Parked at the inland edge of the lot was a CSK-131, China's equivalent of the Humvee. Light flared through the windscreen as a soldier inhaled on a cigarette. Collins maneuvered the drone in an attempt to get a thermal image of how many were in the vehicle, but the glass impeded his efforts. Movement inside indicated at least two in the front seats, but there could be two more in the back. The heavy machine gun mounted on top looked menacing and could tear through a small team in an instant.

"Front and rear night vision cameras," Baldwin whispered. "We'll have to move around them and keep them in mind upon our return."

Each member logged the stationary patrol in their mind, especially as it was parked in a position that covered their entire exfil area. They couldn't take it out now as its absence might be noted and the alarm raised. It was far too early in the mission to risk any hint that the team was ashore.

The drone flew further inland. The airport covered nearly half the island, with a central road running the length to separate it from the administrative buildings and barracks. Halfway up the two-laned paved road sat two additional light armored vehicles. They were facing opposite directions just down the road from the building where the hostages were kept. These were a new addition, having arrived with the extra company of soldiers that had landed. Two guards sat just outside the hostage building, leaning back against the wooden structure.

Baldwin wasn't worried about the two guards, but the vehicles with their armor plating and heavy weapons added a twist in the plan. It was going to be difficult taking both of them out along with the guards without waking up the neighborhood. From what he was eyeballing on the screen, the entire picture looked like a firefight in the making. He'd check the outside of the building for some other way in, but the satellite photos they'd studied hadn't shown any other entrances. There were two paned windows on either side, but those had been shuttered. However, it was worth another look, and he directed Collins to move the drone around the building.

"We have fifteen minutes left on the battery," Collins warned.

The drone footage of the windows only verified what the previous photos had indicated: the windows were a no-go. It looked like they'd have to go in through the front door.

"Bring it back," Baldwin directed.

With the original route to the building compromised by the armored vehicle to their front, Collins brought the drone back along a secondary route the team had plotted. It was riskier because it exposed them more to the tall observation tower overlooking this section of the island, but that couldn't be helped now. He was confident they could make it past, but it was their return with a mob in tow that was a worry.

"Okay, folks. We're moving along our secondary route around the breakwater, up the beach, and across the small bay on the southeastern tip. Then we're going through the fields to approach the building from the rear. We'll be in direct view of the observation tower, so we move slowly. Exfil will be the same route except we'll have to go along the beach rather than swim the bay. That will bring us almost directly under the tower, but we don't have a choice. Welch and Renton will lead and take care of the 131 if the vehicle is still there on our return," Baldwin briefed.

"How are we going to take the building?" Ted Riker, the team medic, asked.

"I'm still working on that one. I'd like to see up close and personal if we can manage a way in through the side or back. If not, then I see us taking out the guards and the vehicle personnel. We'll firm that up once we get closer," Baldwin answered. "If we get into a firefight on scene, then we'll call Banshee minus zero on our way out. That will give us five minutes to get to our exfil and get our passengers away before the fireworks start."

"That's cutting it pretty close," Sam Vangle commented.

"Then we'll have to do our best Carl Lewis imitations, won't we?" Baldwin returned.

"No problem for me, skipper. However, as an old man..."

"You can fuck off with that. I'll make you think you're standing still."

"If you say so...*sir*."

* * * * * *

Captain Garner looked out over the dark flight deck. At first glance, it appeared to be a chaos of moving lights as the crews waved wands to direct the aircraft to their positions. However, the more one looked, the more the chaos turned into an intricate yet carefully orchestrated dance. Two F/A-18Fs stood ready at the forward catapults. The code was received that the SEAL teams were ashore and commencing their rescue attempt. Admiral Fablis, the task force commander, broadcast the message to initiate Blue Thunder. Captain John Garner acknowledged receipt and issued the order to his carrier air group commander to commence operations.

Adjacent to the aircraft hooked into the forward catapult, a crew member began spinning a red wand over his head. The pilot moved his throttle forward and flames began to stream from the tailpipes of one of the Super Hornets, the aircraft instantly straining against its restraints. Bathed in the red glow of the sodium lights, the pilot gave his aircraft a final check and then saluted. The spinning wand then abruptly lowered, pointing to the front of the carrier. The pilot and back-seater were thrown back into their seats as the catapult fired. Trailing flame, the attack fighter shot forward and rose into the air.

Seconds later, the second of the two went through the same motions and was soon airborne, the afterburner cutting out shortly after liftoff and the fighters vanishing into the darkness.

Two other aircraft were immediately waved forward to be hooked to the launching system, blasting off from the flight deck shortly afterward to join up with the previous two circling the carrier. As a flight of four, they were directed by the E-2 airborne command post and climbed to their assigned altitude and stations. This process was repeated numerous times from both the *Roosevelt* and the *Nimitz*, the night skies filling with aircraft laden with a variety of weaponry.

In the combat information center, Admiral Fablis watched the carefully orchestrated plan form up. EA-18 Growlers orbited at low altitudes and airspeeds, ready to race in and jam radio frequencies and radars as necessary. Hawkeyes and the attack packages circled over the horizon of Fiery Cross Island, waiting for the signal to be unleashed.

* * * * * *

Just outside of the manmade channel serving the island harbor, the delivery vehicle held its position close to the coral reef rising from the sea floor. Six sets of eyes focused on the nearby dark shape sliding past. The hull of the Chinese corvette patrol boat cut through the gentle swells, its slow-moving propeller pushing the craft toward the deeper waters of the South China Sea. As the Chinese vessel slid past, Petty Officer Joel Infelt guided the SEAL delivery vehicle in its wake and slipped into the entrance to the lagoon.

David Hawser, the Blue Team leader, knew that Gold Team was easing onto shore at this very moment. David knew that LTJG Baldwin and his team had the more difficult assignment, but this one wasn't going to be a cakewalk either. He kept reviewing his mental map of the island, knowing that there were three observation towers on the spit of land just to his left, or east. There was another one located to the west near the command centers located on the northern tip of the island next to the radar farm that was his team's target. Those posts looked over the entire northern section of the island, and there weren't too many locations that couldn't be directly observed from the towers.

Entering the harbor proper, Infelt brought the SDV around and parked it next to one of the freighters docked at the concrete pier that ran the length of the northern waterfront. Other piers lined the entire lagoon, turning it into one large harbor for offloading supplies. Sealing the craft, the six SEALs floated upward.

Coming up next to the hull of a freighter, Hawser lifted his head above the surface just high enough for his eyes to come clear. He didn't spot any movement nearby or on the opposite spit of land, and there was only the sound of the sea slapping against the metal hull. With one hand on the ship, he guided himself round the vessel and glided through the water toward the rocks lining shore. Timing the small waves lapping the pier foundations, David crawled onto the breakwater and began peeling off his scuba gear. One by one, the other five of his team, their dark shapes silently knifing through the waters, emerged to do the same.

Lining the dockside were stacked containers, lifted from the ships by two cranes poised like praying mantises waiting patiently on twigs. Slipping back into the water, the team swam past the pier to a location closer to the radar farm. The scuba suits the team wore protected them somewhat from their body heat showing up in any thermal imaging, but any magnified view through night-vision devices would easily spot them. With that in mind, Hawser and his team were wary of the three observation towers standing tall directly across the water.

Peeking over the lip of the rocky embankment, David stared directly across a paved perimeter road into the mass of radar domes occupying a significant part of the northern tip of the island. Just scant feet away, behind a chain-link fence topped with razor wire, was everything the military installation needed to extend its reach and provide warning of any form of intrusion. Weather radars, powerful search radars, and targeting radars formed most of what lay within.

To the west was a large complex of concrete buildings, their tops festooned with a multitude of antennae. These were the communications and central command centers that directed the island's offensive and defensive capabilities. Some radomes fed into the air traffic control tower at the airport for aircraft sequencing for approaches and departures. According to schematics obtained from some anonymous source, all of the cables leading from the farm were combined into one large conduit that was then fed into the varying complexes. In David's opinion, that was a major design flaw, which he and his team would attempt to exploit. It was imperative to the overall operation that they blind the island and expose their mobile radars. If the radars were still operational when the aircraft arrived, losses would mount.

Petty Officers Bollinger and Infelt covered the road in one direction, while Crimson and Longe covered the other. Rising, Hawser, and Dewey dashed low across the road and slid, coming to rest next to the chain-link fence. With Hawser keeping an eye into the facility, Dewey began to quickly clip the links with a bolt cutter, creating a gate. Hawser slid through.

One by one, each member of the team rose from their position to race across and slide through the opening Dewey held open. With the last one through, Dewey folded the fencing back and fed the broken links into the adjacent ones so that it appeared whole. The team slipped further inside the facility, six dark shapes moving furtively through the array of radomes.

The team worked their way toward the main entrance where the schematics showed the cables coming together. They'd have to dig approximately two feet under the sand, expose the width of the conduit, and then rig it. That sounded easy enough if it weren't for the four guards standing alertly at the entry gate in direct view of where they needed to dig. The question wasn't so much if they could eliminate the guards but whether the sentries had set report times or if the command center requested radio checks. If that were the case and one of those came after the security personnel were taken out, then the team could have a whole lot of attention drawn its way in a hurry. However, there was little choice in the matter. The guards had to go before the team could start their job of locating the mass of cables and rigging them to blow.

With the guards positioned inside the fence, the setup was an easy matter. If it had been otherwise, they would have had to creep closer in order to avoid the sounds or sparks from an inadvertent bullet hitting one of the chain links.

Small strobing flashes of light blinked across the ground and the side of one radome as bullets were sent streaking toward their targets. Hard thunks whispered through the night air as each round found its mark, forcefully impacting the bodies of four unsuspecting Chinese guards. As if a scythe swept through their midst, they fell like stalks of wheat, unseeing eyes staring at the starry heavens above.

In a flash, four of the SEALs were upon the stricken bodies, ensuring they were no longer a part of this world and dragging them back to hide them next to one of the radar domes. The team waited in the shadows, listening and looking for an approaching vehicle. In the blackout, it would be difficult to miss the small flashes of gunfire, but you'd have to be looking directly at it. The radios each guard carried remained silent, as did the surrounding area.

With four team members setting up in a loose perimeter, Hawser and Bollinger oriented themselves according to the schematic. They began digging in the loose soil, scooping armfuls of sand away from the burgeoning hole. The deeper they went, the more compact the sand became and the slower the hole grew.

At a little more than two feet below the surface, Hawser began digging perpendicular to the cable route, hitting metal a short time later. Working quickly, Ken Bollinger, the team's ordinance specialist, cleared the sand away to reveal a thick armored conduit. Wrapping magnesium strips around the tube, he then placed a thick canvas sheet over the hole, creating a tent-like structure. Next, he lit the strips, which flared brightly, but the canvas prevented any light from escaping. It was over in a second, smoke and the smell of burned metal wafting upward once the tent was removed.

Bollinger waited a few moments for the conduit to cool and then checked. They had a nearly complete burn through in two locations. With a sharp tap from a pry bar, the conduit broke through. A minute later, explosive charges were placed around the exposed cable and the fuse rigged to an electronic firing device, which would be triggered remotely. The two men reburied the cable, leaving a thin aerial protruding from the surface. Smoothing over the surface, the team moved to the fence and hid in the shadows prevalent among the radomes. Hawser and the other five SEALs then waited for the call that would prompt them to complete their mission.

* * * * * *

Waves splashed continually over the six figures as they moved slowly up, over, and around the breakwater rocks. Each member of the team was conscious of the night vision capabilities of the vehicle parked a short distance away and made sure to keep below the low concrete wall separating the empty lot from rock.

As they rounded the point of the island, the rocks gave way to a thin strip of beach rising up to a series of large buildings. There the team halted, and again the drone was sent aloft, checking along the upper sands for any sign of patrols or bunkers that had previously gone unnoticed. Nothing showed, and the team slowly negotiated their way along the beach, mindful to keep a path to ensure the surging waves erased their tracks. The buildings and lower level of the narrow beach provided cover from anyone looking out from the observation tower. That shield would change once they reached the inlet.

James Baldwin crouched at the edge of a breakwater jetty that extended into the water at the entrance to the small bay. Waves rolled past on the other side, a constant motion of up and down against the jetty. Rising dominantly at the end of the bay was the first real obstacle, and one that would vie for prominence for the rest of their excursion to the hostages: the observation tower. As James looked at the beach encircling the inlet, he again was conscious of the difficulties he and the team would face bringing the twelve sailors back unseen.

With a nod, the team slithered their way over the top and into the water on the other side. There they started side-stroking in order to disturb the seas as little as possible, rising up over crests and down into troughs. Suddenly, a bright light stabbed through the night, the seas lighting up around them. Diving immediately, they strove for the bottom only a few feet away. Latching onto coral, they held both their positions and breath, hoping to become just another dark spot under the waves. With waves rolling past overhead, the six members of the team swayed back and forth with the current as if they were strands of kelp.

Baldwin looked up toward the surface. Through the water, the bright light shimmered, dimming as the waves slid over the top of him. He was listening for the tell-tale sound of a boat motor approaching. One minute passed and he knew their time was running out. At best, they had another minute before they would need to resurface. Overhead, the spotlight moved back and forth.

One minute, thirty seconds, and his lungs started the complaining that would very soon rise to a scream for air. One minute, forty seconds. He was already calculating his ascent in order to barely extend his mouth above the surface as best he could in the rolling waves for a breath of fresh air. One minute, fifty seconds and the light winked out, darkness returning to the surface overhead. James let go and pushed off, his head poking above the seas where he was rewarded with an inflow of oxygen. He held his breath as the waves rolled over him only to gasp for air again on the other side. Slowly, his body recovered and the six figures again started across the bay, swimming underwater for the most part, rising only for air.

Crawling out of the water on the other side, they quickly crossed a narrow stretch of sand and made their way into grass-covered dunes. The sound of a vehicle rose above the backdrop of waves cresting offshore. The team kept their heads down as the vehicle slowed and a beam of light shot across the dunes, searching the nooks and crannies. On the backside of the short dunes, six team members lay in the shadows created when the spotlight swept over their positions. The light eventually winked out and the vehicle moved on, but to the six SEALs, it was obvious that they had somehow piqued someone's attention.

I suppose if I held American hostages and knew that there were two carriers somewhere out in the darkness, or knew that we existed, then I'd be a little nervous as well, Baldwin thought as he gave it a few more minutes before moving on.

Leaving the dunes, the team skirted across a road that ran along the perimeter beach and down the spit on the east side of the island. There they entered open terrain with a sports field and freshwater pond. As they rounded one of the corners of the pond, the night was again interrupted by the violent intrusion of a high-powered light emanating from the observation tower. The last man made it over the edge and hugged the small embankment as the beam swept over their positions.

Again, the sound of a vehicle moving up the perimeter road grew louder. The armored vehicle stopped in nearly the same spot and added their spotlight to the one roving about from the observation post. Together, the two lights covered every inch of the field without once finding the six men hunkered below the pond's embankment. After a couple of minutes, one and then the other winked out, and the vehicle commenced moving back up the road.

It was now beyond obvious that the tower sported some kind of radar that could detect movement close to the ground. Without animals or a whole lot of traffic to interfere with the readings, they could remove the ground clutter filters and operate much like the ground control radars at busy airport terminals. However, they weren't yet so alert as to do more than send motorized patrols to quickly scout whatever the radar had picked up. If they had sent foot patrols, they would have eventually found the team, which would have forced them into an engagement that would have negated any attempt to rescue the sailors.

The SEALs would have to watch their movements and make sure they weren't the tallest objects in the area. Operating in a radar environment like they were would add an even greater level of difficulty to the exfil of the hostages. They'd have to operate either terribly slowly or move very quickly. James would evaluate their options on the way to the building. However, they had to first rescue their fellows before having to run the gauntlet of their return.

Remaining low and slow, the team crawled the rest of the way to the targeted building. It had taken them a little longer than anticipated, but they had arrived. Peeking around one of the rear corners, James could see a Chinese CSK-141 parked just up the road. This was a troop-carrying version of the 131, basically an elongated and up-armored version of the Humvee. The 12.7mm turret could put some heavy firepower downrange in a hurry. James knew that the vehicle could withstand hits from his 7.65mm with ease. The vehicle in view wasn't something that could be messed with in a direct engagement.

Around the other corner sat a CSK-131, this one also with a 12.7mm manually operated turret. Each of those .50-cal equivalent rounds could tear through anything on the island with the possible exception of the concrete bunkers along the western beaches. If they hit flesh, there would be chunks of meat and bone flung away from a pink mist. With Welch and Renton covering the corners, Baldwin huddled with the others at the back of the building.

"The windows are indeed shuttered and still a no-go, and I don't see any way to enter anywhere else quietly. With the night-vision cameras and the positioning of the vehicles, it's going to be a hard go taking out the front guards and conducting any kind of rescue without being noticed," Baldwin briefed.

"So, we have to figure out a way to either take out the vehicles or draw them away," Riker commented.

"I'm afraid so."

"Well, we had them spooked and they still didn't move these away, so I doubt any kind of distraction will get rid of them," Riker said.

"That's my thinking as well. I think we have to take them out," Baldwin stated.

"And without the tower seeing us."

"That's the long and short of it. And then there's the return trip and the radar to think about," Baldwin responded.

"So, you're thinking to take out the guards and vehicles, quickly retrieve the hostages from inside, and move them to Kitchen via the trucks?" Riker inquired.

"Kind of. We move quickly enough to stay ahead of any response. Take out the vehicle parked in the lot and defend the location until the Ospreys arrive. Then we vanish, hopefully ahead of the incoming fire," James suggested.

"I say let's do it. I'm tired of ducking that fucking spotlight anyway," Collins replied.

The rest of the team gave their input and the plan was a go.

"Give everyone a heads up that we'll exfil on the run with a minus zero option on the code."

The word went out in a flash message and the team readied themselves. Somewhere out in the night skies beyond the horizon and below the swells, hundreds of men and women were poised for the signal of six men in the middle of the lion's den.

Tyler Welch and Scott Renton crept to their respective front corners of the building. Peeking around the corners with signal mirrors, the two men observed that the two guards at the front door remained in nearly the same positions they were when they were first recorded. Light flared from one as he brought a flame up to torch the end of a cigarette. The other leaned back against the building, his head lolling to the side as if he were sleeping in an upright bed.

Behind the two leading men were the rest of the team, their focus zeroed in on their respective trucks. Baldwin was teamed with Sam Vangle and was responsible for the larger of the two armored vehicles, while Riker and Collins would take care of the CSK-131. There would be little room for error. Keying the mic, he whispered a single word.

"Go!"

Welch and Renton rolled around their corners, knives flashing out from their sheaths. They were upon the two guards before their presence was noticed. Warm liquid poured down long blades to soak into gloves as the two SEALs buried their knives deep, their free hands coming up to cover their victims' mouths. With a twist of the blades, the Chinese guards stiffened from the intense pain, their attempts to scream muffled by the firm pressure of gloved hands. The bodies then relaxed as they died, slumping against the two professional soldiers who eased them slowly down to the ground. Any sound died out before it had traveled three feet away.

At the same time, Baldwin and Vangle dashed forward, keeping low. They came at the larger CSK-141 at an angle, hoping to keep out of the sight of the rear-facing camera. Grass whipped at their legs as they closed in, their eyes focused only on the vehicle.

Vangle led and was the first to arrive at the rear side doors. Crouched low beneath the windows, it appeared they had made it without being observed by anyone inside. Baldwin crouched with him and nodded quickly. Vangle reached up and grabbed one of the handles, yanking it open. Baldwin rose and was met with two heads in the front seats in the midst of turning in his direction. His short-barreled suppressed M4 was already to his shoulder and he fired point-blank into the driver's head. A quick strobe of light was the only indication that a subsonic round was on its way. Smacking into the soldier's head, the bullet tore through bone and tissue, exiting the other side. Blood and meaty chunks splattered against the far window and windshield, the pieces of flash slowly peeling off to fall to the floor. The driver fell against the door, blood dripping from the hole in the side of his head.

Without hesitation, James switched targets, firing into the

back of the passenger's head. More blood and brain tissue were added to the windshield as the man rocked forward, his head coming to rest against the dash. Baldwin added a third round to the passenger as the man's nervous system triggered a rapid flailing of his legs, the appendages thrumming against the floor. With the shot, the man stilled. Vangle was already checking for others in the rear of the armored vehicle, but there were only the two.

"Vehicle two, clear," James radioed.

"One clear," came a reply from Collins. "Two gomers down."

There wasn't any spotlight flaring from the tower just up the road, so it appeared all eyes up there were focused elsewhere. Both sets of men climbed inside the vehicles and tossed the bodies into the back, cleaning up the mess as much as possible. The motors were running, so there was no need to start warming the diesel engines.

At the building where the hostages were being kept, Welch wedged a small pry bar behind the swing latch that had been installed on the building's entry door. The wood splintered as the latch gave way and the two men quickly entered, their weapons up and ready. The building was an open area and obviously a cafeteria of some sort. However, the tables had been moved and cots arranged against the outer walls. Heads rose from pillows as the two men entered, their barrels searching the near and far corners of the room for the smallest inkling that armed men were within.

* * * * * *

President Winslow could feel the nervous tension eat at his gut, the coffee and sandwiches he had consumed churning into a volatile mix. The large screen at the end of the room depicted a high-definition black-and-white top-down view of Fiery Cross Island. Even though the moon was supposedly down, he could see faint white lines of the incoming waves encircling the island.

As if appearing from thin air, six bright blips appeared in the waters off the southern tip of the island. Winslow leaned forward as the camera view magnified and the screen showed six figures moving through the low surf next to some structures extending into the water.

"Sir, those men wading ashore are one of the SEAL teams. This one is Gold Team, assigned to rescue the hostages," stated General Warner, the commander of the Special Operations Command.

The men stopped moving and the screen pulled back, showing two Chinese fighter aircraft taxiing in the direction of the men. The planes turned the corner seemingly feet away from the men working to get ashore. Spouting flame behind them, the fighters zoomed down the runway, picking up speed. They gracefully left the runway, the afterburner cutting out seconds later as the aircraft flew out of the picture.

Winslow's attention focused back on the men. He had sent them there, his wishes and words taking on reality as these men marched into danger. As much as he tried to visualize what it must be like for the six beacons in the dark, he couldn't even begin to fathom what they must be going through. Here he was thousands of miles away, tense to the point of losing the contents of his stomach.

The rest of the men in the room, most of them in uniform, were quiet as they watched the progress of the mission. The only sound was General Warner describing the environment the men were moving through. On the northern tip of the island were six additional beacons.

"That would be Blue Team. They're assigned to the destruction of the radar capabilities in order to reduce the threats for the incoming aircraft," the general had briefed.

Sweat began to form under Winslow's arms; the clock and teams moved relentlessly slow. If the SEALs were found out, the ramifications would be disastrous. Not only would they lose any chance to have the sailors returned anytime soon, but the number would increase. In all likelihood, the twelve SEALs would be lost and there would be additional losses to the attacking fleet aircraft if those radars weren't shut down.

A bead of sweat trickled down the back of his neck as he contemplated losing face on the world stage. America's vaunted special operations teams would be compromised and the fear the carrier groups exuded would be diminished. His mind went back to President Carter's Tehran hostage rescue and the humiliation of the nation when it failed before even really leaving the ground. That could not be repeated here. His legacy wouldn't be one of failure. The mission unfolding before his eyes must not fail.

The screen split into two separate views. Each side held one of the teams as they progressed toward their objectives. On the north side, Frank watched as the six men, depicted in greater clarity than he'd known was possible, exited the water and ran across a road. There they worked through the fencing and into the network of radomes.

As he switched his gaze to the other team, his breath caught in his throat. A light stabbed out across a small bay and played out across where the SEAL team was located. He expected a storm of gunfire to follow, but the beam started moving from side to side as if searching for something they knew was there.

"Can they not be seen," President Winslow asked, releasing his inheld breath.

"Sir, as we can only see their beacons at this time, I can only assume that they've gone underwater," General Warner replied.

All in the room were mesmerized by the scene playing out. Frank found himself internally chanting for the team's safety and that they remain hidden. Time ticked by one slow second at a time, the beacons representing the SEAL team members seeming to hover motionless. He felt it had been so long that he wondered if the team members carried small personal air tanks. On the northern shore of the bay, a vehicle drove up and added another spotlight to shine across the water. Both the additional vehicle and the spotlight from the tower indicated that the team had somehow been found.

As suddenly as they appeared, the inlet again darkened as the lights winked out. The armored vehicle that had parked along the shore began moving back up the spit of land. The beacons began moving and turned into the shape of men swimming. Frank felt an ache in his fingers. Looking down, he saw that he had been holding a folder in a death grip without realizing it.

The president still felt the tension riding deep inside as the men began crossing an open field. There, the spotlight from the tower again reached out into the darkness, probing the ground for movement it knew was there.

"It looks like they have ground radar built into the observation towers. We were wondering if they had this capability, and I guess now we know," General Warner stated.

"What does that mean for our men?" President Winslow asked.

"It means they'll have to slow their approach to the building, sir. They're almost there, so our forecast timetable won't be affected much. However, the return with the hostages will be hampered."

"Meaning they may not make it to the pickup zone?" Frank questioned.

"We have an excellent team with an exceptional leader out there, sir. If anyone can make this happen, it's them. They'll have to improvise a route back and somehow take care of the vehicle overwatching the zone, but I have every confidence they'll safely extract our men and women," General Warner answered.

Frank nodded, wishing that he had the same confidence that the general was portraying. The SEALs hadn't seemed to travel more than a city block or two and had triggered a spotlight twice. To him, that didn't seem like great odds for the team making it back, let alone rescuing anyone. But he had seen the results of what special operation teams could accomplish previously; maybe this was just normal for them.

The spotlight again blinked out, returning the terrain to darkness. For the second time in seemingly as many minutes,

Frank found himself releasing his held breath. He didn't know why he was so tense watching the operation unfold. There had been many nerve-racking moments during his tenure, but this one felt ten times worse for some reason. Perhaps because the ramifications of failure were so great. If they were caught, then it would be a long while before they could be recovered.

As the general said, the team started off again but moved much slower. They arrived at the building without further incident. This part looked like watching a video game as the men moved into positions near one corner. They then moved, very faint flashes showing from their positions. Two guards posted at the door dropped to the ground, their heat signatures slowly dissipating as their bodies cooled.

Four other members of the team darted for two vehicles parked nearby. Again, faint flashes of light were the only indications that more people had just lost their lives. Frank leaned forward, his fingers again gripping a folder as two men entered the hostage building.

*   *   *   *   *   *

"US SEALs. Not a word from anyone, and no one move," Welch called into the room. "Remain where you are."

Covered bodies rose up to their elbows but no further, twelve sets of eyes following the two special operations men ensuring that the building was clear of hostiles. Once they were sure, the two men fished pictures out of plastic wrappings and went around the room, comparing photos with the people awakened from their slumber. Information on the back of the pictures was asked of each individual; once their identities were verified, they were told to gather in the middle of the room. Other than the softly spoken verifications, not a word was uttered, each hostage knowing that they were still in the middle of a hostile area.

"Twelve eggs verified and ambulatory," Welch radioed.

"Copy. We're ready outside. Once you leave the building, move quickly," Baldwin replied.

Welch turned to the twelve sailors dressed in a variety of civilian clothes brought by the Red Cross.

"Okay, folks. There will be two vehicles parked on the road, one to the left and one to the right. Once we're outside, we're moving quickly to the one on the right, the larger one. Pile in as best you can. I'll alert you now that there will be blood, bodies, and non-pleasant odors. You're going to have to ignore those. It's imperative that we move fast. That means we have to load up quickly and get moving.

"Once we've done that, we're going to drive you down the road where we'll be met by two aircraft that will bring you to a carrier waiting offshore. Do as we say when we say it and I assure you that we'll get you out of here safely. But it's vital that you listen and immediately comply. Before we move, is there anyone here who doesn't understand exactly what we're doing?"

Twelve pairs of wide and frightened eyes met those of the SEAL, but to a man and woman, they all nodded.

"Okay, good. You follow me, and Renton there by the door will come along behind us. Take a deep breath ... ready ... let's go," Welch said.

Renton cracked the door and peeked out, and then swung the portal wide open. Welch led the way outside and angled for the larger of the two light armored vehicles. Behind, the sailors followed in line, with Renton closing the door and swinging into a trail position, both as a watch on their six and to shepherd any who wandered in the darkness. Although there wasn't any moon to light the night landscape, the stars were enough to make out the darkened objects of the vehicles and other buildings. Several of the sailors stumbled in the grassy area's uneven terrain, but righted themselves quickly and continued.

At the CSK-141, Baldwin waited at the rear door and "assisted" the arriving navy personnel into the rear of the vehicle. They clambered over the two bodies lying in back, some slipping in the blood, but not a one cried out, although a couple started gagging from the smell of emptied bowels.

"Deal with it for two minutes and then we'll be out," James stated, closing the door after the twelfth one was shoved into a compartment meant for ten.

The team leader then rushed to the driver's side and climbed behind the wheel with Vangle climbing into the back to man the 12.7mm turret. Welch hopped in the front passenger seat while Renton crammed himself into the rear.

"Okay, we're good to go back here. Collins, make the call," Baldwin ordered.

Collins acknowledged and switched frequencies.

"This is Mother Hen, en route to the Kitchen with a dozen eggs. Banshee," he radioed. "I repeat, Banshee, minus zero."

The radio call was relayed via satellite to Raven One, an E-2 Hawkeye circling beyond the horizon.

"Copy Banshee minus zero and Mother Hen is en route," Raven One acknowledged.

*   *   *   *   *   *

With that call, the other pieces of Operation Blue Thunder were freed from their constraints.

The "Banshee" call whispered in Hawser's ears. He heard the minus zero addendum radioed by Gold Team and then repeated by Raven One broadcasting on all channels. Petty Officer Hawser sent an electronic signal, and a short distance away, the ground trembled as the explosives wrapped around the thick bundle of cables detonated. In the same moment, Bollinger and Infelt dashed over to the scene, finding a hole with sand flung to the side. Buried within, two ends of multiple cables poked through, the ends clearly separated.

"I guess that'll do it," Bollinger commented on his handiwork.

"I doubt that's going to go unnoticed," Infelt replied, both men glancing over to the prominent tower across the water and then the one nearby.

"Yeah, it's time to get the fuck out of Dodge."

Hawser had an urge to comment "to the fence, and beyond" upon hearing that their part of the mission was successful. Instead, he ordered his team out of the complex without adding the personal touch. As one, the six men dashed through the dark and scuttled through the fence opening. Just on the other side, a spotlight coming from the near observation tower pierced the night. Radomes became brilliantly lit golf balls as the light rolled across them. A second light joined the first from the tall structure across the water.

Without hesitation, the team members raced across the perimeter road. Running shadows materialized on the pavement as far spotlights caught up with the team sprinting for the water. Tracers quickly spat out of the installation, zipping across the water. Sparks flew from where the heavy rounds hit the asphalt and careened into the night sky.

Instead of the angry bees David Hawser had heard in the past, the sound of these near misses was the roar of freight trains. He knew that the team wasn't merely dealing with 7.65mm incoming fire, but .50 or heavier. The six men launched into air at the top of the breakwater rocks, tracers zipping along in the wake of their passage.

The second light began to swing in their direction as the men hit the surface of the lagoon. Towers of water launched into the air as the heavy slugs tore into the bay. Hawser saw several trails of rounds zip past as the force of their momentum carried them deep underwater.

The six frogmen swam under the resting hull of the ship, coming up in the more deeply shadowed area between ship and shore. Spotlights bathed the ship and surrounding waters in their beams, the bow becoming starkly defined, but no light could reach the SEALs. As the staccato sound of heavy machine-gun fire echoed across the base, the men quickly donned their scuba gear and dove back under the surface. The delivery vehicle was readied and they slowly made their way out to sea, where they met up with the USS *Santa Fe*.

*   *   *   *   *   *

Stars glittered through the plexiglass, a dome of a thousand jewels shining on a cloth of black velvet. The lower edges ended where the inky void of the seas met with the heavens. Spread across the night sky were nearly two hundred aircraft, riding the cold currents seven miles above the South China Sea.

Even though his mind was on the upcoming mission, Lt. Chris Thompson never failed to appreciate the beauty of the world through the cockpit. It lent a different perspective on life, as if he left the worrisome parts of himself on the ground when the wheels tucked into their wells. In the same motion, he knew that the freedom he had attained would be over once he extended his landing gear. And when he hit the deck or runway, all that he had left behind would come back in a rush.

"Banshee," Raven One radioed. "I repeat, Banshee."

Fuel sprayed as F/A-18F disconnected and fell away from the tanker. Chris was the last one of his flight to refuel. With the other three aircraft spread in a loose formation, Thompson retarded the throttle and the Super Hornet's nose dropped. Four aircraft flowed through the night, each carrying a pair of AGM-88 HARMs (High Speed Anti-Radiation Missiles), designed to be fired from a distance and home in on enemy radar signals. In addition, they had AGM-84 SLAMs (Stand-off Land Attack Missiles) slung on hardpoints. These missiles were remote-guided precision weapons that could be redirected in mid-flight. Out on the wingtips were the sleek AIM-9 sidewinders for air defense should they encounter Chinese fighters at low level.

The four aircraft plunged for the sea's surface, pulling up a scarce hundred feet over the top of the swells. Together, with others hidden in the darkness, the Super Hornets raced for the island and the people responsible for sinking one of their ships and killing many of their shipmates.

* * * * * *

Fifty miles off the shore of Fiery Cross Island, the USS

Ohio moved silently through the shallow waters. It had been a quick passage, the risk of being found offset by the need to be in position prior to the operational order being transmitted. The captain and his crew had checked and rechecked that the correct targeting coordinates had been input. Sonarmen sat with heads pressed against earphones, intently listening for any telltale signature of a Chinese sub loitering nearby or for the presence of ASW forces.

"Captain, sonar reports all clear. They're picking up some screw noise, bearing two one zero, that sounds like a Chinese Luyang-class destroyer. However, it sounds like it's out at the second or third convergence zone," the XO reported.

"Very well, bring us up to sixty feet. Maintain heading and speed," Commander Gambino ordered.

"Sixty feet, aye, captain. Bow planes up ten degrees, set your depth at sixty feet."

Slowly, the large, quiet sub eased up through the waters of the South China Sea. It always caused a degree of anxiety in the crew whenever they neared the surface, where there were too many ways of being found. There could be aircraft overhead with MAD (Magnetic Anomaly Detection) gear, which could easily find the SSGN submarine in the shallow waters. The goal was always to avoid being detected and having enemy ASW forces converge.

At sixty feet below the rolling swells, the boat leveled, heading southwest at five knots.

"Boat is level at sixty, sir. Sonar still reports all clear."

If it were daytime, Commander Gambino would raise the periscope to just under the waves to search for shadows. However, during the night, he wouldn't see anything.

"Very well. Raise the ESM mast."

On top of the conning tower, a door slid silently open and a mast began to rise through the depths. Cresting the surface, the crew began recording any electronic signals that might be floating through the air. The mast was only up for a second or two before it was lowered on the order of the captain.

The signals were run through and analyzed without

finding any search radars or other electronic emissions in the vicinity. Fairly sure that they were the only ones in the area, the captain ordered the comms mast raised. He and the crew then initiated the missile launch checklist.

"Conn, comms."

"Go comms," the XO responded.

"Sir, I have 'Banshee.' I repeat, I have 'Banshee.'"

"Copy, Banshee," the XO acknowledged. Turning to the captain, he repeated the radio call.

"Comms mast down. Open missile doors one through twelve," the captain ordered.

"Aye, sir, opening missile doors one through twelve," the XO echoed, relaying the order.

A short time later, the executive officer added, "Missile doors one through twelve open, missiles ready to fire."

The captain nodded. "Fire one."

Chapter Nine

The calm sea was suddenly interrupted by a boil of water, through which a geyser erupted toward the night sky. The metal cylinder rose through the tower of water like a creature awakening from the depths. As the missile cleared the surface, a roar echoed across the forlorn sea, a tail of fire turning water to steam. Gaining speed, the missile arced through the night, the flame from the solid propellant lighting the area like a welder's torch.

As abruptly as it appeared, the fire winked out as the Tomahawk cruise missile deployed its wings and ignited the turbofan engine that would carry it the rest of its way to the target. Deployed, the missile descended to a hundred feet and sped forward at five hundred miles per hour. Behind, the sea was just beginning to calm as another missile burst through the surface."

"Missile doors closed, boat secured from firing action."

"All ahead flank. Turn right heading three, three five, descent to four hundred feet," the captain of the USS *Ohio* ordered.

* * * * * *

The USS *Lake Erie* knifed through the water with almost surgical precision, the ungainly topside not matching the elegant lines of her hull. The front of the superstructure looked like it should be smashing bugs on an interstate, not housing the latest in American technology. Bow waves crested as they splashed away from the vessel. Behind the Ticonderoga-class cruiser, the wake caused by the twin screws was almost phosphorescent beneath the jeweled heavens.

From her aft deck, flame abruptly shot skyward. Plumes of smoke were illuminated by fire as a missile rose from one of the many cells of the vertical launch system. The smoke spread out as the tail of the Tomahawk cruise missile cleared the deck. Gaining speed, the rocket arced into the night until, like the others fired from the USS *Ohio*, the flame winked out and the missile transitioned to its stealthier mode. More followed, the roars of ignition and launches a constant echo across the waters of the South China Sea.

* * * * * *

Riker sat in the driver's seat of the lead vehicle, staring through the windscreen toward the white observation tower that loomed ahead. The road led directly underneath the tall structure, and unless the Chinese occupying its heights were blind, they were sure to see the two vehicles depart their positions. At the very least, the move they were about to make would draw attention toward the team and hostages. It was the opposite thing they wanted and far less than ideal, but the choices were limited. Beside him, after finishing with his radio call, Collins scrambled into the back seat and climbed through the open hatch to man the heavy machine gun mounted on top.

In the larger vehicle, LTJG Baldwin waited for everyone to settle in as well as they could. Once the last SEAL was aboard and the door closed, he turned the CSK-141 around and gave the order to move out. As the two vehicles started down the road and approached the tower, the radio came alive with Chinese voices. Each subsequent call was a little more adamant than the last.

"I'm pretty sure they're trying to talk to us," Welch commented.

"If they have something to say, they can come right on down and say it to my face," Baldwin replied.

"Let's just hope they don't actually do that."

The vehicles, gaining speed, passed the building. Displayed on one of the monitor screens inside, the rearview camera showed activity to the north. Spotlights beamed out from two observation posts, along with red tracers spitting out from the tops.

"Looks like Blue Team is catching hell," Welch stated.

"That probably means we're next up to bat," Baldwin

responded. "Riker, see if that thing has a turbocharger."

"If I press on the accelerator any harder, I'll be Flintstoning it," the lead vehicle radioed back.

Through the windshield, Riker saw the empty lot emerge out of the darkness, along with the armored vehicle parked at the edge. Even though he was expecting it, the heavy chattering from the machine gun over his head startled him. Tracers reached out into the darkness and slammed into the armored truck. Sparks erupted along its length like fireflies playing at the edges of grasslands. Glass shredded under the heavy fire, the bodies inside torn apart as the 12.7mm rounds ripped into soft flesh and bone.

In the light of his NVGs, Riker saw wisps and then a column of smoke blossom from the stricken vehicle. The gunfire ceased and the lead vehicle raced past into the lot. The calls on the radio ceased and a bright beam of light shot out from the top part of the tower, bathing both vehicles in white. Riker pulled the CSK-131 around and parked it at an angle to the observation post. Baldwin, driving the larger truck, shot past, heading for the far edge and breakwater.

From the top of the tall structure, tracers pierced through the night, reaching out for the team. The heavy machine gun mounted above began chattering again as Collins engaged the tower, tracers passing each other in the dark. Riker imagined more than saw chunks of concrete tumble groundward as the .50 caliber rounds hit the structure. Collins guided the outgoing tracers to intersect those incoming and the machine gun atop the tower stopped firing.

Baldwin whipped the truck around near the edge of the lot.

"Everyone out! Welch and Renton, stay with them and keep below the rim of the concrete barrier," Baldwin ordered.

Doors opened with SEAL and sailor alike spilling out. Welch and Renton guided the twelve over to the rocks and hid them as best as they could. With Vangle on the mounted weapon, Baldwin drove over to near where Riker had parked and angled his vehicle in the opposite direction. Collins kept his weapon trained on the tower while Vangle searched the roadways ahead and to the left toward the airfield.

* * * * * *

General Quan slowly sat up at the persistent ringing, rubbing his eyes as he answered the phone. Less than two minutes later, he was in the combat information center. There he learned that the radar systems had gone offline. Quan was a by-the-book officer who had replaced the previous gung-ho personality of General Tao. The general command didn't want another incident with the Americans and had chosen someone who may lack initiative, but was reliable and unlikely to make mistakes. That was exactly what they needed in the current crisis.

The general ordered a systems check to include a complete reboot of the search and targeting systems.

"Sir, Tower One reports movement at the edge of the radar farm," one soldier manning the comms reported.

"Get Tower Three on it as well. Dispatch a patrol to the area," General Quan ordered.

"Tower One firing on soldiers running for the harbor."

"Get people over there. Alert Tower Four and get a report from the prisoner guards," the general said, suddenly aware that a rescue attempt from American special forces may be underway.

"Sir, Tower Four reports that the vehicles guarding the prisoners are moving south down the road. The vehicles aren't responding to any attempts to contact them via radio."

"I want a platoon sent over to the prisoner building immediately. Put another platoon north to locate the others. Send the rest of the new company after the vehicles. Tell Tower Four they are cleared to open fire. This is a rescue attempt and we are going to stop it in its tracks."

General Quan thought about the situation more. Any rescue would entail an airborne element — the prisoners weren't going to be transported by sea. That would be too risky and they definitely weren't going out underwater, as the prisoners weren't trained for something like that. So, taking out the radars may have been a move to hide the incoming airborne rescue contingent.

However, removing the radars could also hide any incoming raid from the American carriers thought to be operating in the area.

"Let's get the mobile radars online and alert the airbase of a potential incoming attack. Let's get our aircraft airborne," General Quan ordered.

* * * * * *

"Eagle flight, execute," Raven One radioed.

Lt. Chris Thompson eased the stick back on his Super Hornet. The aircraft left the confines next to the surface of the South China Sea and ascended into the night. Beside him, three other F/A-18Fs climbed with him. They were seventy-five miles from Fiery Cross, within the range of their HARM missiles.

"I have one targeting and acquisition radar coming online," LTJG Enquist stated from the back seat.

"Copy."

"There are several more coming up now. I'm designating targets, standby to fire."

Sam Enquist busied himself in the cockpit, selecting targets and assigning them to the others in the flight. It took only a moment. A warbling tone came through the helmets of both pilots.

"We're being painted," the back-seater updated.

"Copy that. How much longer?" Thompson inquired.

"Almost there."

The tone changed to a steady one.

"Okay, they locked onto us. Two radar-guided missiles are heading this way."

There wasn't much Thompson could do at the moment as they had to remain in the radar environment until they had fired their own anti-radiation missiles.

"Okay, we're locked up and ready to go," Enquist said. "Firing."

Lt. Thompson ensured he had the correct weapon selected and then pressed the trigger on the stick. On command, a missile dropped from one of the hardpoints on his wing and ignited. It then raced away from the jet, fading in an instant from a tail of flame to a glowing spot in the sky. Having locked onto its prey like a jungle cat, the HARM headed toward the island at 1,420 miles per hour. It would make the seventy-five-mile journey in a little over three minutes.

One after another, missiles left the shelter of their wings to seek out targets. Lt. Thompson then thumbed the chaff missile countermeasures. Canisters ejected from their racks and deployed thousands of foil strips in the wake of the aircraft. Chris then eased the stick forward and the Super Hornets of his flight headed back for the deck and out of the envelope of the radars now coming online. From there, they'd climb again if more radars came online, turning in slow orbits until that happened.

The missiles fired from the island base lost their lock on the aircraft as they descended below the horizon. Instead, some of them found juicier targets in the chaff clouds, flying into them and detonating. Others that lost their lock were unable to locate other targets and fell harmlessly into the sea.

* * * * * *

Far offshore, a pair of EA-18G Growlers lit off their electronic packages and closed in on two Chinese destroyers patrolling the waters near enough to Fiery Cross to be a threat. Their intent was to keep the ships blind and unable to transmit until the strike was complete. The operational plan relied on keeping the upcoming battle quiet for as long as possible. With so many aircraft out on strike packages, the task force was vulnerable to any land-based strike the Chinese may muster.

Additional electronic aircraft would add their measure to the fight once the radars were taken care of. The island and its environment would be immersed in a bubble with information neither getting in nor out.

* * * * * *

Out of the dark, the sirens began low and rose to a crescendo that was soon blaring across the Chinese base. Anyone in the world who heard that sound would recognize it as a warning that something dangerous was approaching. Those living in "tornado alley" of the United States would immediately cease what they were doing and dash for the storm cellar. Gulf coast residents hearing that sound would know that 150 mile per hour winds would soon touch their shores. Anyone living near a nuclear power plant would turn worried eyes toward the cooling towers rising prominently above the landscape. A Chinese base on an island that had recently attacked and sunk an American warship would instantly fear that an American reprisal was inbound.

Hearing the noise radiate through the night, Welch turned to his teammate helping guard the hostages. "Well, I guess shit's about to get interesting."

"Let's hope it stays in the interesting range and the meter doesn't head into the 'Oh Shit' scale," Renton replied.

"I'd be good with that."

At the airbase, the doors of the various squadron ops buildings flew open. Fighter pilots wearing survival vests and carrying helmets streamed out, running across the ramps. Bomber crews ran for the vehicles that would take them to their laden aircraft. Scrambling up ladders, jet pilots crawled into their cockpits and began to go through startup checklists, aiming to get their aircraft off the ground as quickly as possible and engage any enemies striking for the island base.

Vangle and Collins steadied their respective weapons, their long barrels aimed down the road that ran the length of the island and into the night. Coming their way were several dimmed headlights, just strips of illumination that barely lit the pavement.

On the other side of the island, streaks of fire vaulted from the ground and arced high into the night. Batteries of anti-air missiles had found targets and were fired against the incoming attackers. Volley after volley launched from their rails with loud whooshes, the rockets quickly gaining speed and racing toward their targets at faster than Mach speeds.

Tracers sped out of both barrels as the two SEALs opened fire on the incoming vehicles. Streaking down the street, the 12.7mm rounds slammed into the lightly armored vehicles, tearing through metal and glass alike. Steam shot skyward from the leading trucks as radiators were punctured, the hood of one coming undone and being pummeled by subsequent bullets. In another vehicle, the windshield starred as a heavy round tore through it and impacted the passenger's throat. Blood coated the interior as his head was severed from his body. The two leading trucks veered off the paved path and crashed into adjacent buildings, only half of those inside managing to crawl clear of the wreckage.

Behind, the other vehicles of the responding forces peeled around the careening trucks and began to open fire on the SEAL team only to be met with a continued torrent of fire. One lurched to a stop, its engine compartment smoking heavily. Driven by the incoming fire, another turned too sharply. Its front wheel caught and the entire vehicle began to tumble. Bodies were violently ejected through the doors that were jarred open from the impacts.

Amid the scene, Baldwin noticed streaks of light arcing down from the heavens. The trails of fire sped down and vanished from sight. A second later, a ball of roiling flame and smoke rose skyward. The HARMs had begun arriving, their seeker heads finding the radar emissions of their intended targets. Proximity fuses detonated the fragmentation payloads, which engulfed the mobile trucks and trailers, sending shrapnel in every direction. Radars were perforated beyond use, and the trucks disintegrated.

The men, both Chinese and American, flinched as one missile plummeted out of the night to hit a complex next to the empty lot. The white observation tower and buildings were brilliantly lit for a moment as the warhead exploded, the blast wave rising momentarily above the siren blaring at the nearby airfield. One by one, the Chinese base lost its ability to detect and target foes via radar. The missile batteries that survived the initial onslaught would have to be manually aimed and fired.

Crouched by their charges, Welch and Renton heard the drone emerge above the sound of the siren and the waves slapping against the rocks just below. Turning, both men saw dark shapes appear out of the inky void of the night, looking like a strange breed of insect. Out beyond the waves, two Ospreys closed in on the empty lot.

Ignoring the inbound tracers streaking across the field, the two aircraft swooped over guardian and charge alike. Their wings tilted upward, the propellers transitioning to rotors, and the aircraft slowed. They quickly settled to the ground. In a flash, Welch and Renton herded the sailors into the lead aircraft. With barely a pause, both aircraft took to the air and sped off, rapidly blending into the night.

"Twelve eggs away," Welch called.

"Copy that," Baldwin responded. "That's our cue, gentlemen. Let's be away."

* * * * * *

The emergence of bodies from within the building was sudden. Frank and the others in the situation room watched as the figures dashed for one of the vehicles, disappearing as they clambered inside. Together, the vehicles started down the road toward the empty field that was the pickup zone.

"Well, I guess that's one way to do it," Frank heard General Warner chuckle.

To Frank, the method of movement didn't seem very SEAL-like. In his mind, they should continue to be invisible. However, he was at a loss for how they were supposed to achieve that with an additional twelve untrained people. But driving down Main Street was beyond his imagination.

The phone lying in front of Frank rang. Reaching over, the president selected the speaker option.

"President Winslow," he answered.

"Sir, the code has just been issued. Phase two of Operation Blue Thunder has begun," a voice on the other end announced.

"Thank you," Frank returned, hanging up.

"Sir, just to iterate, that means that both submarine and shipborne cruise missiles are firing as we speak. In addition to the pickup aircraft, it means that attack aircraft are now inbound to the island," General Dawson explained.

Frank nodded and turned his attention back to the screen. Streaks of light reached out from the lead vehicle as they neared the empty lot, intersecting with the lone vehicle parked there on overwatch. At about the same time, a spotlight shone from the tower for the third time, this time immediately finding the targets that had been so elusive. The men in the situation room thousands of miles away watched as a firefight began between the tower and the two armored vehicles stolen by the SEALs.

It was a short-lived battle with the tracers from the building stopping almost as soon as they started. However, it wasn't long before fire was being traded with incoming Chinese vehicles closing on the scene. The hostages had been moved to the edge of the field. Two dark shapes abruptly entered the picture with one settling to ground. The Ospreys had arrived. Twelve figures darted from their cover and entered the aircraft. Then, just as suddenly as they appeared, they departed.

General Warner answered his cell phone and hung up after several seconds of listening. "Sir, I just received confirmation. All twelve sailors are aboard and are on their way to the USS *Roosevelt*."

President Winslow felt some of the tension he had held within release.

* * * * * *

More HARM missiles began to hit their targets, taking out any secondary radar sites that the Chinese brought online following the loss of their main mobile sites. Explosions rocked the island, fireballs erupting across the base.

With a last volley from the machine guns, the four frogmen scrambled out of the vehicles and raced across the empty lot with tracers hard on their heels. Joining with Welch and Renton, the team scrambled over the rocks toward their entry point with everything they could muster. They'd awoken a hive that was intent on stinging those who had broken into their home.

Arriving at the approach lighting system, roars whooshed over their heads. The sound startled the team and they crouched. Looking up, the six men barely caught a glimpse of a cruise missile as it streaked overhead.

Four missiles raced down the length of the tarmac, shredding their shrouds and disgorging cluster bomb munitions. The combined-effect bomblets fell among aircraft in varying stages of startup and pilots still being ferried to their planes. Fragmentation bomblets shot holes through wings and fuselages while also ripping holes in and severing the limbs of Chinese soldiers. Fuel tanks were punctured, their contents pouring across the ramp.

Master caution lights flashed red in taxiing aircraft as they were shredded from the now armed and landing bomblets, their engines flinging turbine and compression blades in all directions. Flames erupted from failed engines. Holed canopies were raised and pilots jumped from their cockpits into a maelstrom of shrapnel.

Incendiary bomblets flashed, the fuel running from the tanks catching fire. Soon, great swaths of the tarmac were alight, the aircraft caught in the developing inferno creating explosions of their own. Munitions began cooking off, missiles bouncing around like unguarded fire hoses. Two additional missiles raced down the runway, releasing their ordinance on top of two fighters attempting to take off. The two J-16 fighter jets became masses of flame as they tumbled down the runway, shedding parts until they both came to rest in two pyres.

Additional cruise missiles began arriving, their thousand-pound warheads detonating over the communication and control complexes on the northern end of the island. Gouts of orangish-red flame surrounded white-hot centers as the missiles exploded in the air over the buildings. Others dove into the facilities, showering concrete chunks out to great distances.

On Fiery Cross's eastern side, missiles started slamming into the massive fuel depot. Tanks of fuel ruptured, spilling their contents into holding reservoirs designed to catch spills. Arriving cluster munitions set the whole complex ablaze. The entire island shook from the massive explosion. Pillars of fire towered skyward, illuminating the dense column of dark, billowing smoke. Along with the smoldering fires of the airfield and those rising from the rubble of the various complexes, it was a scene straight out of an apocalypse.

*   *   *   *   *   *

"Tiger flight, turn left heading two six five," Raven Two radioed.

Lieutenant Blaine rolled his F-35C into a smooth arcing turn. There was no need to reply as the airborne command post controlling the air-to-air engagements would see the turn on radar. It was best to keep radio traffic to a minimum lest the maneuvering aircraft be identified from their radio calls. A mile off his wing, another pair of Lightning IIs turned with him, rolling out still abeam in a tactical formation. Kyle knew they were being vectored behind Chinese fighters that were speeding northward as they attempted to burn through the radar jamming. They could then begin in earnest to search for attacking aircraft.

"Eagle flight, turn right heading three five zero, descend to angels four. Accelerate to five fifty," Raven Two called.

Blaine eased the throttle forward as he began a bank to the right. The single-seat, single-engine fighter responded like a sports car, the airframe slicing through the night sky. Rolling out on the new heading, Kyle knew that he and the others of his flight were now closing on the tail of four Chinese J-16s. Those pilots were unaware of the four American jets sneaking up on their six o'clock.

"Eagle flight, four bandits at your twelve, thirteen miles, angels six. Light 'em up," Raven Two radioed.

Kyle reached to his glass display and brought his radar out of standby, also arming the AIM-120 AMRAAM launch-and-leave radar-guided missiles. Instantly, four blips appeared on the radar, one already targeted by the data relayed from Raven Two. Kyle eased his throttle back and waited a second for the tone indicating a good lock-on with the target.

"Fox three," Kyle called.

He then pressed the trigger and a missile launched forward from one of the wing stanchions. Three other missiles left the wings of his flight and raced through the night toward their targets, all of which were now scattering across the skies as radar alerts began warning the Chinese pilots. Four more AMRAMMs left Eagle flight.

The radar lit up as the Chinese pilots began deploying chaff in order to fool the seekers. They then began high-speed maneuvers to come around toward the F-35Cs so they could get radar locks.

Kyle selected his AIM-9X Sidewinder missiles. These were heat-seeking missiles that had a "lock-on after launch" capability that didn't require the pilots to lock onto the heat signature of a target in order to fire. These missiles had a datalink so they could be launched and directed to a target afterward.

The internal weapon bay doors opened and Kyle fired two Sidewinders from the rotary launcher. It was overkill for the number of opposing fighters they were engaging, but they were the only ones identified by the airborne command posts.

The Chinese pilots jinked around the skies, releasing chaff bundles. Several of the incoming radar-guided missiles altered courses toward the clouds of tinfoil strips. One veered toward one such cloud, but then found a fighter maneuvering on the other side, the picture presenting a top-down view of the aircraft as it pulled vertical.

The AMRAAM turned with the aircraft, detonating just behind the left wing root. Shrapnel tore into the trailing edge of the wing and the fuselage, the left engine coming apart from the damage. Parts of the failed left engine were thrust through the armored hull of the other engine, tearing through the compression and turbine blades. Both engines came apart, with shuddering explosions. The aft end of the J-16 shredded and trailed sheets of flame.

The pilot, holding the stick of an aircraft veering out of control, pulled on the ejection handles. Explosive bolts fired and the canopy was whisked away in the slipstream. First the rear and then the pilot's seats launched on their rails, the two crewmen carried away from the plane that was tumbling violently through the skies.

"Splash one," Raven Two called.

A second Chinese fighter yanked hard as an AIM-120 closed in, the pilot trying to make the missile go aft and lose its lock-on. However, a second guided missile sped in and closed the distance, detonating just below the twin air intakes. Shrapnel again tore into compression blades and the engines came apart. Pieces of the missile also tore into the fuselage. The aircraft buckled, separating into two parts. Both pieces tumbled, shredding more pieces of the aircraft as it plunged toward the sea, miles below.

"Splash two."

A third Chinese attack fighter managed to shake off one missile, and the second one was distracted by one of the deployed countermeasures. However, as it rolled out of a hard turn in afterburner, the AIM-9X Sidewinders arrived. One of the heat-seeking missiles exploded just behind and a little under the tailpipe, the 20.8-pound warhead disintegrating the aft end of the engines.

The pilot fought with his J-16 as it began bucking through the skies, the engines slowly coming apart. The aircraft then pitched violently upward and the two crewmen had enough and bailed out, adding their chutes to the two already floating down.

"Splash three."

The pilot of the fourth aircraft activated the afterburner at the first warning tone and dove for the deck. The J-16 quickly passed through Mach and then surpassed Mach 2 as the pilot broke ranks, hoping only to survive what he knew would be a volley of missiles fired from optimum angles and ranges.

Down on the deck, the attack fighter sped along at twenty miles per minute, the AMRAAMs chasing at nearly twice that rate. It took about a minute for the guided missiles to catch up. The pilot, seeing the incoming stream of fire, banked hard just fifty feet over the top of the crests. The missile overshot and slammed into the sea. Seeing the second missile arcing through the night sky as the J-16 turned, the pilot repeatedly jammed the countermeasures and pulled hard in the opposite direction. The missile faltered in the chaff cloud, but then was through it. However, it failed to find another target as the pilot had gone vertical at the right moment, and the second missile also fell into the rolling waves.

The two AIM-9Xs, being slower and with a smaller range, never caught up with the fleeing aircraft. Having avoided the missiles didn't spell safety for the crew, though, as they were low on fuel from the time spent in afterburner and weren't able to make it anywhere close to any of the other Chinese bases in the Spratly Islands. They too had to bail out when their engines flamed out for lack of fuel.

"Splash four."

*   *   *   *   *   *

Waves rolled across the legs of the wetsuit-clad figure as he waded through the incoming surf. Five others behind flopped through the water as they made their way underneath the steel dinosaurs that were the approach lighting system. The tops were illuminated by the flicker of flames coming from further inland with billowing columns of smoke darker than the night sky. The constant explosions from incoming cruise missiles were on pause; now, only the crash of breaking waves offshore mixed with the roar of a conflagration at the fuel farm. With a last look at the partially burning island, LTJG James Baldwin, now waist-deep in the water, dove underwater and made his way to the delivery vehicle with the rest of his team.

The cruise missiles fired by the USS *Ohio* and USS *Lake Erie* had severely damaged the aircraft parked along the tarmac, as well as the combat control facilities on the northern end of the island. The burning fuel farm cast a hue across the eastern section, highlighting the sides of any buildings still standing. Most of the base's air defenses had been rendered useless by the first and subsequent waves of HARM-firing Super Hornets. Fast-moving Chinese patrol boats were in the middle of leaving the harbor, loaded with as many surviving uniformed personnel as they could carry, many of them wounded.

With the last of the cruise missiles, it was time for the various attack packages staged offshore to proceed. The radios came alive with the sequencing of aircraft. At first, flights loaded with stand-off missiles were given targets and the skies began to fill again with fiery trails. AGM-84H/K SLAMs (Standoff Land Attack Missiles) raced across the seas and were guided to targets while AGM-84As Harpoons (anti-ship) slammed into the sides of vessels parked alongside the concrete piers or anchored in the deep lagoon.

Explosions again rocked the island as the facilities that survived the first onslaught began to receive attention. Chunks of concrete were hurled across the ramp, the once pristine lawns, and the now buckled roadways as non-hardened aircraft shelters were struck along with administrative buildings. The vehicles that had been hunting the invaders sought any shelter, many overturning as buildings next to them were struck. Many of the soldiers, their priorities changing from island defense to survival, raced down to the beaches or to the bunkers along the water's edges, all the while wondering if there was an invasion force inbound as they stared out at the darkness that was the South China Sea.

A second pause interrupted the blasts. Smoldering ruins marked where buildings once stood, where booted heels once echoed down hallways. The rubble flickered orange from the large fires still fiercely burning. Cries of those wounded and buried in concrete and rebar could barely be heard above the roaring flames. With their weapons destroyed, souls braved the shifting rubble and the threat of incoming fire to find those in need. Teams moved heavy chunks and pulled survivors from the collapsed buildings, setting up medical facilities in empty fields. Even with the threat looming overhead, generators, lights, and eventually tents were set up so the wounded could be treated.

"Talon flight, initial approach fix, inbound."

Rolling crests showed in the night-vision-enhanced heads-up display as Lieutenant Matt Goldman directed his fighter onto the new course programmed into his flight director system. The four others of his flight all took separate headings in order to line themselves up for their attack runs. Hanging off his wings were a mix of AGM-65F Maverick missiles and JDAM (Joint Direct Attack Munitions) BLU-109/B bombs, the latter 1000-pound bombs used as bunker busters.

Matt received his clearance to proceed and soon called out the final approach fix. Moving the throttles up, the Super Hornet accelerated to 540 miles per hour—nine miles per minute. At that speed, he and LTJG Keene in the backseat would have little time to find a target, lock onto it, and fire.

The magnified view of the island ahead showed the carnage visited by standoff weapons delivered courtesy of the United States Navy. Coming in from the north, Keene was quick to pick out a target, selecting the tall shape of an observation tower. He placed crosshairs on the white building and locked the laser, notifying Matt that he was locked and loaded. Matt quickly confirmed that he had the correct weapon selected, and fired.

Trailing a stream of fire, the Maverick left the rails and sped ahead of the attack fighter. Even as the Super Hornet zipped through the night, Keene ensured that the laser designator remained about a third of the way up the target. The glass-enclosed seeker in the head of the missile received the scatter-back of the laser and guided in on the source. The tower grew quickly in the cockpit screen as the missile homed in, going bright and then dark as it struck the target.

Flame blasted from the tower, showering the area with large pieces of concrete and embedded rebar. The tower leaned to one side and began to topple, speeding up as it neared the ground. It hit with a mighty crunch, causing dust and sand to billow from the impact. The rounded structure collapsed even further, becoming a long line of white-painted rubble. Eyes from those in the open fields attending the wounded looked up as the explosion rolled across the island base, signaling yet another round of incoming fire.

The island raced under the nose as Matt's F/A-18F tore across the northern end. The Gs came on quickly as he yanked the aircraft into a tight turn, countermeasures ejecting from their racks. Flares burned brightly as they arced through the night, their reddish light flickering against the chaff that was also deployed. A minute later, another observation tower tumbled to the ground as his wingman made his appearance on the battlefield.

After each of his flight made their pass, Goldman brought the Super Hornet back around for another attack run. This time, his back-seater selected one of the fortified hangars that had withstood the cruise missiles. Pillars of smoke drifted from the smoldering remains of aircraft parked on the tarmac or caught taxiing out to the runway. Upon hearing that he was ready to go, Matt toggled two JDAMs from their hardpoints. The bombs were originally designed as glide bombs, but bolt-on attachments turned them into precision-guided munitions. They had a high-altitude launch range of fifteen miles. However, targets were hard to come by at this stage of the operation, so Matt had to opt for close-in attack runs.

The two bombs hit the top of one hangar and tore through six feet of reinforced concrete before detonating their five hundred pounds of explosive. Two bombers parked in the expansive interior were riddled with shrapnel, turning them into useless hunks of metal. One of the large aircrafts' main gear collapsed and its left wing slammed into the ground. Fuel tanks were perforated and torn apart, spilling jet fuel across the hangar floor. Fumes rapidly filled the interior and exploded. The secondary explosion blew a larger hole in the hangar, through which black smoke poured.

One after the other, the hardened shelters and any remaining structures on the island were hammered under this third attack. Not a single tracer or missile arced into the skies. The navy crews enjoyed complete control of the air over the stricken island. Follow-on attacks sought targets of opportunity, but eventually those disappeared as well. Without being told to do so, no one targeted the lights set up in the middle of the open fields. Perhaps it was because they knew what was going on there, or maybe they decided it wasn't worth the cost of their ordinance.

Admiral Fablis listened and watched the events unfold without any input. He left direction to those with the expertise in their fields, but closely monitored the action. His job was to say when it was time to quit, whether that be due to external forces or because he felt the operational objectives had been accomplished. The ASW patrols were out in strength, ensuring the surrounding waters were free of threats, especially Chinese ones. The last thing he needed during this whole thing was to have anti-ship missiles materialize out of nowhere.

In addition, E-2 Hawkeyes were out on the perimeter searching for any sign of incoming bombers or cruise missiles from mainland China. All of the Chinese naval vessels were plotted and monitored for any hint that they were about to fire missiles. So far, it appeared that the jamming was effective and no one knew what was transpiring on Fiery Cross.

The admiral listened as pilots searched for new targets but were coming up increasingly empty.

"Okay, let's bring our boys back home," Admiral Fablis ordered.

The combat information center came alive as instructions

were sent out. The airborne command posts called off ongoing attack runs and began sequencing aircraft to the tankers and for the return back to their respective carriers. Patrol aircraft forming a defensive perimeter tanked up and remained stationed, awaiting the time when their replacements could be sent aloft. At the moment, the decks were being prepared for returning aircraft that had directly participated in the operation. The first waves were already on deck, but the subsequent ones had night landings to complete before their missions would be finished. The decks were busy with landing F-35Cs and F/A-18Fs, the aircraft being guided into their parking places and stowed within.

The returning aircraft left behind a smoldering island. All of the buildings that had been neatly arranged along the streets were now piles of concrete and rebar. All of this was highlighted by gouts of flame still shooting skyward at the fuel farm. There wasn't a building, aircraft, or defense system left intact. Ships lay partially submerged or rolled inverted at their berths. Several now graced the bottom of the harbor, still attached to their anchor chains.

* * * * * *

"Clear the flight deck. Standby to receive hostages," the loudspeaker blared.

The flight deck was awash in the red glow of the sodium oxide lights, illuminating the crew members and aircraft as the former sought to park the latter. Noise was a permanent fixture on a carrier recovering aircraft, the ear-protected crew relying on hand signals to conduct their business.

Out of the dark, two insect-like Ospreys materialized, coming to land on the flight deck. Taxiing forward and parking near the island, the lead aircraft shut down one engine. A door swung open and the twelve rescued sailors began to emerge. Medical orderlies were immediately on them, checking that they weren't seriously injured. Two lines had formed between the Ospreys and a hatchway leading into the carrier's interior, where crew members of the USS *Theodore Roosevelt* welcomed their fellow sailors back with applause, cheers, pats on the shoulder, and handshakes. At the end of the line, Admiral Fablis personally welcomed each one back with a salute and a firm handshake. The twelve rescued were the only ones remaining from the USS *Preble*. Soon, they were ushered into the medical bay for a more thorough examination.

From there, they were flown to Japan where they received additional welcomes and an in-person video call from President Winslow. Families were flown out to be reunited with their loved ones.

*   *   *   *   *   *

Far below, scattered clouds drifted across the night sky, slowly disappearing under the nose and wings of the giant bomber. Through holes in that layer, the ocean seven miles below appeared as an inky void. The clouds partially glimmered in the starlight. The darkness below gave Major Wayne Blythe the illusion that he was skimming the edges of a black hole, the clouds the remains of a star torn apart by the immense gravitational pull.

Above, the heavens winked and sang as they did every night, each star without a thought or pause for what was occurring on this tiny planet sailing along with the rest of the galaxy as it gradually made its way closer to the center. They were oblivious of the four B-52 bombers flying over the Pacific Ocean, their wing pylons loaded with destructive power. Of course, what the four aircraft could deliver was far, far less impressive than the powers exerted by even the tiniest of celestial objects. But that wasn't on the major's mind at the moment as his copilot began going through the missile launch checklist.

"Pilot's munitions consent panel LOCK/UNLOCK switch?" the copilot said over the intercom.

Major Blythe squirmed in his seat to get more comfortable. They had departed Minot Air Force Base hours ago, flying halfway across the country and then again nearly all of the way across the ocean. He had forgotten exactly how many tankers they had hit on their way, but Wayne was ready to get this mission over with and get home. Of course, there was a little thrill that this was an actual mission and not merely an exercise. That's what kept him alert.

"Unlock," Major Blythe returned.

"Master Fault Light?"

"On," said the radar navigator.

"WCP LOCK/UNLOCK Switch?"

"UNLOCK," the radar navigator replied.

Master Fault Light?"

"OFF."

"Fly to?"

"Entered."

Missile Status?"

"Go," the navigator responded.

"Program?"

"Entered," the navigator said.

"Missile launch mode switch?"

"Auto."

"Launch Countdown?"

"Monitored," the navigator replied.

"Missile status indication?"

Outside of the aircraft, one of the twelve AGM-158B joint air-to-surface standoff missiles dropped from its nestled position on the pylon of the left wing. Stubby wings clicked into position and the turbojet engine fired. The extended-range cruise missile slowly pulled ahead of the BUFF as it accelerated to .75 Mach, descending to its cruise altitude of one hundred feet. It was the start of an hour-long, five-hundred-plus-mile journey to a remote island situated in the southern reaches of the South China Sea.

"JASSM missile one away," the radar navigator stated, reading the message at the bottom of his display.

A second cruise missile dropped from its position, dropping out of the night sky to chase its brother across miles of ocean.

"JASSM missile two away."

Over the next minute and a half, twelve missiles drove away from the B-52, the other two of the flight also delivering identical payloads. Major Blythe stared past the windscreen. Somewhere out there, thirty-six missiles would deliver their thousand-pound bunker buster payloads onto a tiny island. In an hour, it would be determined whether an island could sink or not. Having seen what damage a single one could do, he didn't relish anyone on that tiny island receiving thirty-six of them.

"Egress Maneuver?" the copilot called.

Major Blythe turned the wheel and eased the eight throttles forward. The huge bomber reluctantly rolled into a bank, coming to a new heading 180 degrees out from the launch heading.

"Performed," Wayne replied.

"Missile launch mode switch?"

"Standby."

The crew continued with the post-strike checklist and then settled in for the long flight home. They were the last piece of Operation Blue Thunder.

The island had been quiet for a little over an hour, the surviving Chinese personnel thinking the attacks were finally over. Some organization had started. Bunkers along the beaches were manned in case of an amphibious assault. The wounded were treated as well as they could be with supplies salvaged from the hospital. Many sat in the dark, smoking what cigarettes they could locate and waiting for the dawn to hopefully catch sight of rescuing forces. No one had been able to get a message out, but several sat in the wreckage of vehicles attempting to get radios operational.

Terrified eyes looked up when the last batch of cruise missiles began to arrive. The first slammed into the northern end of the base, the missiles diving deep underground before exploding. Towers of sand, seawater, and chunks of concrete rose from the blast, the explosion rolling across the island.

Seconds later, the second one arrived, this one diving into the northern end of the runway.

Any remaining windows shattered. Over the next minute and a half, the island was rocked by thirty-six separate blasts, starting in the north and working south. Deep holes were torn, slowly turning the island back into the shoals it once was. The fires raging at the fuel farm spread out over the sea as the bunker busters tore into the island, the immense craters filling with seawater. The many months of work creating the island and then more to construct the buildings and other base workings were destroyed in ninety seconds. The question was answered. An island couldn't be sunk, but it could be converted to a semi-submerged sandbar. It would take considerable effort and a good amount of time before the island base could be reconstructed.

Offshore, the SEALs had stored their delivery vehicles and were aboard their respective boats, starting their two-week journey back to Pearl Harbor. The task force recovered their aircraft and turned north, choosing to remain in the South China Sea. Considering the close proximity of China, it was either a courageous or ridiculous decision. But the United States had demonstrated its strength, sending a message that it wasn't going to cut and run.

Operation Blue Thunder
9-10 June, 2021

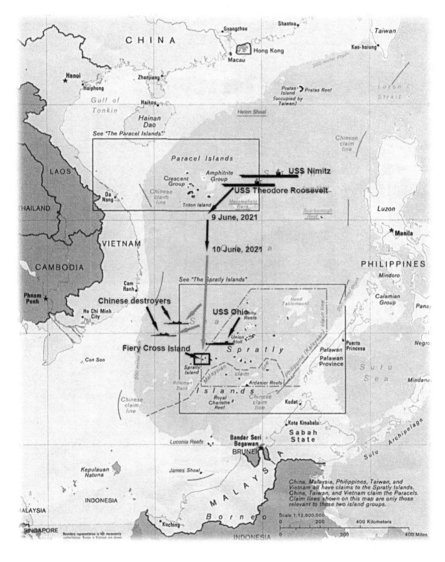

Hostage Rescue

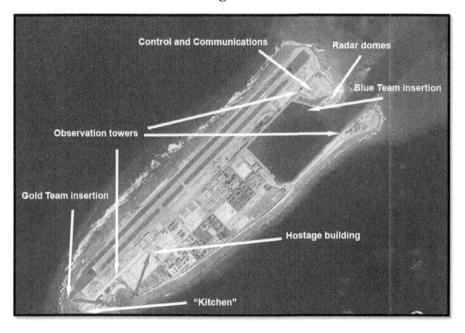

Chapter Ten

White House Situation Room
Washington, DC
10 June, 2021

President Winslow and the others seated with him watched as Fiery Cross Island was systematically taken apart. Large and small columns of smoke rose from the varying complexes on the island. Every minute or two, carrier-borne aircraft would streak into the picture and just as quickly exit the field of view. Behind them, more fire and smoke would erupt from additional explosions, adding to the rubble that was once a fully functioning military installation.

With each new bomb detonating on the island, Frank saw the political clout the United States had gained burn away like the spreading fires. The number of Chinese dead would most certainly be greater than the American loss of life from the USS *Preble* sinking. Even though an American warship was illegally fired upon while in international waters, the focus of the world would now turn to the destruction of the base. The only advantage they could hope to hold onto was that China had illegally held American sailors and conducted an unprovoked attack on an American warship. However, Frank believed they'd be lucky to come out even on the sympathy front.

With the battle now fully underway, the speakers hidden in the ceiling of the situation room broadcast the various radio traffic, providing an immersive experience for the administration and general staff. Frank heard the order to cease operations, and soon there weren't any more aircraft zooming across the screen. The base was completely destroyed, the fuel storage facility casting an eerie orange glow across the entire island. The room was completely silent for a minute.

"Sir, as you heard, the aircraft are now returning to their respective carriers. With the exception of defensive patrols, all should be landed within the next hour and a half. The twelve sailors are aboard the *Roosevelt* and will be transferred to

Yokosuka naval base once they've been medically evaluated," General Dawson broke the silence.

"I want a teleconference with them set up once they're comfortable," President Winslow responded.

"I want to remind everyone here that Operation Blue Thunder hasn't been completed," General Dawson continued. "Right now, we have aircraft over the Pacific that have released additional bunker buster cruise missiles. Those missiles should reach the island in about thirty minutes. That should complete the island's destruction."

"Very well; thank you, general. I think we should take the time and discuss the likely Chinese reactions," Frank said.

"Well, first off, they'll want revenge. This could create a division within the central committee. The military will want to strike back at our carriers while they're in the South China Sea. President Hao's position will be weakened, but I think he will retain enough power to prevail. We'll see a push on the diplomatic front just as we did. If they opt to conduct a reprisal strike, then that will be viewed as an escalation. Considering their positioning lately, I don't think they can afford to be viewed as aggressors at this stage," Secretary of State Stevenson replied.

"Does everyone else agree with this reasoning?" Frank asked the others around the table.

"No, I think they'll conduct a limited strike somewhere. I don't see them just letting this go. They can't be viewed as weak, for the reasons Secretary Stevenson mentioned," the CIA director cautioned.

"I'm not sure about that," Secretary Stevenson responded. "In my mind, it depends on how they prioritize their goals. I expect them to continue pursuing their economic endeavors. A large-scale retribution will erase any advantage they may gain from this."

Views were exchanged around the table with the consensus being that the Chinese would eventually be forced to strike back in some fashion. It was the same as the United States had done. Explore the diplomatic front, but when that played itself out, they'd have to strike back in order to save face. That is, unless they had a major breakthrough along the financial lines, but the United States would fight tooth and nail to prevent that from happening.

No one around the table reached a conclusion as to where the Chinese would hit, but it was decided that the carriers would remain in the South China Sea for the time being.

* * * * * *

Almost as soon as Alpha Platoon disembarked from their respective submarines, they were driven to the hangar where they had trained for the operation. A large monitor was positioned at the front of the old briefing area. The teams were tired and ready for a beer or three followed by a twenty-four-hour coma. However, they shuffled to the front and settled in their seats, curious as to this different kind of debrief.

Lieutenant Newsome, dressed in his summer whites, stood next to the monitor, greeting and welcoming the two teams of his platoon. Chief Petty Officer Fields leaned over and whispered something in his ear, to which he nodded.

"Room, atten-*shun!*" Newsome's voice rang out and echoed across the empty hangar.

The sound of chairs shuffling backward followed the reverberation as twelve SEALs scurried to attention. The monitor flared to life and showed the presidential seal.

"Gentlemen, the president of the United States."

President Winslow came onscreen. "Please, sit down and relax. You men have earned it."

The SEALs looked behind to relocate their chairs and eased back down into them.

"I won't keep you long as I know you have other things on your mind. I just want to personally thank you for what you did. The country owes you a tremendous debt of gratitude. Now, you may just comment that it's your job, but not to a specific few. I have here several letters from family members, some of them directed toward you fine group of sailors. I'm going to read a couple of excerpts so you can truly know how much what you did meant to others.

"This one is from the mother of one of those you rescued…'I don't know specifically who you are, but I hope this letter makes it to you. There isn't much to say other than my son is alive because of you, so thank you from the bottom of my heart.'

"This is another one from a father…'I thought I had lost my daughter and had begun to accept my fear that she would be held for years to come in a Chinese prison. I can't tell you the joy it brought to my heart hugging her at the airport. Thank you for returning my daughter.'

"And here's one from one of the sailors you rescued…'I can't tell you how scared I was each and every day. Each day held the fear that I would be a prisoner for years to come. My mother is ailing and I didn't think that I'd be able to see her again. I will forever hold the image of the two big men entering the room and going from bed to bed, calming everyone there. I thought I had been forgotten, so thank you. Oh yeah, I was able to see my mom just yesterday and that is all thanks to you.'

"So, gentlemen, again, the nation owes you a debt of honor. As I said before, I won't keep you. I will add, however, that mountains of pizza and refreshments are on the way, courtesy of the United States government."

*   *   *   *   *   *

Beijing, China
11 June, 2021

The theater and fleet commanders all stoically watched as the ministers threw words and blame around as if they were playing tennis. The foreign affairs minister blamed the national defense minister for his inability to keep the Americans from taking the prisoners and demolishing the base. In response, the defense minister shot back that they should never have followed his advice to keep the American sailors prisoner. Both blamed the minister of state security for the failure of the intelligence community to see that the carriers were moving into striking positions.

The generals and admirals knew that they had provided the answer some time ago—that letting the American carriers roam free in the South China Sea had been a mistake. They should have struck before this disaster, but they also knew that this wasn't the time to tell the powerful men sitting around the polished table that they were wrong. In their minds, keeping the prisoners had been a mistake that could only lead to one conclusion: the retaliatory attack that was still being analyzed.

Overflights had shown that the island had been reduced to nearly what it had been before construction efforts had begun. Pockets of fuel still burned, but those were mostly oil slicks that extended down current from the island that had been Fiery Cross. The island and all that was on it was a total loss, with only sixty-three survivors found when rescue forces finally arrived.

The sight of the destruction caused anger to surge through the general staff each time the pictures or video were displayed. Their initial reaction had been to launch everything they had at the carriers, but they'd been overruled. That the cabinet wouldn't do what obviously needed to be done angered those with stars on their shoulders nearly as much as the smoking ruins.

The American carriers were now hundreds of miles north, still steaming in the South China Sea without any indication of departing. To the general staff, each chest adorned with rows of medals, that wasn't the best decision, considering the forces that China could bring to bear. But it was a matter of what the men in expensive suits wanted to do and how far they were willing to go to protect their resources. At the very moment, the Americans were sailing with impunity. However, the military general staff had to continue to hold back for the moment, biding their time for when their input might be received in a better light. Yes, the moment would come and they'd be ready. The gleams in their eyes and firm set of their jaws said as much.

"Enough!" Paramount Leader Hao shouted, slamming his hand down on the hardwood table. "We would make greater progress if we stopped bickering among ourselves. There is much blame to go around and we all hold our share of it. We can do nothing about what already happened except to take the steps necessary to ensure it doesn't happen again."

"If we would have had more warning from our intelligence apparatus, we could have had forces ready to meet the attack," National Defense Minister Zhou stated.

"I said enough! We need to come together to determine where to go from here and what our response will be," President Hao said firmly.

Minister Zhou nodded in deference and then stated, "We must retaliate in order to save face. We cannot let this transgression go unpunished or we'll lose ground with our allies and those we hope to bring to our side. If we do nothing, they will not look to us for protection and we might as well give the keys to our country to the Americans."

"I have to side with the good defense minister on this one," Finance Minister Lei agreed. "If we do not send a strong message, then any hope we have of making the yuan an international fund will vanish on the wind."

"There is a lot of talk about retaliation around this table, but let's clarify exactly what we mean by that. As I see it, there are three possible avenues. The first is financial, the second is diplomatic, and the third is a military response. So, let's not talk abstracts here, but delve into each one so we can see what they'd look like. Let's start with the financial," Hao contended, directing order into the room.

Finance Minister Lei cleared his throat, knowing that the conversation had slid into his arena. "The Americans still have our assets frozen, and there's not much we can do about that. If they unfreeze them, we can pull our investments out, which will send their stock market into a downward spiral. As we discussed before, this will also hurt us, but it is an option.

"So, the first thing we can do is to continue our push to make the yuan an international trading currency. I believe we'll be able to make more headway with this in the current situation. We'll see world opinion swing back to our side, so we should take full advantage of that.

"We can also initiate tariffs on the United States while continuing to pursue free trade agreements with our eastern Asian neighbors. Although the switch is beginning to be made to move pharmaceuticals into Canada, we still have them as a major bargaining tool for the time being. This solution, though, will bring our two economies back into the same trade war we had before all of this began."

President Hao nodded, expecting the answer he received. While they may be able to make more headway into the financial markets, there just wasn't much more they could do in that area. The Asian countries surrounding the South China Sea may be more amenable by reason of proximity to negotiating a defense pact, but that wouldn't have much impact on trade. Nevertheless, Hao would add that to the list.

"I think that about covers it for the financial possibilities that we can pursue. We will reimpose tariffs on some of their scarce commodities and push for greater acceptance of the yuan. I believe that we should hold off on a general tariff increase for the time being. If they release our assets, then we can further discuss pulling out our investments," Hao stated. Turning to the foreign affairs minister, he continued. "Enlighten us on the diplomatic options we should contemplate."

Minister Liu took a drink of water from the crystal goblet and stood, shuffling and straightening the piles of paper lying in front of him.

"With the extent of their actions, the Americans have thrown away any political sympathy they held, and I foresee the scales shifting in our favor, providing we successfully navigate the turbulent waters. Had they merely rescued the prisoners, then they would still hold an edge in world opinion. However, with the extent of the unwarranted devastation and tremendous loss of life, we now have the opportunity to swing the court of world opinion to our advantage. I believe we can even start sowing the seeds to remove the dollar as the world's currency, but that path will have to be delicately tread. It will take time, but the notion is more possible today than it was yesterday. After all, what the Americans did will frighten many.

"We will appeal to the United Nations, seeking to identify ourselves as yet another victim of American bullying. The world must rein in this reckless and dangerous behavior, striking sovereign nations with impunity. At least that will be the message we portray to the world. Nothing will immediately come of it, but it should swing more nations toward our embrace."

"Make sure we're placing a counter-suit in the World Court, asking for restitution for the damages and loss of life the Americans caused. Also ask for the one they've filed to be dropped, considering they more than made up for the loss of life and damage caused by the sinking of their ship," Hao stated.

Liu Xiang nodded and then took his seat. "I'll see to it personally."

"Very well, I agree with your proposals. We now have two avenues of action. I know most of us here are waiting for the one that will matter the most, and that is what military response will we take, if any. So, as this discussion will most likely be lengthy, and perhaps heated, let's break for a meal first," President Hao proposed.

The others seated around the conference table knew they didn't have a choice, that the paramount leader's suggestion was more than that. In response to an unseen gesture, waiters flocked quietly into the room from hidden doorways. They marched around the table and, as unobtrusively as they could, began laying fine linen napkins, silverware, and crystal glassware. Once places were set, plates and first courses were brought and placed at intervals along the rich wooden table. Subdued conversation drifted around the table as the members ate, some with gusto, others taking slow pleasure with their meals, while the remainder seemed to have no appetite.

Hao Chenxu burped and wiped his lips as the last dish was drawn away. He would have rather spent the rest of the day contemplating other affairs of state, perhaps lazily spending the afternoon drifting from one thought to the next. However, the current tension between China and the United States demanded his attention. Any mistake one way or the other could lead to a larger war that could escalate beyond his control or that of the president sitting in the Oval Office. The waters had to be carefully navigated to achieve their aims without events again spiraling out of control.

"Gentlemen, now we can approach this difficult situation with a full stomach. Defense Minister Zhou, would you be kind enough to lead us through the conversation?" Hao asked.

"Of course, Paramount Leader. I would like to start out by saying that we know that the Americans have sortied their Pacific submarine fleet," Minister Zhou began.

"Wait! I remember our discussion of that matter, but I don't remember hearing that their nuclear missile boats sailed as well. Are you now saying that's the case?" Hao inquired.

"I misspoke, Paramount Leader. It is as we discussed. Their fast attack submarines have left their ports, along with three cruise missile Ohio-class submarines. It is believed that one of those submarines was involved in the attack against Fiery Cross. The Americans are preparing for a limited war with us. I want to adamantly stress that we should not fall behind in our own preparations so we can immediately counter their moves," National Defense Minister Zhou commented.

"And what is it that you are suggesting?" Hao questioned.

The eyes of the admirals lit up just a fraction, a move that was barely noticeable. This was the time to press for their solution. They'd all waited for the moment when the Paramount Leader seemed willing to at least listen, if not act.

"For detail, I would like to turn over the discussion to the commander of our southern fleet, Admiral Lin Zhang," Zhou stated.

Admiral Lin motioned to a guard standing quietly in the shadows. The man walked over to the entry door and spoke with someone on the other side. Soon, several uniformed men entered carrying screens and electronic equipment. It didn't take long for the presentation equipment to be set up as the admiral stood and waited with a laser pointer in one hand.

"First, Paramount Leader, I would like to start out by discussing what a shooting war with the United States would look like. Then we can move into what our moves should be, finishing with recommendations on what we should do immediately.

"It is our belief that any engagement with the United States will be limited, meaning that they will not want any fighting to escalate beyond the South China and Philippine Seas. That means they won't attack mainland China, which will give us a permanent safe haven for our fleet of bombers and missiles. That will give us a tremendous advantage, which I will show you at a later point," Admiral Lin spoke, circling the South China Sea that was depicted on the screen. "Neither will we seek to escalate the conflict by striking at Hawaii or their west coast."

"Does that include Japan?" Hao asked.

"Yes, Paramount Leader. The Americans will treat any attack on their Japanese bases as if we directly attacked their homeland. I will add that any attack against Okinawa will be treated the same way. As for Guam, well, we believe that the Americans will not escalate any conflict in the event of an attack there, even though it's considered a protectorate. If we invade, then that is a different story, but the situation will not escalate if we conduct a limited missile strike against their base," Admiral Lin answered.

"Are you sure about that, admiral?" Hao inquired, his eyes narrowing.

"No, but it is my firm belief that they will not. However, nothing is ever one hundred percent assured, especially when matters of war are involved."

"Very well—continue."

"So, the fighting will be confined to the South and East China Seas, along with the Philippine Sea. As we all know, the United States has us hemmed in by their bases in Japan, Guam,

Okinawa, but the proximity of the conflict to our mainland will be to our advantage. We will hold superiority over the battlefield. The threat of our bombers and missiles will hold their carrier fleets out along the periphery of the outer island ring, therefore rendering them useless. Their fighters from land bases won't be able to reach our patrols, and our satellite coverage over the area will keep us informed as to their movements," Admiral Lin stated.

"If that is true, admiral, then why weren't we warned ahead of time of this strike against Fiery Cross?" Minister Liu inquired.

"Minister, at the moment, we have redundancy of our satellite cover, but there's still a two-hour window where we are blind. We caught the American fleet heading southwest at speed, and then again when they were north of the island. The problem was not in coverage, but in interpretation. Our analysts saw the formations and concluded that the Americans were conducting an exercise. That was because we did not correctly deduce that they would conduct a full-scale attack. That was a mistake that has now been rectified. As it stands, minister, the American fleets cannot travel more than sixty miles between our satellite passes, and they will be far outside of any attack radius due to the measures I mentioned," Admiral Lin answered.

Minister Liu nodded. Admiral Lin took a brief moment to regather his thoughts.

"So, we will have air superiority over the area, and with that, supremacy over the seas. Not only will our aircraft hold the Americans at bay, but so will our numerous boats deployed within this relatively small expanse. With the carriers out of the picture, then the conflict will become a war of submarines. From their sailing attack submarines, it is clear that the Americans see this as well. However, we will be in position before they arrive, giving us the advantage.

"Without them being able to use their carriers and their ASW technological advantage, chiefly from their P-8 aircraft, then we will create a stalemate scenario, which will actually be to our advantage."

"And how will a stalemate be to our advantage?" President Hao questioned. "Explain yourself."

"Paramount Leader, if we are able to keep the Americans from moving about freely—prevent the ability to use their striking power at will—blockade them from the seas, then it will show the world that we are in fact the superior force. We'll more easily be able to extend and enforce our claims to the territories in question. We will show the world that we can meet the Americans head on and come out ahead. It will also show the Americans that these freedom of navigation sorties they are so keen on have come to an end—that we can kick them out of the area whenever we choose.

"The Americans move about freely because of the power they project, but if we are able to push them back and hold them there, then that projection will be diminished. We will show the world that we can hold the South China Sea as the true power there. That will bring Malaysia, the Philippines, and others into our fold. A stalemate is the same as a win here," Admiral Lin explained.

"Thank you for your explanation. I think we all here better understand what we will be facing. I do have another question, though. Will we be able to match the American submarines once they begin arriving in numbers?" Hao asked.

"Provided we sortie our own submarine fleet and get them into position before the Americans arrive, we will hold the advantage. We will be moving quietly at the entry points, listening intently for the Americans attempting to slip through. Our airborne ASW forces will be continuously overhead as well. So in answer to your question, paramount leader, yes, we will be able to match the Americans."

"But we must sortie our submarine fleet."

Admiral Lin nodded. "That is correct. We must be in position before the American submarines arrive."

"Take us through what that would look like."

"First, as mentioned, we *must* deploy our own submarine fleet. The nuclear attack boats will deploy to the Philippine Sea to deny the area to the Americans. They will expect this and move their subs accordingly. We must control the sea if we are to keep the Americans from launching attacks on our other outlying islands, so we'll use our greater numbers to counteract their projected deployment.

"Our diesel-electric submarines will be used to guard the approaches to the South and East China Seas. Again, our advantage lies in our ability to get there first and quietly lie in wait, catching any American sub or fleet attempting to enter. We will effectively close off the seas to their navy, leaving us free to do anything we see fit," Admiral Lin commented.

"And their latest class of submarine—will we be able to hear them attempting to come through?"

"The Virginia-class fast attack submarine. They are very quiet, but we will supplement our boats at the entrances with lines of passive sonobuoys and ASW patrols from our destroyers. We can put up formidable defenses that they will find difficult to penetrate."

"Difficult, but not impossible."

"No, not impossible. However, let the Americans lose a couple of their precious advanced submarines and they'll be reluctant to send more. I want to be clear: this is war, and not every exigency can be foreseen. But, with the United States unable to send their ASW forces into the area, specifically the P-8s and drones, then our subs will remain practically undetectable. We will hold every advantage in a conflict.

"Also, keep in mind that the American supply chain will be longer than ours. They will not be able to maintain any superiority beyond the range of their carrier aircraft, which again will be pushed away from any battle. We will be able to exert superiority across the board, therefore negating the striking power of their fleets. If they poke their noses into the seas, then they will be overwhelmed by the offensive power we can throw at them from our mainland forces."

"Very well, admiral. I think you've made your point. What are the thoughts regarding our surface fleet, particularly our two carriers? Do we keep them safeguarded and pull them back into port or leave them on the open seas?"

"We will need the fighters on the carriers, so we maintain them in open waters. However, they will remain hidden behind our screen of submarines, keeping them beyond the reach of the Americans. They will be able to launch long-distance cruise missiles from their own bomber fleet, but the distance will limit their effectiveness. If we surround the carriers with destroyers supplied with air defenses, we will be able to shoot down any they launch."

"Okay, you mentioned deploying the submarines was the first step. What else are you thinking?" President Hao asked.

"Well, paramount leader, it is our belief," Admiral Lin started, his roving eyes and gesture indicating that he was speaking for the entire general staff, "that we must strike at their carriers while they are still vulnerable operating in the South China Sea."

This statement created a rustle and several sharp intakes of breath. Attacking an American carrier fleet would certainly constitute an outright act of war, one that may not be so limited in nature.

"We must weaken them and show them and the world our own resolve," the admiral continued, ignoring the hostile looks shot in his direction. "We now not only have a valid reason to do so and still hold favor with world opinion, we have the ability to do so. We can inflict considerable harm with a first strike, which, combined with our other acts, will give the Americans pause. If we can eliminate two of their carriers, that will make them much more cautious with their usage."

Having laid out the generalities of his proposed battle plan, the admiral again took his seat.

The room sat in silence for several seconds as those around the table contemplated the enormity of what the admiral offered.

The foreign affairs minister cleared his throat. "Well, um, thank you for that, Admiral Lin. While we need to think about this, I suggest something … less dramatic. I agree that we need to strike back, but we should mediate our response to something between doing nothing and launching a direct attack against American carriers. I'm thinking of something similar to what the Americans did at Fiery Cross. Perhaps a missile attack against one of their smaller bases? That will show our resolve without bringing us to the brink of an all-out war. We discussed several other potential targets. Attacking their fleet will squander any diplomatic gains we hope to make."

"Begging your pardon, minister, but wouldn't an attack against one of their bases also squander the gains you speak of?" the national defense minister inquired.

"Not necessarily. If we limit our response to a few missiles, then we save face and show the world that we won't kowtow to the Americans. It will also demonstrate restraint, unlike their attack. That can only serve to increase our stature and gather additional allies along the way," Minister Liu answered.

"So, minister, what is this base you suggest striking at instead of the plan laid out by military staff?" one general asked.

"Admiral Lin mentioned that the American base on Guam could be hit without escalation. Don't I remember hearing that they pulled their bomber fleet out? So the damage inflicted will not be as great," Minister Liu replied. "I agree that they will not escalate beyond that, especially if we ask the United Nations to intervene in a timely fashion."

The admirals and general staff seated around the table all mentally shook their heads. Once again, the civilian ministers were shying away from what needed to be done. This was a chance to show the world that China was a military power in both firepower and strategy. It would also send shockwaves through the American military. It would prove that China shouldn't be trifled with.

"I feel it is my duty to add that gaining superiority in the aforementioned seas would allow us to finally unify Taiwan. And if we can convince North Korea to move while the Americans cannot reinforce or conduct strikes from their carriers, then we can also remove one of the locations from which the Americans keep us hemmed in," Admiral Lin said.

At the mention of Taiwan, eyes turned toward President Hao. This had been one of the foremost goals of the Chinese government, and a major thorn in their side.

"You make an alluring proposition, admiral," Hao responded. "But, I have decided that we will not attack the American carriers for the moment. However, I want that option kept open, along with Taiwanese reunification. If our actions in other arenas are successful, then we can effectively blockade Taiwan and force them back into our fold. But, make no mistake, if what we are attempting to accomplish fails, then we will revisit your plan.

"For now, we will reinstate the tariff measures against the United States. In addition, Minister Liu will have our ambassador denounce this American attack to the United Nations and ask for reparations for the loss of lives and material. We will stress that the territorial boundaries be upheld in our remaining islands. Militarily, I want plans drawn up for a missile attack on the island of Guam. I want to limit the damage to the installation, but it should also be a show of power," Hao ordered.

The paramount leader held up a hand, forestalling the south sea commander who had leaned forward with the intent of commenting.

"Furthermore, I will authorize the release of our submarine fleet to counter the Americans. Ensure that they reach their positions before the Americans arrive," Hao added.

"And what are their orders should the Americans arrive?" Admiral Lin inquired.

"For now, nothing. Sinking one or more of their submarines will cost us our advantage before the UN. It won't be long before we are able to determine if our measures are successful. Thank you for your time," President Hao stated, ending the meeting.

Yulin Base
Hainan Island, China
12 June, 2021

Captain Tan Chun paused to survey the massive underground chamber. Bright lights hung on long cables from the roughly hewn stone ceiling high overhead. Other lights, both portable and permanent, added their illumination. Noise echoed in the immense underground structure—metal being hammered, voices shouting orders, and welding torches sending sparks in all directions. In quieter times, Chun knew that he'd hear the slap of water as it lapped against the long concrete piers lining the waterfront. Now, there was only the glare from the lights against the oily black water to denote that most of the underground chamber was actually part of the sea. Looking past the work, past the low crests of the saltwater, Chun could see the cavern's entrance far away, just a dot of brighter light showing from the single exit.

Pulling his uniform jacket closer, Captain Tan again began to walk along the pier. The dark shapes of nuclear attack submarines nestled close, held by thick ropes anchored to craft and shore alike. Gangways ran from the dock to the submarines riding high above the water, all bustling with sailors. The boats were being stocked with food and other sundries necessary for the long months submerged at sea. Some were still in the process of loading weaponry, the torpedoes and missiles being carefully hoisted. Captain Tan knew he was witnessing a major effort to get the submarine fleet out to sea, and also that the same thing was underway at submarine bases up and down the Chinese coastline.

His heels clicked on the concrete as he passed boat after boat, mentally ticking off the names of the other captains like himself as he strode by the line of Type 093 subs. The tone of his steps changed as he marched onto the gangplank leading to his own submarine, *Changzhen 17*, a Type 093 nuclear fast attack submarine supposedly comparable to the American LA-class boat. Saluting as he came aboard, Captain Tan felt his arm go light as a sailor relieved him of his seabag. The sailor smiled and then vanished into an open hatch on the fore deck just ahead of the conning tower. The captain again paused to stare up at the low conning tower rising above the black tube that housed the submarine's components. The two hydroplanes mounted at the front looked small in comparison.

Knowing that he didn't have much time if he was to conform to the scheduled orders, Captain Tan followed the crewman down into the depths of the submarine. He immediately went to the control room, aware that his bag would be lying on his cabin bunk when he had a moment to himself. Entering the control room, his second-in-command briefed him on the boat's condition and readiness. Weapons had been loaded and stored, the six torpedo tubes stocked with two YJ-18 supersonic anti-ship missiles and two electric torpedoes. The other two tubes would remain empty, waiting to be filled with whatever was decided once the sub was underway. All other supplies had been loaded and were in the process of being stored. They would be ready to be underway inside of an hour.

Captain Tan acknowledged the report and retired to his bunk for his last minutes of solitude before being the first of the base subs to deploy out to the Philippine Sea. There he knew he would have to combat American LA- and Virginia-class submarines, but being there first would allow him to loiter quietly and listen for the intrusions he knew would be coming. He didn't have any shooting orders as yet, but knew that they wouldn't be far behind. Since the attack on the Chinese island of Fiery Cross, everyone knew that a conflict with the United States was inevitable. With that in mind, Captain Tan set his crew to be extra vigilant about getting the vessel ready for sea.

Shouted orders rose above the general clamor of the underground submarine base. Sailors heaved on the thick ropes, tossing them over the side where they hit the water with a heavy splash. Crews on the dock pulled, coiling the dock ropes next to the stanchions. As the sailors made their way below decks, Captain Tan ordered a single blast from the boat whistle mounted on the conning tower. *Changzhen 17* eased away from the pier with tugs nestled alongside guiding the submarine out into the internal harbor.

"Slow ahead, right standard rudder. Come right to heading 170 degrees," Tan ordered.

The water behind the attack submarine churned slightly as the seven-bladed propeller engaged and slowly began revolutions. The boat moved through the dark oily waters, waves slowly rolling across the top deck and away from the slow-moving vessel. In the distance, sparks showered outward from one of the Type 093G cruise missile subs as it underwent modifications to its vertical launch system. The captain navigated his boat toward the exit, leaving the noise of the docks behind.

The light of the exit tunnel grew larger and brighter as *Changzhen 17* neared. Waiting for the submarine were two additional tugs that would help the fast attack submarine navigate the narrow exit. A faint shadow momentarily dimmed the light coming from the entrance as a destroyer passed, searching the waters for any indication of an American submarine. A blast from another berthed submarine reverberated throughout the underground facility, indicating that it was departing its mooring and heading for the open depths.

Standing atop the bridge, Chun watched as the expanse of the interior narrowed and the rough stone closed in above. Morning sunlight touched on the black hull as the sub nursed its way through the exit and edged into the open. Once away from the exit, a steady breeze graced the crew atop the bridge, with a light chop splashing against the coated hull. Captain Tan felt the chill against his bare cheeks as he watched the tugs ease away.

"Ahead half, make your course two one zero," he ordered.

The captain barely felt the increase in vibration through his rubber soles. The water rode over the hull with an increased urgency as the sub picked up speed, the bow swinging around for the gap in the breakwater barriers nearly stretching around the entire outer bay. It took only a minute to reach the barrier, where the sub sailed past the mussel-encrusted rocks. Waves rolled against the outer stones; strings of kelp waved back and forth. Trailing two destroyers, *Changzhen 17* was quickly past the barrier to deeper water under her keel.

"Prepare to dive," Tan ordered.

The bridge quickly emptied, boots ringing faintly on the steel ladder rungs. The upper and then the inner hatches were closed and the light boards checked to verify proper sealing.

"Diving stations manned, lights green, captain. We are ready to dive," the second-in-command relayed.

"Very well. Maintain speed and heading. Make your depth two hundred feet."

The black hull eased lower into the swells, the long shape being swallowed by the sea. With a last splash of a wave cresting against the conning tower, the sub slid below the surface and entered the domain for which it was truly born. A moment later, *Changzhen 17* made a course correction, heading for its patrol zone in the Philippine Sea. Behind came a long line of Type 093 nuclear fast attack submarines.

One might wonder just how an entire fleet could be deployed with only twelve hours' notice. The answer to that question might be found in the numerous dispatches and phone calls sent from the defense ministry hours after the American attack.

*   *   *   *   *   *

"Screw noises bearing three zero zero, range three thousand yards, moving right to left. I make their speed at ten knots and they're actively pinging," sonar called. "It sounds like two Luyang destroyers. I'm labeling these two as targets Alpha One and Two."

"It sounds like they're looking for someone," Lieutenant Commander Munford remarked.

"Do they have us?" Commander Ackland inquired.

"I don't think so, sir," sonar replied. "The bearing changes remain constant."

"Very well," Ackland responded. Turning to his executive officer, he commented, "I don't like these shallow waters. What do we have loaded?"

"Tubes one and two are loaded with Mark 48 torps, tubes three and four with Harpoons," Munford replied.

"I want those two targeted with the Harpoons, one apiece should do it. With recent events, I want everyone to treat this like the real thing. Who knows what they're likely to do if we're discovered."

"Aye, captain."

"Another set of screws behind the first two, captain. Bearing three zero three, range three thousand yards, moving right to left. Speed ten knots. This one sounds like a Type 093 submarine. Yep, definitely one of their nuclear attack boats," sonar stated. "This one is target Bravo One."

"Must be coming out of the underground facility," Lt. Commander Munford commented.

"I would guess so. Plot time and course," Ackland ordered.

The USS *Texas*, a Virginia-class fast attack submarine, continued to lie quietly near the bottom while destroyers sectioned the seas above, their active sonar gear pounding the depths in search of them. The sub and its crew listened for additional ships leaving the special harbor that was chiefly restricted to the Chinese fleet of submarines.

Ten minutes after the first submarine departed, sonar reported another Type 093 submarine sinking into the South China Sea, and then recorded one every ten minutes over the next forty minutes. Once the fifth left for the open seas, the waters around the loitering boat quieted, the escorting destroyers returning to their stations inside the harbor breakwaters.

The crew of the *Texas* waited patiently, listening for the return or the exit of any additional enemy submarine.

"Make your depth sixty feet," Commander Ackland ordered.

The sleek and deadly submarine rose silently upward.

"Steady at sixty feet," the XO reported.

"Raise the comm mast."

A tube rose through the waters, the top barely cresting the surface. As soon as it cleared, flash radio traffic was sent and the mast lowered. The exposure was less than three seconds. Just as silently, the USS *Texas* eased back down into the dark waters off Hainan Island, China.

At other submarine harbors, nearly identical actions took place. Flash traffic began arriving at ComPacFlt headquarters from station keepers positioned outside of the various Chinese naval ports. The communications were all the same, and when taken as a whole, it spoke a single message—the Chinese had sortied their submarine fleet.

# # #

About the Author

John O'Brien is a former Air Force fighter instructor pilot who transitioned to Special Operations for the latter part of his career gathering his campaign ribbon for Desert Storm. Immediately following his military service, John became a firefighter/EMT with a local department. Along with becoming a firefighter, he fell into the Information Technology industry in corporate management. Currently, John is writing full-time.

As a former marathon runner, John lives in the beautiful Pacific Northwest and can now be found kayaking out in the waters of Puget Sound, mountain biking in the Capital Forest, hiking in the Olympic Peninsula, or pedaling his road bike along the many scenic roads.

Connect With Me Online

Facebook:
https://Facebook.com/AuthorJohnWOBrien

Twitter:
https://Twitter.com/A_NewWorld

Web Site:
https://John-OBrien.com

Email:
John@John-OBrien.com

Printed in Great Britain
by Amazon